"You're so scared of being hurt, you keep everyone at arm's length, especially me."

"Aw, Kenz—" Raw pain was in his voice, in his eyes, as he looked at her.

"I think there isn't any need to keep me at arm's length. I am not going to take your son away from you."

"So you're saying I shouldn't keep you at arm's length," he went on slowly. Without waiting for her to answer, and before she could think of a suitable retort, he slid his hands over her hips.

"Know what?"

"What?"

"You're right. That's much too far away."

"Ross," she breathed as he brought their bodies oh so close.

"Know what else I think?" he added, his lips hovering barely an inch above hers.

"What?"

"That you *are* a threat. To my peace of mind. To my sanity…

"Let me show you what I mean."

Dear Reader,

It's spring, love is in the air…and what better way to celebrate than by taking a break with Silhouette Special Edition? We begin the month with *Treasured*, the conclusion to Sherryl Woods's MILLION DOLLAR DESTINIES series. Though his two brothers have been successfully paired off, Ben Carlton is convinced he's "destined" to go it alone. But the brooding, talented young man is about to meet his match in a beautiful gallery owner—courtesy of fate…plus a little help from his matchmaking aunt.

And Pamela Toth concludes the MERLYN COUNTY MIDWIVES series with *In the Enemy's Arms,* in which a detective trying to get to the bottom of a hospital black-market drug investigation finds himself in close contact with his old high school flame, now a beautiful M.D.—she's his prime suspect! And exciting new author Lynda Sandoval (look for her Special Edition novel *One Perfect Man,* coming in June) makes her debut and wraps up the LOGAN'S LEGACY Special Edition prequels, all in one book—*And Then There Were Three.* Next, Christine Flynn begins her new miniseries, THE KENDRICKS OF CAMELOT, with *The Housekeeper's Daughter,* in which a son of Camelot—Virginia, that is—finds himself inexplicably drawn to the one woman he can never have. Marie Ferrarella moves her popular CAVANAUGH JUSTICE series into Special Edition with *The Strong Silent Type,* in which a female detective finds her handsome male partner somewhat less than chatty. But her determination to get him to talk quickly morphs into a determination to…get him. And in Ellen Tanner Marsh's *For His Son's Sake,* a single father trying to connect with the son whose existence he just recently discovered finds in the free-spirited Kenzie Daniels a woman they could *both* love.

So enjoy! And come back next month for six heartwarming books from Silhouette Special Edition.

Happy reading!

Gail Chasan
Senior Editor

Please address questions and book requests to:
Silhouette Reader Service
U.S.: 3010 Walden Ave., P.O. Box 1325, Buffalo, NY 14269
Canadian: P.O. Box 609, Fort Erie, Ont. L2A 5X3

For His Son's Sake

ELLEN TANNER MARSH

▼ *Silhouette*®

SPECIAL EDITION®

Published by Silhouette Books

America's Publisher of Contemporary Romance

SILHOUETTE BOOKS

ISBN 0-373-24614-5

FOR HIS SON'S SAKE

This edition published by arrangement with Harlequin Books S.A.

® and TM are trademarks of Harlequin Books S.A., used under license.
Trademarks indicated with ® are registered in the United States Patent
and Trademark Office, the Canadian Trade Marks Office and in other
countries.

Visit Silhouette Books at www.eHarlequin.com

Printed in U.S.A.

Books by Ellen Tanner Marsh

Silhouette Special Edition

A Family of Her Own #978
A Doctor in the House #1110
For His Son's Sake #1614

ELLEN TANNER MARSH's

love of animals almost cost her readers the pleasure of experiencing her immensely popular romances. However, Ellen's dream of becoming a veterinarian was superseded by her desire to write. So, after college, she took her pen and molded her ideas and notes into full-length stories. Her combination of steamy prose and fastidious historical research eventually landed her on the *New York Times* bestseller list with her very first novel, *Reap the Savage Wind.* She now has over three million copies of her books in print, is translated into four languages and is the recipient of a *Romantic Times* Lifetime Achievement Award.

When Ellen is not at her word processor, she is showing her brindled Great Dane, raising birds and keeping the grass cut on the family's four-acre property. She is married to her high school sweetheart and lives with him and her two young sons, Zachary and Nicolas, in South Carolina Low Country.

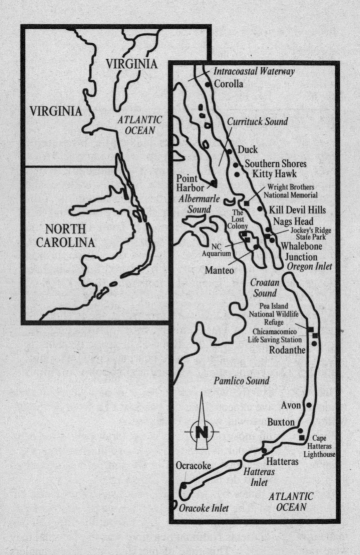

Chapter One

Love at first sight. If anyone had told Kenzie Daniels that it was about to happen to her she would have hooted with laughter.

Two people who'd never met before didn't just take one look at each other and go all soft inside. Outside of the movies it didn't happen like that. Not with a total stranger, not coming face-to-face in the middle of nowhere—and certainly not if the other person happened to be a seven-year-old boy.

But that's exactly what happened, and in a place Kenzie would never have expected: on the beach not far from her house, while lying on a towel reading a magazine.

She'd been up most of the night before drawing—as an artist you worked when your muse was awake—so this morning she'd gone out after breakfast to lounge in the sun before heading to the grocery store to do her weekly shopping.

Crossing the dunes by way of the boardwalk, she spread her towel in the sand. The tide was low and the waves washed lazily onshore. One of the things Kenzie loved about the beaches that made up Cape Hatteras National Seashore was the fact that they were rarely crowded. This time of morning only a few anglers stood casting their rods into the shore break while a group of teenagers waxed up their surfboards nearby.

Of course, in a few hours families would come spilling from the houses lining the dunes behind her, loaded down with beach chairs, umbrellas and toys. After all, July was peak season on North Carolina's Outer Banks, and every town from Nags Head south to Buxton, where Kenzie lived, was crowded with vacationers.

But the sheer length of the Outer Banks' shoreline meant that there was always plenty of room for everyone. And for the time being few people were around to disturb the peaceful morning hours.

Taking off her shirt to expose the slim, one-piece swimsuit underneath, Kenzie rubbed on sunscreen, then stretched out on her back and reached for her copy of *Newsweek*. Already she could feel the tension in her neck and shoulders seeping away. She'd spent too long hunched over the drawing board again, but inspiration had struck just before bedtime and she now had two good drawings to show for the sleepless night.

How long had she worked anyway? At least until three o'clock. She grimaced ruefully, picturing her mother nagging her for keeping such hours. Good thing she wasn't living at home anymore. And good thing she hadn't heeded her mother's advice by advertising for a roommate. This way she could burn the midnight oil as long as she wished, play the music as loud as she wanted, never worry that she was running afoul of someone else's privacy, feelings or sleeping habits.

You were wrong, Mother. You, too, Brent. Living alone definitely has its advantages.

So did the fact that she and Brent hadn't gotten married the way they'd planned.

Had that been the case, "I'd have gone out of my mind by now," Kenzie muttered aloud. Better to be an artist out here on the isolated cape than surrounded by the people, the press, the staff and obligations that went with marrying someone like senator-to-be Brent Ellis.

Brent was definitely running for the senate this year, because her mother had told her as much the last time she'd called. Grinning, Kenzie tried to imagine herself as a senator's wife but couldn't. In fact, the only thing she knew for sure was that she would have made a lousy one. Not that she wasn't well schooled in the ways that Washington's political wheels turned. Heck, she'd practically come of age at Republican party fund-raisers and embassy receptions.

But she had never embraced the lifestyle her parents preferred, the one that Brent, now that he'd been made a full partner in her father's prestigious law firm, intended to claim as his birthright. Lord knows she wasn't cut out to play the obliging Washington hostess at his behest. To stand loyally at Brent's side while he climbed the political ladder toward—what? A bid for the presidency somewhere down the road?

A vision of herself as First Lady made Kenzie snicker aloud. And at the same time wince, remembering a presidential campaign that she alone had brought to ruin a little more than a year ago.

Her heart cramped. No. No way she was going there with her thoughts right now. She'd promised herself during those awful days when the fallout was just beginning that she wasn't going to dwell on something she couldn't change, that she wouldn't have changed even if she'd known in advance about the storm of controversy she was unleashing over her family's heads.

As for her father...

"That's enough, Kenzie!" No way was she going to let thoughts of her father screw up her morning off. Or drive her to talk aloud to herself the way little old ladies did when they'd been living alone too long.

She sighed deeply. Forced herself to relax.

At the moment she wanted nothing more than to lie here soaking up rays. Take a nap. Be left alone like Greta Garbo in—

"Look out!"

The warning yell came from right behind her. Startled, Kenzie lifted her head. A sharp, crackling sound came from high above, and in the next second something big and billowy fluttered down on top of her.

"Hey!" Kenzie flailed at the colorful nylon streamers tangled around her legs, at the brilliant green body of the kite that had crash-landed barely an inch from her head.

"Oh, no! I'm sorry! Are you all right?"

The kite's owner was running toward her, rolling up the string as he went. A boy of no more than seven in bathing trunks that reached to his knees. "I'm only just learning. Did it hit you?"

Kenzie looked up into his face, preparing to give him an irritable lecture. But that was before she saw that his eyes were bright blue and his hair a thatch of black curls. He was chewing his lip apprehensively, but when their gazes met he grinned at her shyly. Dimples appeared in his cheeks, and his freckled, upturned nose crinkled charmingly.

Instantly, stupidly, Kenzie felt something inside of her melt. No doubt about it, the word *cute* had been invented for this little guy.

"No harm done. It barely touched me."

"I thought for sure it was going to hit you on the head. I'm ever so relieved it didn't."

Not only was he cute, but she'd just noticed he had an accent. That, and his choice of words made him adorably grown-up and sophisticated sounding. Was he English?

Kenzie smiled at him. "I'm fine. Really."

His grin widened in response, revealing a missing front tooth. "My name's Angus. What's yours?"

Angus. Even his name was adorable. She resisted the urge to tousle his curly black hair. "Kenzie."

His brows drew together. "What sort of name is that?"

"Short for MacKenzie."

He beamed. "Oh, that's a proper Scottish name!"

She laughed. "Glad you approve."

"I'm Scottish, too. At least my grandfather was. I was born in Norfolk."

"Not the one in Virginia, I assume."

He nodded approvingly. "Do you know where *my* Norfolk is?"

"That would be in East Anglia. Somewhere north of London, I think."

Angus's dimples deepened. "Not many Americans know that."

Kenzie felt both flattered and amused by his obvious admiration. "Lucky for me I've traveled a bit. Are you renting a house in Avon, Angus?"

He pointed over his shoulder. "We're staying in that one there."

The rooftops of several beachfront cottages were visible over the dunes, but Kenzie didn't bother turning to look. They were all pretty much alike: sturdy wooden dwellings built high off the ground to withstand the flood tides and storms that frequently lashed the Outer Banks.

Angus untangled the kite's tail and picked it up from her towel. Kenzie saw that it was nearly as big as he was. "First time piloting one of those?"

Angus looked sheepish. "It's hard to steer."

"Piece of cake once it's aloft. The trick is getting it airborne."

"Do you know how?"

"Um, it's been a while...."

The dimples reappeared, dazzling her. "Oh, please, could you show me?"

She glanced back toward the houses. "Your folks won't mind you spending all this time out here alone?"

"My dad said I could come down, as long as I didn't go in the water. Please, Kenzie?"

How could she refuse? "Hand me the string. Let's give it a try."

Ross Calder closed the cover of his laptop with a snap. Annoyed, he sat back on the couch, running his hands through his hair. While the Internet certainly made it possible to stay on top of his work while on vacation, it wasn't the same as being at the office. Meeting clients face-to-face. Engaging in the dialogue with colleagues so important to an attorney with too many cases on his hands.

Lousy time to take a couple of weeks off, what with the Fitzpatrick trial rescheduled for early August, in addition to a thousand other, equally important cases and meetings and tiresome loose ends.

Growling, he set the computer aside and crossed to the glass doors opening onto the back deck of the house. Why not phone in? Ask Delia if she would—

His thoughts skidded to a halt. No way. Delia had reminded him emphatically just before he left Friday afternoon that she wasn't going to take a single one of his calls until Thursday at least. That she would not return his e-mails, no matter how much he hounded her to respond. And she'd instructed everybody else on staff to do the same.

"It's for your own good, Ross," she'd said in her sweetly maternal way—the old busybody. "I insist you take at least five full days to unwind. Naturally I'd rather you didn't pester us for the entire fortnight you'll be gone, but I'm well aware it's the only way to reach a compromise. Please, Ross. It's the first vacation you've taken in six years."

Her voice had softened and she'd laid her hand on his arm, ignoring his scowl and the rigid muscles beneath her fingers. She'd been his business manager for more than five years now and had stayed with him when he'd left his old firm. And she was as adamant about overseeing his mental health and well-being as she was the running of his office. "You need to have some time with your son."

Sliding back the glass door, Ross wandered onto the deck. Propping his hands on the railing, he stared out across the ocean. Delia was right. He had his son to think of now.

His son. As usual, the words caused an icy chill to settle around his heart. As usual, they brought to mind other, scornful words not intended to hurt but doing so anyway: "What on earth makes you think you know how to raise a seven-year-old?"

"I can figure it out," Ross had responded stubbornly.

"How?" his brother, Alex, had shot back, furious. "Using who as a role model? Not *our* father, I hope!"

Ross deliberately pushed his brother's words to the dimmest recesses of his mind, back where all the memories of his father were stored and rarely, if ever, taken out. Poor Alex was six years older than he was, which was why he had a lot more memories of the father who had abandoned them and their mother when Ross was only three. Ross's memories were vague and few in number. And unlike Alex's, they didn't have the power to wound.

His thoughts turned again to Angus, the boy Alex so adamantly insisted he wasn't qualified to raise. Angus was the one who had begged Ross to take him on this trip, the one who'd chosen to come here to Hatteras Island before the new school year started.

Not Hatteras Island, specifically. Anywhere on the Atlantic seaboard would have been fine with the boy. Born in England, a country literally surrounded by water, he'd never even seen the ocean before.

Or his father, for that matter, until April of this year.

There was that rock-hard lump in Ross's chest again. A knot of frustration and worry—okay, maybe downright fear—whenever he thought of his new responsibility. This boy he had inherited upon his ex-wife's death only four short months ago—a boy he hadn't known existed until just a few, short months before. Penelope had been killed in a plane crash. Once again his throat tightened with the guilt and anger he hadn't quite come to terms with yet. The anger he'd felt at Penelope for keeping Angus a secret from him—and his guilt for having been a complete stranger to the boy until now.

Ross's eyes blazed. Not a boy, damn it, *his son.* They'd been together for weeks now—why couldn't he learn to think of Angus as his?

And you didn't *inherit* a kid, for crying out loud. He'd had a darned important part in Angus's creation, after all, even though he hadn't played a single role in the boy's life afterward. The important thing to remember was that he was now Angus Calder's legal guardian. His father.

Ross unclenched his jaw. Forced himself to let go of the knot in his chest. Over the dunes he could hear the breakers crashing. Angus was down there somewhere flying his kite.

Maybe he should join him. Suggest a walk on the beach or something. Only, Ross wasn't fond of the beach. Born and raised in upstate New York, he preferred the freshwater streams and lakes of New England to the salty sea.

But Angus was another story when it came to the ocean. From the moment he'd seen the Atlantic from the airplane window on his way to America he'd wanted nothing more than to set foot in it.

But a weekend trip to Long Island or the Jersey shore wasn't what he'd had in mind. Instead he'd fetched the atlas from Ross's library and traced his finger down the coast south along Delaware, Maryland and Virginia, sounding out the different names of seaside towns until he hit Norfolk.

"Look! That's where I'm from!" he'd said excitedly, as if Ross didn't know. Then, in the next moment, the North Carolina town of Nags Head had caught his eye.

"Why d'you suppose they call it that?"

It was the first unsolicited question he'd ever directed at his father.

The explanation Ross had uncovered for him had lit the boy's eyes with excitement. Not for a minute did Ross himself believe the tale of North Carolina pirates hanging a lantern around the neck of a nag and walking the dunes in the dark trying to make ships run aground so they could plunder them.

But Angus did. And of course he wanted to see the place for himself. Fortunately for him, he'd made the request in Delia's presence—they'd stopped by the office after eating lunch together—and an hour later a ream of colorful pages, downloaded and printed from the Internet, had appeared on Ross's desk.

One look at the points of local interest had convinced Ross that Nags Head, North Carolina, was too crammed with mini-golf, pizza parlors and outlet malls for his tastes. Undaunted, Delia had gone back to her computer and brought him another set of downloaded images, this time of Cape Hatteras National Seashore on Hatteras Island, with its miles of empty beaches and dark green water.

Angus and Ross had arrived the day before yesterday, flying into Norfolk, Virginia, and renting a car for the two-hour drive south to Avon. Angus had been on the beach practically every waking moment since.

And Ross couldn't deny that it was doing the boy—his son—a world of good.

Where the heck was the kid anyway? Ross checked his watch. Quarter to ten. He'd told Angus to stay no longer than twenty minutes, and he'd left the house at nine. Scowling, he descended the steps and headed for the boardwalk that crossed the dunes.

At least Angus had kept his word about staying out of the water. Relieved, Ross spotted him right away sitting in the sand on the other side of the boardwalk steps, looking up at the sky and laughing.

Ross tipped back his head. The kite they'd bought yesterday was dipping and curving in the deep blue of the sky above.

But Angus didn't have hold of the strings. Who did?

"Here you go, sport. Your turn."

A woman was walking toward his son, reeling in the kite string. She was wearing sunglasses and a navy-blue one-piece bathing suit. Shoulder-length blond hair was pulled back in a ponytail that swung below her sun-browned shoulders.

Ross stopped in his tracks. He'd made a point of shying away from serious relationships since he and his former wife, Penelope, had parted ways—and not on the best of terms. Heck, he'd made a point of shying away from women altogether, but this woman wasn't the kind any red-blooded male could ignore. With tanned legs that seemed to go on forever and curves in just the right places, she had the knockout good looks that could set any man's pulses racing. But it was more than sex appeal. There was something about her, in the way she was smiling at Angus, in the way she tossed her head and set her ponytail dancing, that seemed sweet and natural and irresistible—even to him.

"Here, hold them like this."

The kite was controlled by a pair of strings attached to bright red handles, and the woman was showing Angus how to hold one in each hand, then change the kite's movement by slowly raising and lowering them.

"Look at me! Look at me!"

Angus was crowing with excitement as the kite responded. Ross had never once seen the boy look animated since first laying eyes on him at Penelope's parents' house in London.

It shamed Ross to remember that he and Angus had shaken hands at that meeting, Ross feeling truly out of depth for the first time in his life. He remembered wondering awkwardly whether he was supposed to hug the kid or not. Scared that if he did, Angus might burst into embarrassed tears or, worse, push him away.

And Angus had seemed equally ready to do either—or both.

There was that pain in his chest again.

He left the boardwalk, frowning. "Angus! You were only supposed to stay twenty minutes!"

Startled, Angus and the woman turned. Ross had been standing up in the dunes where neither could see him. Now he stalked across the sand toward them, brows drawn together.

"Is that your dad?" Kenzie whispered to Angus. "He looks mad."

"He hates when I'm late." There was a thread of panic in

Angus's voice. "Kenzie, I don't even know when twenty minutes is."

And why should he? He didn't even have a watch.

Kenzie turned, steeling herself to take the offensive. There was no doubt the man striding toward her was Angus's father. Those blue eyes and untidy black hair were definitely the same. But Angus's sweet, smiling expression was infinitely preferable to that rugged, unpleasant look. He was wearing jeans, expensive boat shoes and a worn T-shirt, the kind you bought from Eddie Bauer or J. Crew to make you look outdoorsy.

Only, this man didn't need to invent an image for himself. He already had a style of his own—in spades. He exuded the aggressive maleness of a man in control of his world, a man not used to being ignored. Kenzie made the conscious effort to keep her mouth closed so her jaw wouldn't drop as she stared.

"Where have you been?" Ross demanded.

Angus lowered his head. "Sorry," he mumbled. "I didn't know I was late."

His father folded his arms across his chest. Definitely not a conciliatory stance. "Then I guess you have no business coming down here by yourself."

This time Kenzie's jaw did drop. "Excuse me?" she blurted, astounded by his tone. "I'm confused as to who's at fault here. Angus seems a little young to be allowed on the beach alone."

"Does he?"

Was there a crack in that tough-guy veneer? Even though he'd shot the question back at her, Kenzie thought he suddenly sounded uncertain. She turned to the boy. "How old are you, Angus? Six? Seven?"

"I'll be eight on Wednesday," he told her proudly.

"There aren't any lifeguards out here," Kenzie said firmly. "And there's usually a rip current running along the shore break."

"Angus knows the rules." She could almost feel the heat of the man's glare. "He's not to go near the water."

But Kenzie could be tough too. "A seven-year-old should have an adult with him when he comes down to the beach, Mr.—"

"Calder. Ross Calder."

He might not be too thrilled to have her lecturing him, but at least he was civil.

Kenzie reached out to shake the hand he extended. "I'm MacKenzie Daniels."

Ouch! He'd squeezed too hard—deliberately, she wouldn't doubt, as though wanting to let her know he was still in charge. She gritted her teeth to keep her smile from wavering. At the same time, she removed her hand slowly, resisting the urge to snatch it away. Not because he'd hurt her, but because of the way the contact between them had run like a physical jolt up her arm and through her body. His big hand had almost swallowed hers in a very masculine way.

But he was still a jerk. And too tough on his kid. Hopefully Mrs. Calder was nicer. "Here's your kite, Angus."

Angus took the handles from her. The kite, ignored, had landed in the sand behind them. "Thanks," he said glumly.

"Keep practicing. You were doing great."

"Was I?"

She resisted the urge to put her arms around him. To stick out her tongue at his father for being such a spoilsport. "Absolutely."

"Will you help me tomorrow?"

"If I'm out this way, maybe. But I live down in Buxton."

"Where's that?"

"The town with the lighthouse. I just happened to be here today because I needed groceries."

Avon had the only chain supermarket south of Nags Head. Every now and again Kenzie skipped the offerings at Buxton's mom-and-pop grocery stores and drove the few miles to Avon to do her shopping.

"Okay. Maybe I'll see you." Angus was looking at her as though he was miserable. Why?

She gave his father a hard look. "Nice meeting you, Mr. Calder."

"Likewise, Ms. Daniels."

She watched them disappear over the dunes. So much for a sunbath. She was much too worked up to relax now. At the way Angus had changed the moment his father had shown up, like a dark cloud blocking out the sun.

And the way she had reacted to Ross Calder's handshake.

Instead of being furious at his unspoken message of superiority, she'd found herself reacting to it on a purely physical level.

Nuts.

Gathering up her things, she went back to the car.

She'd parked in one of the National Park Service turnouts that dotted the highway running south from Oregon Inlet to the end of Hatteras Island. The neighborhoods that made up the southernmost part of Avon ended here, where Cape Hatteras National Seashore parkland resumed. The boardwalk to the parking lot led past the last few cottages on the edge of town.

Angus had said he was staying in one of them. Kenzie scanned the decks for a sign of him, trying to look as if she wasn't. But all of them were empty.

She sighed. Just as well. Even though something about that blue-eyed boy had touched her, she didn't need to run into him again. Or his father, either, thank you very much.

Chapter Two

But Avon was a small town. Running into acquaintances was the rule, not the exception. Only, Kenzie didn't expect to see Ross Calder and his son again quite so soon—like that very evening.

She had spent the afternoon inking her drawings and preparing them for mailing. Afterward she'd gone down to the dock behind her house to check on the minnow traps. They were filled with fish, including one or two good-sized spots and a croaker, but as usual there wasn't enough for all the hungry mouths she had to feed. So she'd driven up to Avon to spend some of her precious cash at the bait-and-tackle store.

She was walking back to her truck when someone called her name. Shifting her packages to one hip, she turned. "Angus! What are you doing here?"

"Going to the movies."

He was wearing a navy T-shirt with "England" written on it in red and white, khaki cargo shorts and high-topped black sneakers. She'd forgotten how cute he was. Or how good-looking his father was. Ross Calder was wearing khakis, too, and a denim shirt with rolled-up sleeves. He folded his tanned

arms across his chest as he came around the car he'd just locked.
The movie theater was right across the parking lot.

"Good evening, Ms. Daniels."

"Hi." Kenzie looked beyond him for Angus's mother, but
the two of them were alone.

Angus was hopping excitedly in front of her.

"What's in the bag?"

"Angus," his father warned.

"No, it's okay," Kenzie said quickly. "Minnows."

The boy's eyes widened. "Can I see?"

Obligingly she opened the container. As he leaned over it, she
caught his father's eye and smiled. Was there anything more
endearing than a curious seven-year-old? Besides, it gave her an
excuse to look at Ross, because he was certainly what you'd
call easy on the eye.

Only, Ross didn't return her smile. The expression on his
rugged face was that of a man looking at a...a specimen under
a microscope or something. It was a probing look, as though he
was trying to figure out what made her tick.

"Are you going fishing with those?" Angus was obviously
fascinated with the contents of the foam container.

"I'm going to feed them to my birds."

"Wow!" he breathed. "What kind of birds eat minnows?"

"Shore birds, mostly. Like herons and egrets."

Could those blue eyes get any wider? "Do you own a heron,
Kenzie?"

She laughed and felt something wicked stirring inside her.
Maybe because Ross Calder was standing there looking so impatient, as though letting Angus talk to her was the last thing
he wanted. "Tell you what. If you'd like, and your father says
okay, you can come over to my place tomorrow and see for
yourself. I think you'll be pretty impressed."

Angus whirled. "Can we?"

"We?"

"I can't drive myself, can I?"

Kenzie bit her lip to keep from grinning. He was a cheeky
little Brit all right, and more of his father's son than had been
evident at first.

"We'll see." Ross's tone didn't hint at what he was thinking.
But his expression made Kenzie wonder if maybe he wasn't

having trouble making up his mind. He almost appeared to be feeling uncertain about whether to give in to the boy's wishes or tell him no outright. Surely an odd reaction coming from a man who seemed as self-confident as Ross Calder?

"Please?"

"Angus. We can talk about it tomorrow. Right now we're late for the movie."

"Better hurry," Kenzie agreed. "It's the only theater around and it fills up fast. Come on over after ten, okay?" She gave them directions to her house, said goodbye and walked off feeling pretty pleased with herself for having made up Ross Calder's mind for him.

Okay, so maybe she shouldn't have. After all, she wasn't stupid, and she strongly suspected that Ross Calder didn't want to have another thing to do with her. You'd have to be blind to miss the body language. He was obviously used to giving orders and having them followed. And his orders were clear: Keep away from my kid.

Not that Kenzie didn't respect those wishes. But it irked her that he could be so standoffish when Angus was so much the opposite.

Besides, she hadn't given him a single reason to dislike her, had she? Was she sending out the vibes of an ax murderess or something?

Oh, the heck with Ross Calder. Angus's reaction when he saw her birds up close would be well worth his father's unwilling participation. Kenzie had joined the local shorebird rescue society about a month after moving to Buxton. Her whitewashed cottage had had an aviary in the back, and when Kenzie's landlord had told her that the former tenants had been rescue volunteers, Kenzie had immediately decided to do the same. The moment she had been given her first orphaned baby bird to hand feed, she'd been hooked. Now she had more than a dozen feathered orphans under her care, and a tour of the aviary was a real treat for any youngster. Kenzie ought to know—she'd hosted Hatteras Elementary School field trips often enough.

But even as she stowed her bags in the back of her pickup, Kenzie's thoughts returned to Ross. Why did he act so uptight all the time? If he wasn't careful he'd wipe that sunny smile off Angus's face for good.

"I should know," Kenzie muttered ruefully.

But she wasn't going to think about her own father right now. No, sir. She'd only end up feeling as grumpy as Angus's dad.

It was a beautiful evening and she intended to enjoy it. Once she got home and finished her chores, she was going to sit on the dock, dangle her feet in the water of Pamlico Sound and watch the sun go down. And she would pretend she didn't have a care in the world.

Which, at the moment, she hadn't. She'd finished enough drawings to meet publication deadlines until the end of the week, and she didn't have any appointments in Norfolk until Thursday. That meant she was free to do whatever she wanted tomorrow, a delicious thought after all the work of the past few weeks, when she'd sat up all night waiting for the drawing muse to hit and enduring harassing phone calls from her editor, because Maureen hated missed deadlines.

As for Ross and Angus Calder, if they didn't show up tomorrow she wouldn't be at all surprised.

Only, to be honest, a little disappointed.

I must be crazy, Ross was thinking to himself. Taking Angus to a strange woman's house to look at her birds. What on earth did the kid want to do that for? After all, he'd spent nearly an hour that morning tossing bread crusts to the seagulls on the back deck. Surely Kenzie Daniels's birds couldn't be as interesting as those dive-bombing scavengers that had made the boy laugh out loud for the first time since coming to America? Or worth a drive in the growing heat of the day?

But here he was, easing the rental car onto the highway heading south toward the town of Buxton.

"Hey, look!" Angus pointed to the black-and-white Cape Hatteras lighthouse on the horizon. "Is that the one we climbed yesterday?"

"Sure is."

A few years ago the lighthouse had been moved several thousand feet inland, away from the eroding beach where it had stood for more than a hundred years. Ross had enjoyed studying the photos of this engineering phenomenon at the small National Park Ranger Station nearby, but Angus had been more excited about the climb itself.

They had made it all the way to the top without stopping, Angus ducking beneath the legs of the tourists puffing along ahead of them in order to be there first. He hadn't wanted to go back down again for the longest time, and Ross had allowed him to look his fill of the ocean, the beach, the rooftops of the houses far below, pleased to see him so animated.

Admittedly it was the first time Ross had felt a little bit at ease with his son. Not worried that he was going to say or do something to make the boy withdraw into himself, the way he had when they'd first met in England after Penelope's death.

What a bleak meeting, Ross thought, recalling how awkwardly he had stood in his former in-laws' icy drawing room while Angus, led in by a servant, had ducked his head and refused to say hello. Penelope's parents weren't even there. They had flown to Majorca, hoping the sunshine would help them get over their only daughter's death, which had occurred several weeks earlier when Penelope's commuter plane had crashed while carrying her on holiday. They had left no message for Ross, although they had known he was coming to take his son to America—nor, apparently, had they told Angus about it, either.

Angus had been unaware of the recent upheaval in his life—that his father, having only recently learned of his existence, had tried to see him, only to be denied visitation rights by his mother. When no amount of pleading, arguing or, finally, threatening had swayed Penelope from her stubborn stance, Ross had reluctantly resorted to intervention from a court of law.

A lot of good that had done him, he thought briefly. Not only had he unleashed a media frenzy thanks to the Archers' well-known name, but Angus had been spirited away to some isolated Norfolk estate. And Penelope, pleading a fragile constitution, had flown off to Naples with some millionaire boyfriend, providing even more fodder for the gossip columns.

Grimacing at the memory, he massaged the tight spot in his chest. He didn't like thinking back on those days or dwelling on how little progress he and Angus had made since then.

On the other hand, Angus seemed to have had fun being with

him yesterday and there was no reason things should be different today. Maybe a visit to MacKenzie Daniels's birds would re-capture a little of the spontaneity they'd felt while touring the lighthouse together.

That, in effect, was why he'd agreed to take Angus to Buxton.

On the other hand, he had to admit that he, too, was a little bit curious. Not so much about MacKenzie Daniels's birds, but about the woman herself.

Of course, his curiosity was purely academic. It had abso-lutely nothing to do with the fact that he felt guilty at how curtly he'd treated her on the beach yesterday. He'd not meant to do so, of course. But when she'd pointed out to him how dangerous it was to let Angus go near the water by himself he'd all but panicked at the thought of what might have happened, and at how absolutely ignorant he was of the commonsense rules of parenting. So he'd retreated behind a facade of rudeness, telling himself that he resented Kenzie Daniels for the sweetly easy way she treated his son—and the way Angus responded to her.

Okay, so maybe he did resent her a little. Ross didn't care to admit it, but you'd have to be blind not to see how much more relaxed and outgoing Angus seemed in Kenzie's presence. Far more so than he'd ever been with his father.

Ross thought back to the way Kenzie had lectured him for letting Angus go down to the beach alone, and a cold hand settled once again around his heart. Had she been right in saying Angus was too young to be trusted near the water? But how was he supposed to know these things?

Cripes, it was proving harder to be a father than it was to practice law! Maybe Alex hadn't been entirely wrong. There were so many rules to learn and so many things you had to figure out intuitively. How on earth was he ever going to get the hang of it?

"Kenzie's lucky to live here," Angus said suddenly.

Ross realized the sand dunes on either side of the highway had given way to the small shops and filling stations of Buxton. "Think so?" Ross hadn't been too impressed with the town yesterday although, to be fair, they'd turned off at the lighthouse without seeing much of it. But looking around now he wasn't inclined to change his mind, except for liking the fact that Buxton was less developed than Avon, crowded as it was with rental houses, restaurants and souvenir shops.

"What kind of birds do you think she has?" It was a question Angus had been asking pretty regularly since last night. Even the comedy he and his father had seen at the theater hadn't held his interest as long as the thought of Kenzie's birds.

"She said something about herons and egrets," Ross reminded him. Although why anyone would want to keep one of those as a pet was beyond him. He didn't like animals in general, and certainly couldn't see anyone owning anything more exotic than a goldfish.

"Look, isn't this where she said to turn? Right after the fire station?"

The road sign read Soundside Lane. "Good eye, son."

Angus grinned shyly. "Thanks."

The car bumped down a narrow paved road past thinning trees and marshland. In the distance the waters of Pamlico Sound shimmered in the sunshine. The road ended at a curving shell driveway. Ross recognized the old black pickup truck he'd seen outside the bait-and-tackle shop last night.

"Looks like this is it."

A sandy path led to the house, which was built at ground level, not elevated like newer ones designed to meet federal flood regulations. Its age showed in the weathered white siding and tin roof. A gnarled oak tree shaded the front deck. Ross had noticed yesterday that, unlike Avon, Buxton had a number of older cottages like this one, which must have been built by the original families who had populated the island. They had probably planted the trees, too, because the oak in this front yard had obviously been around for half a century or more.

Was MacKenzie Daniels a local of long standing? She didn't talk like a rural North Carolinian.

"I'm going inside." Angus was already unbuckling his seat belt.

Ross watched him race up the path toward the house, showing none of the painful uncertainty he usually exhibited in new situations.

"What is it about that woman?" he muttered in despair.

From her kitchen window, Kenzie saw the car turn into the driveway. A sudden wave of panic overwhelmed her. "Oh, my gosh, they're really here!"

After drying her hands at the sink, she hurried into the front room. "Thanks for the warning, guys," she scolded the dogs lolling on the rug.

Both of them thumped their tails on the floor but made no move to rise. If they were aware of her panic they didn't show it.

Kenzie froze as she reached for the doorknob. Was there time to brush her hair, check her makeup for smudges? She hadn't really expected them to come, although she had taken the precaution of getting up early to run a vacuum over the floors and cart the newspapers out to the recycling bin. And just in case they did show up and were hungry, she'd driven down to the Gingerbread House in Frisco for doughnuts and almond bear claws.

But there wasn't time to take a final look in the mirror. Through the front windows, she saw them coming up the walk, Angus in the lead. Kenzie switched her gaze to Ross, noticing the way the sun painted chestnut highlights in his dark hair. The way he had thrust his hands casually into the pockets of his jeans. He was wearing a faded blue T-shirt, which was stretched tight over his wide shoulders and chest.

A totally unfamiliar feeling of shyness crept over her. What had she done, inviting this man into her house? Her home was her private domain and she'd never asked a stranger to come in before. Not a darkly virile man like this one, at any rate.

She looked around as though seeing the place for the first time. What would he think of the cluttered rooms, the shabby furnishings? The peeling paint on the windows and walls? She had the feeling that Ross Calder lived in a decidedly more... genteel environment than this one.

Instantly sanity returned. She had no reason to be embarrassed by the bare wooden floors of her living room, the slouchy slipcovers on her sagging sofa, the shells and driftwood lining the windowsills.

Besides, Ross Calder and his son were here to see her birds, not to judge her for the kind of housekeeper she was.

Her skittering heartbeat slowed as she opened the front door and saw Angus clattering up the steps. She returned his bright smile, resisting the urge to sweep him into a hug. "Hi! I wasn't sure you were coming."

"I told you I wanted to see your birds, didn't I?"

Kenzie looked past him. Ross was still standing on the path below her, she on the deck. Their eyes were level as she looked a challenge at him. "How about you? Are you here under protest or as a willing participant?"

Her directness startled him. But then the corners of his mouth turned up. "Guilty as charged, I'm afraid."

Kenzie had never seen him smile before. Good grief! Did the man know he was armed and dangerous when he smiled like that? Her heart started tripping again and she could feel herself blushing. This was ridiculous! Good-looking men had smiled at her before—her former fiancé wasn't exactly homely, either, but even Brent hadn't caused this fluttering awareness of his masculinity deep inside her.

"To which charge are you referring?" she asked tartly, glad for something to say.

"To the latter. Rest assured, Ms. Daniels, there's nothing I'd rather be doing than bringing my son here to visit."

She'd never wonder again where Angus had come by his charm. When Ross Calder chose to turn it on, it hit you like a ton of bricks. And he seemed to mean what he said—unless he was a superb liar, like her father.

"Please. Just Kenzie." Again she was glad for something to say and for the fact that her voice sounded calm.

"Hey, Kenzie! Who are they?"

The dogs were sniffing at Angus through the screen door, tails wagging.

"That's Zoom and Jazz. And you should be honored. They don't get up for just anybody."

"Can I let them out here on the porch with us?"

Kenzie motioned Ross through the gate at the top of the stairs, then closed it behind him. "Go ahead."

"They look like tigers! What kind are they? Are they nice?"

"They're greyhounds. And yes, they like everybody. That orange-and-black color is called brindle."

Angus stroked the dainty heads while the dogs' tails wagged harder. "Which is which?"

"Jazz has more black in his coat."

"Retired racers?" Ross asked.

Kenzie nodded, surprised he knew.

"They're racing dogs?" Angus breathed.

"They were. In some parts of the country greyhounds are raced for sport, like horses. Zoom and Jazz ran on a track in Florida. When their careers were over they needed a place to live. I got them from a friend who runs a greyhound rescue near Disney World."

"Do they still like to run?" Angus was clearly fascinated.

"You bet. That's why I never let them outside without a leash. They'll take off like a shot. But most of the time they sleep. They're couch potatoes, really."

His freckled nose wrinkled. "Couch potatoes?"

Ross grinned. "An American word. They like to lie around watching TV."

Angus brightened. "So do I."

Ross and Kenzie both laughed. And all at once warmth bubbled inside Kenzie's heart. No doubt about it, she liked being on friendly terms with Ross much better than being at odds with him, like last night in the parking lot, when she couldn't figure out what she'd said or done to make him seem so distant toward her.

Angus turned to his father. "Could we have a greyhound?"

"When you go to college."

"That means no, doesn't it?"

"I'm afraid so."

But Angus didn't seem to care. He whirled back to Kenzie. "Are the birds here in your house?"

"They're out back. C'mon."

Leaving the dogs on the deck, she led Angus and Ross through the yard. The boy danced excitedly beside her, while Ross followed more slowly. Kenzie opened the padlock on the screen door to the shed. "This used to be a garage. Now it's kind of a hospital for sick birds."

Angus's eyes were completely round. "A bird hospital?"

"That's right. So you'll need to be quiet. These are wild birds, not pets. They'll be scared of you, so don't move too fast or get too close, okay?"

"Okay." His voice had dropped to an awed whisper.

Grinning, Kenzie's eyes sought Ross's. Didn't the guy *know* how adorable his kid was?

Apparently not. Instead of smiling indulgently at his son, he was studying the sagging roof of the shed, probably wondering, Kenzie didn't doubt, if it was safe to enter.

Her mouth set. "Come on in. It won't collapse on you."

The front half of the shed was crammed with boxes, cabinets and mismatched drawers. Two refrigerators and a chest freezer took up one wall. Ross looked around at the cluttered workbench with its scale, storage bins and stacks of kitchen and medical utensils. Heavy leather gloves were draped over the sink. It was cleaner than he'd expected, and apparently structurally sound after all.

"Oh, wow! Look at that!"

Ross turned. Angus was pointing at the back wall, which was divided into rows of cages, as well as pens that opened into fenced outdoor aviaries. About a dozen birds were staring back at them, some uneasily, some calmly. Ross recognized a pelican, a hawk and an egret. The rest escaped him.

Angus was tugging at Kenzie's arm. "Kenzie! What kind of bird is that?"

"A red-tailed hawk. Don't get too close. He's just getting over being sick. If you startle him he'll try to fly away and hurt himself on the wire. Do you know what that one is?"

"A pelican?"

"Right."

"What happened to him?"

"His bill got tangled in fishing wire and he couldn't feed himself. He was half-starved when he came here, but he's gained a lot of weight since then. I may set him free tomorrow."

"But why would he want to leave? He's got his own swimming pool!"

They were both whispering. Still, Ross noticed that Angus was practically shaking with both excitement and the strain of not showing it so he wouldn't scare the birds. Ross had seen him this overwhelmed only once before—when they'd gone to a toy store in Manhattan and he'd been allowed to operate a model train by himself. He was usually so withdrawn in public, but right now he certainly didn't look like a kid who was shy or scared or had recently lost his mother. Right now he was looking at Kenzie with his eyes glowing a bright, happy blue.

"I'd keep him if I were you. He's the prettiest bird in the world!"

Even Ross had to laugh at that.

"Don't you like him?" Angus demanded.

"It has to be the ugliest thing I've ever seen."

"That's not true!"

"Oh, yes it is. He reminds me of...of some throwback to the dinosaur age."

Ross had been teasing, but Angus glared at him tearfully. "You don't like anything!"

Ross turned away, but not before Kenzie saw the glimmer of pain in his eyes. "You've got to admit they're a little bizarre," she said quickly. "And there's nothing pretty about that bill when he decides to use it."

"Do pelicans bite?"

"Oh, my, yes."

Angus backed away quickly.

"How'd you get into this business?" Ross asked, determined to ignore Angus's outburst. "Are you a veterinarian?"

"Just a volunteer." Kenzie opened the chest freezer and began rummaging inside. "When they run out of room at the raptor refuge up in Manteo they send them down here. I'm sort of an overflow center."

"How long have you been doing this?"

"About a year. I had to learn the ropes the hard way. Like what to do with a vomiting owl and how not to get your eyes gouged out by a heron. Want to feed them some fish, Angus?"

"Could I really?"

"Sure." She leaned deeper into the freezer, unaware that she was giving Ross a clear view of...well, of a very firm, muscular body. White shorts and long, tanned legs. A cropped T-shirt that rose higher as she leaned over farther, revealing more sun-browned skin.

Ross's hurt at Angus's remark seemed to fade at the simple pleasure of admiring Kenzie's sweetly sexy curves. She seemed so wholly unaware of her appeal. Surely she had to realize the affect she had on every man who met her? And what about the way she was affecting him? Much as he disliked admitting it, he was starting to view Kenzie Daniels in a far more personal light than he wanted to. Yes, he was aware of the sweetness and warmth that Angus had responded to so readily, but this purely sexual pull of attraction was more than he'd bargained for—and something he certainly didn't welcome. He had enough to worry about just dealing with his son!

"Eeeww!" said Angus, pulling Ross back to the present.

Kenzie had pulled a glassy-eyed fish from the freezer.

"Change your mind?" she asked with a grin, dangling it in front of the boy.

"Um—"

"Would gloves help?"

"Oh, yes, thanks." Angus looked relieved.

"Don't blame you, sport. I hate touching slimy stuff, too."

She helped him pull on the heavy gloves while Ross watched, then showed him how to feed each of the birds. Angus didn't even flinch when a gannet with a long, pointy bill lunged forward to snatch the fish. And he whooped aloud when a great blue heron swallowed its meal whole.

"Did you see that? Did you see that, Kenzie? It went down his throat *sideways!*"

"Pretty amazing," she agreed, laughing.

When Angus had given each bird a treat, Kenzie led him away to wash up while Ross followed without speaking, muscular arms folded in front of his wide chest. Pushing a footstool up to the sink, Kenzie lifted Angus onto it, chatting unconcernedly all the while. "Let's scrub that smell away, okay? Here, use plenty of soap. How about something to drink? Are you thirsty?"

"Uh-huh."

"And hungry? I've got pastries in the house."

"Ooh! What kind?"

She twinkled at him. "We'll have to go see. Wait, wait. You missed a spot."

He scrubbed quickly at the offending hand she'd tapped, then jumped off the stool and rushed outside without asking his father's permission.

Kenzie hung away the towel. "Hope you don't mind him having sweets."

"How do you do that?" Ross countered gruffly.

She turned to look at him. "What?"

"Make it seem so easy."

Her hand stilled. He was standing there with his thumbs hooked in his belt, his expression unsmiling and oddly vulnerable. She'd never noticed before, but his eyes were a darker blue than Angus's.

Something in her heart seemed to turn over. No way, she told herself firmly. No way was she going to start feeling sorry for this man!

But she wasn't going to pretend to misunderstand him, either.

"Because it *is* easy. With a boy like that—"

"I don't mean just Angus. You've obviously been around a lot of them. How many children do you have?"

She blinked. "I—I don't—I'm not married."

"Oh." He was silent for a moment, then looked at her with something very close to helplessness. "Then how do you do it?"

Kenzie bit her lip. Something obviously wasn't right here. While she had no idea what it was, her heart had started aching in a funny way. "It isn't anything you can explain," she said softly. "It's just something you know. In here." When she touched her heart, his expression changed, and she knew for sure now that what she saw in his eyes was pain.

"I wouldn't know about that," he said roughly.

Heaven help her, but some strange compulsion was making her reach out to cover his big hand with hers. "I wouldn't be so sure about that."

"What do you mean?"

His fingers had closed over hers and the heat rushed to Kenzie's cheeks because of the way he was looking at her—as though so much depended on her answer.

"I mean that deep down you *do* know the right things to do for Angus. It's supereasy when you...um...you love somebody."

For some inexplicable reason that word—*love*—stuck in her throat. She'd never minded uttering it before. The heated color in her cheeks deepened and she snatched her hand away before Ross noticed. What in heaven's name was wrong with her?

"Kenzie?" Angus was peering around the door at her. Those blue eyes, that cute grin, made her feel instantly in control again.

"What is it, sport?"

"Would you hurry up, please? I can hear those pastries calling me from your kitchen."

Lost in thought, she followed him across the yard. Something was definitely not right between Ross Calder and his son. They seemed uncomfortable with each other, as though they weren't used to—or even liked—being together. And Ross was so up-tight around Angus that the tension was almost a physical thing humming through him. And as for that oddly vulnerable moment they'd just shared...surely that had been an unspoken plea for help?

Kenzie tried to ignore the painful squeezing of her heart. She knew all about bad relationships between parents and their off-spring—she and her father hadn't spoken for more than a year. In fact, the last thing he'd said to her was that he didn't consider her his daughter anymore.

But Angus was only seven. How could you get on bad footing with a kid that age?

And where did Mrs. Calder fit into this?

Unless Ross and his wife were divorced? Or in the process of divorcing? That would explain her absence and the awkwardness Ross exhibited around his son. Maybe Angus resented him for the breakup, and this trip to the Outer Banks was Ross's way of trying to make up for it.

A weekend father. Kenzie knew the type: caught up in their careers, they took no part in raising their own kids and in fact were little better than strangers to them. Then the marriage ended and they found themselves on the outside of the fence, trying desperately to squeeze a loving relationship into those brief, alternate weekend visitations.

Which didn't always work.

Poor Ross! And poor Angus!

She opened the back door for the boy, resisting the urge to ruffle his dark curls. Her heart ached, imagining how he felt, knowing how hard it was to mend a damaged relationship. Sometimes impossible.

"The doughnuts are on the table. Help yourself. I'll pour you a glass of milk."

Ross came in through the screen door behind her. He nearly filled the small kitchen, reminding Kenzie that he was more the rugged male type than the vulnerable man of a moment ago. "Coffee?" she asked quickly.

"If it's not too much trouble."

"No. I've already ground the beans."

Ross looked around the room while she fetched cream and sugar and arranged the pastries on a plate. An old farmhouse sink, a few lopsided cabinets painted white, a laminated countertop straight out of the 1940s. Nothing like the sleek Corian-and-stainless-steel condo kitchen he once owned in New York before leaving his old law firm at the beginning of the year, when the battle over Angus had started heating up overseas.

Clearly whatever Kenzie Daniels did for a living didn't pay much. Granted, you didn't need a lot to live like this.

By now Angus had made himself at home at the oak table. The boy's short legs dangled from one of the mismatched chairs as he munched on a buttermilk doughnut and looked around him with the bright interest of a typical seven-year-old. Again he seemed not at all shy in his surroundings.

"This place reminds me of Norfolk," he announced.

"Your grandfather's place?" Kenzie asked, much to Ross's surprise. What did she know about Angus's family?

"Yeah. Everything's old there, too." He talked around a mouthful of doughnut. "I like it."

"Did you spend a lot of time in Norfolk?"

Angus hesitated a moment, then said with a shrug, "Summer holidays and Christmas, too."

Kenzie set a mug of coffee in front of where Ross was standing. "Why is it that Angus has a British accent and you don't?"

"I'm American, he's not."

"Oh. Then Angus's mother—"

"My wife...my ex-wife is...was English."

Kenzie caught her breath. Was?

"She passed away earlier this year."

The shock of those words jolted her. She glanced quickly at Angus, who sat with his eyes glued to his plate. "Oh, Angus, I'm sorry."

"It's okay." But he wouldn't look at her and she saw his little Adam's apple bob convulsively as he swallowed. Her heart contracted and she glanced at Ross, who was studying his son with the same pained intensity.

"Maybe we'd better go, Angus," Ross said quietly.

"But I haven't drunk my milk yet!"

"And you haven't had your bear claw," Kenzie added meaningfully to Ross.

"What's a bear claw?" Angus asked, immediately intrigued.

"It's like a turnover, with almonds in it."

Angus scrunched up his freckled nose. "I'd rather have another doughnut. Please?" he added, smiling shyly.

The awkward moment was over. Kenzie handed him the plate. "Eat all you like, sport."

Ross sat down at the table, the tension draining out of him. This had been the first time Penelope's death had been mentioned to a stranger, and Angus had handled it much better than he'd thought. So had Kenzie, by knowing better than to ask more questions the way other people probably would have.

"If I had your birds I'd try to make pets out of them," Angus said to Kenzie, a milk mustache painted above his lip.

Grinning, she tossed him a napkin. "So you wouldn't mind pelican poop all over your room?"

"Yuck. I hadn't thought of that." Balancing his empty glass on his plate, he set both next to the sink. "I think I'd rather have a dog. They go outside when they need to use the bathroom and...hey, Kenzie! What are all these drawings?"

Through the opened door leading from the pantry, he had caught sight of her workroom and quickly went in.

"Angus, don't poke——" Ross warned.

"No, it's okay. Look at them, if you like." She rose to pour more coffee into Ross's mug. "How about another bear claw?"

"They're hard to resist," he answered with a smile.

"Tell me about it. I'll have to run an extra mile this afternoon."

Ross had already decided that she was a runner—a serious one from the look of her. He realized he liked that about her, because he was one, too. "How often do you run?"

"Every day, if I can."

"On the beach?"

"Not always. The sand is too soft. I prefer the trails near the lighthouse." Kenzie thought about asking him to join her, suspecting he was a runner, like her, then instantly squelched the idea. Much as she liked having company on her jogs, she didn't think he would agree. Besides, who would look after Angus in the meantime?

She stole another glance at Ross to find him looking at the water outside the window. His face was a dark contrast to the brightness outside, and she couldn't help admiring his profile; his straight nose, his lean cheeks, especially the sensual curve of his mouth. Quickly she dropped her gaze. Why on earth was she studying Ross Calder's mouth?

Angus's head appeared around the door. "Hey, Kenzie, are these cartoons?"

She looked up, relieved. "Yes."

"How come they don't make any sense?"

She laughed. "Because they're for grown-ups. They're supposed to make grown-ups think about things that have happened around the country recently. They're political cartoons," she explained, catching Ross's eye.

"They're all over the place! Come see. Wow! She's got a cool computer, too!"

Time to reel in his overinquisitive son.

But Ross, too, stopped short in the doorway, staring. Angus was right. There were black-and-white ink drawings all over the walls, some framed, some pinned or taped, many of them only half-finished. There were more on a huge drawing table in the corner, which was crammed with art supplies, along with a computer and sophisticated scanning equipment. Two televisions were set up nearby, one tuned to CNN, the other to a local news broadcast. VCRs were recording both.

Kenzie appeared behind them.

"Did you draw these?"

She nodded.

"For work or pleasure?"

"I'm the political cartoonist for the *Norfolk Messenger.*"

"Wow!" Angus breathed. "I've never met a cartoonist before."

Neither had Ross. Thumbs hooked in his pockets, he studied the sketches spread out on the cluttered stand. A few of them dealt with the current administration's proposal to step up offshore drilling near Point Edwards Bay in Alaska, a controversy that had been commanding front-page headlines when Ross and

Angus had left New York two days ago. They were extremely well drawn, politically astute...and cuttingly funny.

Intrigued, Ross studied the ones hanging on the wall. Most of them seemed to deal with local officials he didn't know, poking not-so-gentle fun at their foibles, while others made scathing statements about political leaders across the nation— especially in Washington.

"You drew these?"

Kenzie's lips twitched. "You seem incredulous. Why? Do I come across as that much of a dumb Southern blonde?"

"Trust me, Ms. Daniels, you do not come across as *any* sort of stereotype."

Kenzie frowned. Was she supposed to take that as a compliment? Being unique, if that was what he meant, could be a good thing...or very bad. It was impossible to tell, because although he was looking at her he wasn't smiling.

She felt her breath catch on some odd pain in her throat. Why did he always seem to be so darned...vulnerable to her? As though he hadn't been given much reason in life to smile? Had his wife's death hurt him that badly? And why the heck did she care?

Fortunately Ross had turned his attention back to the drawings. "You've got a very keen eye for politics, Ms. Daniels. But you seem to think extraordinarily poorly of lawyers."

"Doesn't everybody?"

The sudden sharpness of her tone surprised him. Turning, he saw that her mouth was set in a hard line and that her eyes were snapping. He'd never noticed before that they were light blue and had flecks of gold in them.

"You don't, ah, care for lawyers?"

"In general, no. If Washington were a cesspool—and sometimes I think it may be—they'd be the bottom feeders."

"Oh, really?"

"Yes, really," she said with unexpected heat.

"That seems rather harsh."

Her chin tipped. "But accurate."

"My father's a lawyer," Angus piped up helpfully.

Kenzie's gaze flew to Ross's intractable face. "Is that right?"

"It is."

A totally inexplicable feeling of betrayal washed over her. She should have known! He wasn't vulnerable or hiding some sort of inner pain! She'd misread those feelings, hadn't realized that his reticence was really an air of superiority and that the inscrutable expression he wore whenever he spoke to her was actually a habit perfected in the courtroom, where it could prove a huge disadvantage if the other side of the bench knew what you were thinking.

No wonder Angus wasn't entirely comfortable with this man! Not to resort to stereotypes, but all the lawyers Kenzie knew— and being from Washington she knew plenty—weren't exactly the warm and fuzzy, touchy-feely type. Furthermore, they were rarely cut out to be loving fathers.

Like her own.

Oh, yes, Kenzie knew exactly how hard it was to have a decent relationship with a coldhearted lawyer for a father. And the situation was made even worse for Ross and Angus, who were obviously grappling in different ways to come to terms with the former Mrs. Calder's death. Grief, instead of bringing them together, was driving a wedge between them.

"Kenzie? Can I let the dogs in? I hear them crying on the porch."

Her expression softened as she looked down at Angus. The poor kid, she thought, aching. I know something of what he's going through. "Sure you can, sport."

When Angus grinned his thanks at her she smiled back, her cheeks dimpling. The gesture was absolutely pure and natural, and Ross, watching them, felt jealous longing flare like a white-hot brand inside him. How come Kenzie never smiled like that at him? And why wouldn't he share the intimacy between them? Why did he feel himself the outsider here? Okay, so Kenzie Daniels seemed to have made some kind of favorable impression on his son. How could he not admire her bird hospital, her career as a cartoonist, a house on an island and a pair of tiger-striped dogs? With no vested interest in their relationship, she could also treat the boy with the easy familiarity Ross didn't dare to. Maybe Angus was even beginning to feel some sort of displaced maternal affection for her.

Good God! The thought was enough to make any single father panic.

"Come on, Angus. We've got to go."

His harsh words made Angus look so stricken and Kenzie so disappointed that he had to grit his teeth to resist changing his mind though he didn't want to admit it, Angus wasn't the only one falling victim to the warmth of Kenzie's smiles. "We appreciate your hospitality, Ms. Daniels, but it's getting late."

Angus hung his head. "Thanks, Kenzie," he mumbled. "I had fun."

Kenzie was tempted to yell "Objection!" but knew better. Just like a lawyer, she thought furiously, taking no notice of anybody else's feelings!

"You're welcome, Angus." She squeezed his shoulder, then hastily shoved the remaining doughnuts into a bag. "For later," she whispered.

Straightening, she found Ross's eyes nailing into her. Almost defiantly she tipped her chin. Without another word, he turned and walked out of the door.

She watched the car bump down the driveway and shook with anger. How dare that man treat his son that way? The kid had just lost his mother, for crying out loud! Couldn't Ross see that what Angus wanted—craved—was simply a little love and warmth?

"Fat chance he'll get it from the likes of him," Kenzie muttered, shutting the front door none too gently.

Zoom and Jazz, aware of her anger, lifted their heads to look at her. Kenzie knelt to fondle their ears. "Settle down, guys. I'm not mad at you. I'm just obsessing."

About the wrong thing. If she was going to fret about a damaged father-child relationship, she'd be better off worrying about her own.

Yeah, right.

And as for the conflicting emotions Ross Calder aroused within her—well, he happened to be good-looking, even sexy, and it was understandable that she, as a healthy young woman, would respond to that. But never mind that there might be a perfectly good explanation for him bolting out of her house like that, dragging poor Angus along with him, or that there were other, kinder emotions burning beneath his icy demeanor. He was still a lawyer, a bottom feeder of the lowliest kind, and she'd be darned if she'd respond to him in any positive way or feel the least bit sorry for him. Provided she ever saw him again.

Scowling, she turned to tackle the dishes in the sink.

Chapter Three

"I'm telling you, Delia, he's a different kid around her. Totally open, friendly, eager to please. It's almost a kind of hero worship. Everything she says and does is 'supercool' to him. I don't understand it."

"Do you think she reminds him of his mother?"

Ross tucked the receiver under his chin and pulled the pizza from the oven. Setting it on the counter, he envisioned Penelope, tall and darkly elegant, accompanying him to the opening night of the London symphony in a clinging Halston dress. Then Kenzie Daniels in shorts and a T-shirt, pulling dead fish out of a freezer. If he wasn't so busy brooding, he would have smiled at the comparison.

"Not a chance."

"Maybe she reminds him of somebody else. A housekeeper or nanny?"

Ross had met both women at Penelope's funeral. One had been extremely old, the other dumpy and dark. "No way."

"Maybe she just has a natural way with kids."

"Meaning I don't?"

He could actually hear Delia hesitating over the phone line.

He gripped the receiver hard, dreading her answer. Bad enough that Delia had taken it upon herself to call and check up on them, and even worse that Angus had told her all about Kenzie the moment he'd answered the phone. Gushed on and on about her, actually, so that Delia had asked Ross for clarification when it was his turn to talk.

Now he was going to have to listen to things he didn't want to hear and to admit things he didn't want to acknowledge.

"He misses his mother, Ross. And maybe, in a way, he's blaming you for her loss."

His heart cramped. "Now wait a minute—"

"It's totally unfounded, I know. But he's a little boy, Ross. Kids tend to look at things differently. They really don't know how to weigh what's fair and what's not. And you took him away from his home, his grandparents—"

"Who are even more cold and unloving than I am." He tried to sound as if he was making fun of himself, but his voice was flat. He'd never felt less like joking.

"Give him time, Ross. And you, too. It's only been a few months! He'll warm up to you once he gets to know you better. After all, you've been a stranger to him all his life, and I wouldn't be surprised if Penelope said unkind things about you to him when you first sued for visitation rights."

Which had happened just before she'd died. Did Angus blame him in some way for that? Ross wondered suddenly. But who could have known that Penelope would be killed in a plane crash while locked in a bitter legal dispute over the son she had never acknowledged to Ross?

For God's sake, some strange lump was forming in Ross's throat as he wondered if his chances with Angus were doomed. He closed his eyes only to feel them stinging. Were those tears? It was definitely time to get a grip.

"Is that your closing statement, counselor?"

But Delia wasn't about to let him off the hook. "Please, Ross."

"Okay, okay." Damn! Now he'd burned himself on the pizza tray. Cursing inwardly, he held his thumb under the faucet. "Look, gotta run. Supper's ready."

"Just remember what I said. And relax, will you? Stop trying so hard."

"Always have to get in the last word, don't you?" he countered, but this time he succeeded in sounding as though he didn't mind.

Delia chuckled. No doubt she was relieved that he'd chosen to lighten up—though in reality Ross's heart couldn't have been heavier. He wished she'd never called him, wished she'd refrained from overstepping professional lines to discuss such personal matters with him. "Gotta run," he said again, and was relieved that this time his voice didn't waver. "I'll check in with you at the office tomorrow."

"Not until Thursday, Ross. You promised."

"Okay, okay."

He hung up to find Angus lying on his stomach in front of the TV watching cartoons. Handing him a slice of pizza, Ross gestured toward the characters cavorting on the screen. "Who are they?"

"That's Johnny Savage and his friend, Major Stanton."

"Oh? What do they do?"

"Fight aliens. Most of the time they're humanoid. But that one's an octopus. He's a bad guy. His men squirt ink on people to capture them."

"I see," said Ross, who didn't. What had happened to the simple cartoons of his childhood? Elmer Fudd hunting wascally wabbits? The Road Runner foiling Wile E. Coyote?

His brother's words came back to haunt him. *What makes you think you can raise a seven-year-old?*

Ignorance, obviously. Would he ever get the hang of this parenting thing? Not just learning how to look after a kid, feed him, clothe him, keep him from harm, but find common ground for a relationship? And did he have it in him after all this time to embrace a whole new culture?

Ross wasn't sure.

And at the moment he felt very much alone.

"So," he said with forced gaiety when the cartoon ended. "Given some thought to what you'd like for your birthday? I need ideas, you know."

Angus's eyes widened. "Is it Wednesday already?"

"Day after tomorrow."

"And you—you want to give me a present?"

"Why not?"

"I heard you telling someone on the phone that you'd already gotten me something."

"When was that?"

"The morning we left to come here."

That must have been Delia, calling to remind Ross about Angus's birthday; offering to buy a gift and send it to their beach house in the event he had forgotten.

But Ross had already bought the model train set Angus had fallen in love with at the toy store last month. Because of its size he'd brought along only the engine for Angus to unwrap on Wednesday, plus a few other things he hoped the boy would like.

Now he frowned, wondering if he should remind Angus not to eavesdrop on telephone calls between grown-ups. Surely this was a good time to drive the message home?

But the memory of how the boy had withdrawn from him in Kenzie Daniels's aviary earlier that day stopped him cold. Back then he'd only mentioned his dislike of pelicans, not chastised the boy for bad behavior. Still, he didn't want to be the cause of the boy's frustrated tears again. The thought made him ache inside.

"So obviously you know you'll be getting presents on Wednesday," he said instead. "So much for a surprise. But you also get one birthday wish."

"A wish? What kind of wish?"

"The best kind. You can ask for anything you like. Within reason, of course. Something special you've been wanting very badly."

"For real?"

The boy's eagerness tore at Ross's heart. If only it was always this easy. "Sure. My mother started the tradition when I was just a bit younger than you. Each year my brother Alex and I were allowed to make one birthday wish, which Mom did her best to fulfill. She always said it was better than blowing out candles and just hoping it'd come true."

"That never happens," Angus agreed.

"I know."

"Did your dad help make those wishes come true?"

My dad was the wish, Ross thought, then cleared his throat. "He sure did. So go ahead and tell me. What would you like?"

Angus's eyes widened. "I can wish for anything?"

"As I said, within reason."

"Can we go out to dinner?"

"On Wednesday night? Is that your wish?"

Angus nodded.

"Sure we can. Is that all you want?"

"Um, well..." Angus looked down at his sneakers. "Can we take Kenzie along?"

"What?"

He must have spoken sharply, because Angus's face fell.

"You said I could have a wish," he mumbled. "And I want to have dinner with Kenzie."

Ross set his plate aside and drew in a deep breath. The last thing he wanted was to encourage further contact with a beautiful-but-lawyer-hating woman his son seemed to be unnaturally drawn to. "Are you sure that's what you want?"

Angus nodded.

"Not that inflatable kayak at the hardware store across the street?"

Angus shook his head.

"Or that fishing trip on Pamlico Sound?"

"No, thank you." He was still mumbling and he wouldn't look at Ross.

"Or that train set you saw at Garrison's Toy Store?"

He saw the struggle on his son's face and realized he was being unfair.

"Angus, wait a minute—"

"No, I told you what I wanted. I want to have dinner with you and with Kenzie."

Those weren't Penelope's vivid blue eyes staring back at him all at once. They were Ross's own, and they were too darned determined. The tilt of that chin was all too familiar, as well.

"Okay, okay. We'll invite her to dinner." Ross took a deep breath and struggled to make his tone lighter. "Got a restaurant in mind?"

Angus brightened. "There's one on the sound near the place where we turned to go to the lighthouse. It has a deck on the water. Can we go there?"

"Did you happen to notice the name?"

Disappointed, Angus shook his head.

"Would you recognize it if we drove by again?"

"I think so. Does that mean we can eat there?"

"If we can find it."

"Can we look now?"

Ross glanced out of the windows. The sun had set, but there was plenty of daylight left. He drew another deep breath. Anything to make the boy smile again. "Come on."

Following Angus down the steps, he couldn't help thinking how unfair it was that the one thing that seemed to make Angus happy was the one thing he would have preferred to deny him: more time in the company of one MacKenzie Daniels.

For God's sake, he didn't want Angus getting emotionally attached to someone he'd never see again once they returned to New York! And he himself definitely didn't want a woman cluttering up his life, not even for the week and a half that remained of his vacation. After Penelope, it was the last thing he wanted, ever. Never mind that Kenzie Daniels seemed to be everything Penelope had never been: sweet, unassuming, very kind and generous. Not to mention funny and warm and such a natural with kids that he couldn't help envying her that ease.

In the car, he cleared his throat. "Mind if I ask why you want to invite Ms. Daniels so badly?"

"Because I like her."

"I agree she's nice, but you shouldn't get so intimate with strangers, son."

"What's intimate?"

"Eh...make friends with them so fast. We don't know anything about her."

"But we do! She can fly kites and she rescues birds and has two greyhounds and draws cartoons!"

How to argue with that kind of logic? Ross took a stab at it. "You know a lot about Marty, don't you?" Marty was the handyman at Ross's apartment building.

"Yeah."

"And you think he's nice, too. But you've never asked me to invite him to supper."

"That's different."

Lord, the boy was stubborn. "In what way?"

"He's nice to me, but he's not a friend. I mean, it's different with Kenzie. She doesn't work for you and doesn't have to like me if she doesn't want to...and...and..."

He was clearly struggling to find the right words. Ross racked his brains to do the same, desperate to keep the line of communication open. This was the first time Angus had ever tried sharing his feelings with him.

"I think I see what you mean," he said slowly. "Marty's nice, but he's really just doing his job."

Angus looked relieved. "Yeah. But Kenzie doesn't *need* to be nice to me. She just is. She didn't yell when my kite landed on her, and then she showed me how to fly it."

Ross's eyes left the road to settle on his son. "You hit her with your kite?"

Angus blushed. "I didn't mean to. It fell on her. Well, next to her. But I think it scared her. She was sleeping on her towel."

"Oh." So that was it. Nothing like a disaster to break the ice between strangers. The fact that she hadn't berated him had obviously made a big impression on Angus. And his gratitude had strengthened into liking the more time he spent with her. Ross had to admit that, to a seven-year-old, Kenzie Daniels must seem very exotic and interesting—much more interesting than having a dour old lawyer for a father.

Ross's spirits sank at the thought. Angus certainly hadn't indicated any interest in his father's career the first time he had been shown Ross's office in Queens, where he had been introduced to Delia and the others in the practice. Granted, the run-down warehouse that served as headquarters for Calder & Hayes LLC wasn't much to look at. Not like the glass-fronted high-rise on Madison Avenue, where Ross had practiced corporate law for eight years. Where he had been a full partner, highly paid and widely respected, and had lived only a few blocks away in an elegant town house he shared with Penelope, surrounded by the stores, restaurants and the theater and museum districts she had loved to haunt.

And now? What had the bitter battle for Angus—blown out of all proportion first by Penelope and then by the bloodthirsty English tabloids—cost him? He was no longer a high-powered attorney in a prestigious Manhattan firm, but a partner in a tiny law office that no one in midtown Manhattan had ever heard of, doing more pro bono work than not because most of his clients were the indigent and homeless of the city who couldn't afford to pay. Nowadays he supposed he was barely one step above being a public defender—something Penelope had thought utterly amusing when she'd found out.

"My, my, how far the mighty have fallen," she had said to him at her bitchiest best. That had been at their last meeting, back in February, after Ross had shown up at her parents' elegant London town house to demand one last time that Penelope bring the boy back from wherever it was she had hidden him, to be reasonable, to at least allow father and son to meet, for God's sake! But Penelope wasn't interested in talking about Angus. She had wanted to hear all the sordid details about his downfall, how Ross's senior partners had asked him to step down, that the publicity—the firm had an office in London—was damaging their image, how it wouldn't do for the firm to become entangled in a custody battle between Ross and the daughter of Sir Edmund Archer.

"Hey! Hey, stop! There it is!"

Jerked from his black thoughts, Ross hit the brakes too hard. A horn blared behind him. "Sorry. Where?"

Angus pointed. The Boathouse. A two-story restaurant set back against the sound, the parking lot filled with cars. The wide front porch was packed with people waiting to be seated.

"You sure know how to pick 'em," Ross said with a crooked smile. "Come on. Let's see if we can get reservations for Wednesday night."

They could. And Ross had to admit that the dining room was cheery with its cypress-paneled walls and nautical decorations. The food didn't look bad, either.

"I want to sit at the window," Angus whispered. "Can you ask?"

The hostess, writing down their names, overheard and smiled. "I'll be sure and save the best table for you. You can watch the sun go down over the sound."

Angus smiled back at her shyly. "Thanks."

No doubt about it, the kid was opening up. Maybe Delia had been right. All he needed was to give it time.

"Nice choice," Ross said, giving in to his feelings and tousling Angus's hair in the doorway.

For once the boy didn't draw away. "Really?"

"Really. Kenzie'll love it."

That earned him a shy smile all his own. Side by side they went back to the car, Ross feeling swellheaded with pride. Maybe he was starting to get the hang of this thing after all.

And if Angus's happiness meant being nice to Kenzie Daniels, well, he could do that, too. At least long enough to give the boy a birthday dinner he'd remember.

"I don't believe it!" Kenzie gritted her teeth and pounded her fist on the steering wheel. If the dump truck ahead of her slowed down any further they'd both be crawling. She'd been following him since Nags Head, unable to pass because of all the oncoming traffic. Usually Saturdays were the worst time to try and navigate Highway 12, but this was midweek, for crying out loud.

She downshifted as the dump truck slowed to veer around two cyclists, then glanced at her watch. Ross and Angus were picking her up in an hour and she was still twenty miles from home.

Nothing like a hissy fit to sour her mood even further, she thought. She was already tired and cranky after a morning spent in the *Norfolk Messenger* offices, summoned to a meeting that couldn't wait until tomorrow, when she'd already planned to show up anyway. At least Maureen, her editor, had felt bad about springing the planning session on her without warning and had taken her to lunch—though they'd ended up waiting seemingly forever for their food.

Then the long drive back, with Kenzie starting to feel a little pressured about the time. The situation had worsened when her pickup had stalled just north of the Oregon Inlet bridge, the needle on the temperature gauge buried on Hot.

The radiator, of course. She'd been nursing the old one longer than she should have with a gallon of coolant she kept in the bed. The tow truck had taken too long, the radiator hadn't been in stock, and she had whiled away the afternoon at the convenience store across the street reading pulp magazines and wondering how she was going to afford the repairs until a replacement part was shipped down from Elizabeth City.

Now she was stuck behind a slow-moving vehicle and about

to succumb to a screaming bout of road rage. Didn't the driver ahead of her know she had a date—with two good-looking guys, no less? Couldn't he pull over and let her by?

Angus had sounded so grown-up when he'd called to ask her to dinner. Surprised and flattered, she'd accepted at once. Then she remembered that Ross would be there, too. "Are you sure your dad doesn't mind?"

"Oh, no. He said you should come."

Yeah, sure. Kenzie could picture him agreeing with that stoic lawyer's look that Angus was too young and unsophisticated to read. Still, she was surprised at how much she was looking forward to the evening. She had a number of friends among Buxton's permanent residents and went out with them often. But she'd never been invited to celebrate a seven-year-old English charmer's birthday. Not at the Boathouse, which, after all, was outrageously expensive.

"Eight. Angus is eight as of today," Kenzie reminded herself. She had spent most of yesterday working on his present. She couldn't wait to see what he thought of it. No doubt Ross would find it silly. Like most of the lawyers Kenzie knew, he probably had no sense of humor.

The dump truck put on its blinker, downshifted, and turned into a construction site. Honking and waving her thanks, Kenzie sped away.

She fed the dogs and the birds in record time, then leaped into the shower. After wrapping her wet hair in a towel, she dried herself off and padded into the bedroom. No time to obsess over what to wear. She seized a dress from the closet and pulled it on, whipped out the blow dryer, then raced to put on her makeup.

"Kenzie!"

Crud! She hadn't even heard the car drive up, and here she was still barefoot and lacking mascara. "Come on in! Be careful not to let the dogs out!"

The screen door slammed. Angus's light footsteps sounded, followed by his father's.

"Where are you, Kenzie?"

"In the bedroom. I'll be out in a minute. There's juice in the fridge. Help yourselves if you're thirsty."

She slipped on her watch, fastened a thin gold chain around

her neck, spritzed on a trace of perfume. Her sandals were by the kitchen door. Barefoot, she waltzed out to fetch them.

"Oh, my," she said.

Ross and Angus were at the counter, Ross pouring orange juice into a glass. They turned at the sound of her voice. She stared.

"Angus! You look super!"

He was wearing a new set of shorts and a collared shirt, obviously purchased from a local surf shop. The cargo shorts were sage in color, the Hawaiian shirt a riot of palm trees, hibiscus and exotic birds. His shoes were also new, the slouchy kind of sneakers worn by surfers and skateboarders. His still-damp hair was neatly combed.

"Do you really like it?"

"Way cool. I'm glad I dressed up, too."

She had put on a knee-length sundress with spaghetti straps in periwinkle-blue—her favorite color. She wore her blond hair down. Her only jewelry was the delicate gold chain that nestled in the hollow of her tanned throat.

Shifting her focus from Angus to his father, she felt her cheeks grow warm. Like him or not, you had to admit that Ross Calder was one good-looking man. Angus must have talked him into buying something new, as well, because the fine white muslin shirt he wore was bright and crisp. The sleeves were rolled back in a casually masculine way and the open collar revealed an even more masculine expanse of muscled chest. Kenzie wasn't sure how a pair of ordinary khaki pants could look so sexy, but Ross Calder definitely pulled it off.

She struggled to regain her composure as she slipped on her sandals. Reminded herself that, good-looking though he might be, he was still a member of that greedy, grasping, heartless class of professionals who lived for the thrill of making money, of working a judge and jury until their clients went free whether they knew them to be guilty or not.

Like her father.

Whom she had loved desperately as a little girl but who had betrayed her in the end, and who had turned everyone in her family but her mother against her when Kenzie had courageously exposed him for the man he was.

Even after all this time the pain of it clawed at her.

"Kenzie?"

She had to swallow before she could answer. "Yes, Angus?"

"You look really, really pretty."

She gave a strangled laugh of gratitude and relief and pulled him impulsively into her arms. "Happy birthday, you little goofball! How does it feel to be eight?"

"I feel very grown-up, thank you."

Was it her imagination, or did he look a little disappointed when she let him go? She hugged him again for good measure. Funny, but she'd forgotten how good it felt to hug a kid.

Straightening, she found herself eye-to-eye with Ross. He was wearing his lawyer's look again, revealing absolutely nothing of what he was thinking.

Her chin tipped. "Thanks for inviting me."

"It was Angus's idea."

"Oh." Her heart sank.

"And he's right. You do look really, really pretty."

Heat flooded her cheeks. "Thank you."

"My pleasure."

The way he said it made a shiver flee down her spine. Confused and breathless, she gathered up her purse, sunglasses and a padded envelope from the kitchen table.

Angus's eyes lit up. "What's that?"

"Your present, of course. As if you didn't know."

"It's not very big."

"There are a couple of saying here in America, Angus. Maybe you have them in England, too— Good things come in small packages. *And* curiosity killed the cat."

"My grannie always used to say that to me."

"She probably had good reason to."

Outside, Angus gallantly held open the car door for her.

"But you're the birthday boy. You should sit up front."

He dimpled. "But you're the guest of honor."

Returning his smile, she slid in next to Ross. It was the closest she'd ever been to him. He must have showered and put on aftershave recently, because he had a decidedly pleasant smell about him. Clean and...and sexy. Muscles rippled in his arm as he switched on the ignition. "Seat belts, Angus, Kenzie."

She reached for the strap, glad to have an excuse to wriggle away from him. For some reason she found herself completely unnerved by his presence. Maybe it was the intimacy of their outing together; after all, it was easier dealing with him in the familiarity of her own home. Or maybe it was the fact that he looked so drop-dead handsome tonight. Either way, something about him was doing odd things to her inside.

Angus leaned forward as far as his belt would allow. "Will your birds be okay while you're gone?"

"They prefer peace and quiet."

"Did you let the pelican go?"

"This morning."

"Oh. Too bad. I wish I'd seen it."

"That's okay," she said brightly. "Maybe next time."

"Will you be letting something else go before next Saturday? That's when we leave."

"The blue heron might be well enough by then."

"Oh, good!" He leaned forward to address his father. "Can we watch Kenzie let it go?"

"We'll see."

"It's a pretty neat experience," Kenzie said. "Before I let the birds go I band them with a number so people will know who they are if they're ever caught again. To band them, I have to put their heads in a coffee can."

Angus's eyes went wide. "How come?"

"It may seem cruel, but when you stuff them down inside a can they instantly relax. Then you can slide the band on their feet without a struggle."

"Maybe they're frozen with terror, not relaxed," Ross said.

"Actually, research shows that their heart rates slow dramatically. So they really are relaxed."

Angus bounced up and down in his seat. "I want to watch!"

"We'll see," Ross said again, but he sounded a lot more positive this time.

"Ever been to the Boathouse, Kenzie?" Angus demanded in the next breath.

"Only once, when I first moved here."

"How long ago was that?"

"A little over a year."

"Where did you grow up?"

"In Washington, D.C."

"Washington!" Angus leaned forward to eye his father. "Have you ever been there?"

"A few times."

"Is it nice? Would I like it?"

"You'd probably enjoy the museums and the zoo. Tell you what. I'll be going there on business in October. Maybe you can come along."

Angus's face fell. "I'll be in school then."

"Second or third grade?" Kenzie asked.

"I—I don't know. We had forms in my old school, not grades."

"You'll be in third grade here in America, son."

Had Ross noticed the slight tremor in his son's voice? Kenzie certainly had. Her heart ached, picturing Angus facing his first day at a strange new school with a new teacher and new classmates. She hoped he'd had the chance to meet a few of them already, managed to make friends with them. That he'd been taken on a tour of his new classroom so the place wouldn't seem so strange and scary come September.

Did Ross know enough about parenting to arrange those things?

"Do you and Angus live alone?" she asked impulsively.

"At the moment, yes."

What in heck did that mean?

She waited for an explanation, but none came. Instead Ross switched on his turn signal and pulled into the parking lot.

Kenzie mulled over the comment as she got out of the car. Was Ross planning to get married again? Angus had never mentioned a stepmother-to-be. Not that she cared, of course. She only hoped the woman would be the warm and loving person Angus—and his father—needed so badly.

They were seated at a booth with a huge picture window overlooking the sound. Angus sat down beside her, Ross opposite them. A waitress brought menus, requested drink orders.

"Can we have cocktails?" Angus asked eagerly. "It's my birthday," he added importantly.

"Why, sure you can, honey. How about a Shirley Temple? On the house. You're the best-lookin' birthday boy we've had in here all summer."

Kenzie had to smile. Obviously she wasn't the only female

to fall instantly for the freckle-faced charmer with his proper British accent.

"You'll have to have the same," the waitress added to her and Ross. "We're a dry county."

"They don't serve alcohol," Kenzie explained after the woman had gone. "No hard alcohol. Just beer and wine. It's not uncommon here in the South."

Ross nodded. "Blue laws. I've heard of them. But if you ask me, it's barbaric."

Tonight she was inclined to agree with him. She didn't care much for either beer or wine but she would very much have liked a cocktail to calm her nerves. For some reason Ross Calder was taking up too much room as he sat across the table from her. The booth was too small, too...intimate. Her gaze always seemed to be falling on him no matter where she tried to look. His face, his blue eyes, his unsmiling but strangely disturbing mouth. What on earth was the matter with her?

"Can I see what's in the package now, Kenzie?"

"Gladly." Anything to distract her.

But Ross had spied the waitress making her way toward them. "Let's order dinner first, okay?"

Angus pretended to pout, then shyly volunteered to try the locally harvested clams. Kenzie ordered swordfish while Ross requested prime rib.

"Rare, please," he told the waitress. "We lawyers have a yen for fresh blood."

Even though he wasn't looking at her, Kenzie knew which way he'd aimed that barb. It was so unexpected that she didn't know whether to laugh or throw something at him. Honestly, she'd never let a guy unnerve her like this before!

Casting a glance at him she found him watching her, his blue eyes twinkling. So he *had* been teasing. Good grief, did he know how devastating he could be when he wanted to? She looked away quickly, her pulses humming and the heat rising to her cheeks.

"Can I open my present now, Kenzie?"

"Please," she said, grateful for the distraction.

She watched with bated breath as Angus tore open the envelope. She'd had no idea what to give him, and the shopping was so limited in Buxton and Avon that nothing had inspired her. So she'd drawn him a picture, a cartoon she'd painted in a wash of watercolors. It showed the moment of their meeting, with Angus, dressed in a kilt to acknowledge his Scottish forebears, reeling in a kite that was about to land on the unsuspecting Kenzie's head.

She had drawn herself as a somewhat gawky creature in a blue bathing suit, surrounded by all kinds of birds. Zoom and Jazz stood watch in the dunes.

She needn't have worried. Angus whooped aloud when he saw it. "That's me! Look, it's me, and I have on a kilt at the beach! And there's your dogs and your pelican and the seagulls and herons!"

"Do you like it?"

"I love it! I'm going to hang it in my room."

"We'll have to get it framed first." Ross was looking at her almost wonderingly. "It's very good."

To Kenzie's annoyance, little fingers of pleasure seemed to dance up her spine. The last thing she sought was approval from this man, especially when she'd been thinking violent thoughts about him just a moment ago. "Thanks."

"How come you made yourself look so silly?" Angus demanded.

"Silly?"

"Yes. All skinny and your conk so big?"

"My—conk?"

"Your nose."

She shrugged. "Guess that's how I see myself."

"But you're beautiful, Kenzie!"

"Don't be silly."

"But you are! Isn't she?" he demanded, turning to his father. Ross's eyes held hers. "Yes, she is."

No doubt about it, something in Ross Calder's voice was making her tingle all over. "Thanks," she said lamely, then pointed quickly to the envelope. "Look inside. There's something else."

It was a picture book called *Pirates of the Outer Banks*. On the cover, a menacing Blackbeard shook his cutlass at them. "Blackbeard used to hide out on Ocracoke, the island south of ours," Kenzie explained. "So did Anne Bonney, the lady pirate. They supposedly buried their treasure there, but it's never been found."

Angus leafed eagerly through the pages. Then he frowned. "But, Kenzie, I can't read this! I'm not very good yet."

"No problem. I bought it mainly for your father. So he could read aloud to you."

Startled, Ross looked at her.

Yes, read to Angus, Kenzie silently urged him. It's one of the most wonderful things a parent can do with a child. Don't tell me it's never occurred to you to try!

"Can we go to Okie Coke and look for the treasure ourselves?"

Kenzie laughed. "It's pronounced Ocracoke, sweetie. And, yes, you can. It's a short ferry ride from Hatteras Village."

"A ferry ride! Can we go, Dad? Please?"

Dad. Kenzie suddenly realized that she'd never heard Angus address his father that way before. She cast a swift glance at Ross and her heart squeezed when she saw the startled pleasure in his eyes.

"I don't see why not."

"Will you come, too, Kenzie?"

"Um—"

"You've spilled some Shirley Temple on your sleeve, son," Ross interrupted. "Go wash it off, please."

"Okay." He slid meekly out of his chair.

The moment they were alone, Ross turned to her. "Ms. Daniels."

Even a blind man could have sensed the change in him. She steeled herself for whatever was coming. "Mr. Calder?"

"I appreciate everything you've done for Angus, not only this evening, but also the other day. You've been kind to him and made him laugh, and I'm truly very grateful."

"But?"

Ross took a deep breath. "But I'd rather not encourage further contact between the two of you after this evening." Or with me, he thought silently.

Even though Kenzie had suspected this was coming, she was surprised at the stab of disappointment she felt. "I hope you don't think I've done anything to encourage—"

"Oh, I'm not suggesting as much. And while I'm glad Angus seems to be moving beyond the loss of his mother I don't believe it's at all healthy for him to grow attached to you." He said this without looking at her, knowing better than to allow those big blue eyes to weaken his resolve.

"No, it isn't," Kenzie agreed in a whisper.

"So surely you can understand my request?"

She nodded, her own eyes downcast.

"Kenzie." His hand was on her arm, sending warmth shooting through her. "Look at me."

She lifted her eyes and the crooked smile on his face threatened to undo her.

"Let's enjoy tonight, okay? For Angus's sake?"

She didn't like the feeling that was coming over her. A thank-goodness-she-was-sitting-down-because-her-knees-were-giving-out sort of giddiness that had absolutely nothing to do with the way he was looking at her or with the feel of his big, warm hand on her skin. Nothing at all.

She struggled to say something that would put her back on even footing. Before she fell completely. "For Angus's sake, gladly. Just make sure you keep that in mind yourself, Counselor."

He leaned back, breaking the contact between them. "That sounds like a reprimand."

"In a way, it is," she admitted reluctantly.

He leaned back even farther, striving to look casual although he was feeling anything but. Asking her to stay out of their lives after tonight had been much harder than he'd thought, though for the life of him he didn't know why. "So you have some criticism to offer concerning my behavior toward Angus?"

"Toward Angus, no. Toward me."

"You?"

"If you want this to be a pleasant evening, you're going to have to stop behaving so disapprovingly of me."

"Disapproving!" Ross sounded genuinely startled. Had he been trying too hard to build a fence between Kenzie and Angus—and himself—tonight? But how could that be? His tactfulness was well-known in the courtroom and it shouldn't have failed him here.

"Oh, you've been nice enough, I'll admit. But I have this feeling that deep down you didn't want me to come. That I'm here tonight only because Angus insisted on inviting me."

He sucked in his breath at the stab of guilty pain he felt.

"Ouch. You're very direct, Ms. Daniels, you know that? What a shame you never studied law."

"Did I get all the red off?" Angus had appeared at Kenzie's side, holding out a scrubbed sleeve for her inspection.

"It looks fine." She dabbed it dry with her napkin, then stood up.

He regarded her curiously. "Where are you going?"

"The ladies' room," she said as she left the table.

Once there, she took deep, calming breaths as she leaned against the sink. Thank goodness Ross hadn't noticed her reaction to his casual words. Although Ross had been teasing her, the things he'd said had totally unraveled her composure.

"You plead your case very well, MacKenzie. Too bad you never studied law."

Similar words had been spoken by her father, but in a tone Ross Calder hadn't used with her—a tone which she'd never heard *anyone* use with her until that final, hateful confrontation outside the stately double doors leading to Burton Daniels III's law office in downtown Washington, D.C.

It was the last thing he had ever said to his daughter, after the reporters and news cameras had gone. Although he had been the leading candidate for his party's run for the presidency, he had just announced his withdrawal from the Republican race, citing his wife's recent hospitalization as the major cause.

But thanks to Kenzie, everyone in America knew the real reason behind his decision: those questionable campaign funds he'd received from a European businessman whose bank on Grand Cayman Island had consequently become the target of an international investigation. No one in the States had been aware of any connection between the millionaire Belgian banker and the powerful D.C. attorney—until an unassuming political cartoon in the tiny Maryland publication *Eastern Shore Weekly* had raised the question.

The repercussions were only just beginning when Burton Daniels III announced his withdrawal from the Republican race, and no one doubted there'd be more to come.

As indeed there had been. A subpoena to appear before Congress, a Justice Department investigation, a hefty fine and six months' jail time for Daniels's campaign manager.

But what had whetted the nation's interest more than the sullying of Burton Daniels's once prestigious name had been the fact that Daniels's own daughter had drawn the cartoon that had proved his downfall—her first ever published work. Strange, the wags had whispered among themselves, how Mrs. Burton Daniels's hospitalization for chest pains had coincided with the publication of her daughter's revealing cartoon and her husband's subsequent withdrawal from the Republican race.

Still, much had changed since then. Surgery to install a pacemaker had set Kenzie's mother to rights, and relocation to the isolated Outer Banks had helped Kenzie escape the unending media frenzy. Luckily she had found steady cartooning work at the *Norfolk Messenger*, because she'd not have been fit for any other career after fleeing Washington and giving up her nearly completed doctorate in early childhood education.

On the other hand, she and her father had never reconciled. He hadn't spoken to her or acknowledged her existence in more than a year. And he had seen to it that none of her brothers, their wives or their children had said anything to her, either.

And of course Brent Ellis had called off their engagement the moment the scandal broke. Kenzie had clearly heard her father's words echoing behind the pathetic little speech he had made, and she could well imagine the things her father had said when informing Brent that marrying his daughter meant no chance of keeping his partnership in the Daniels family law firm—which, in true Beltway fashion, had barely been tarnished by the sorry chain of events.

Career or love? Brent hadn't hesitated in making his choice.

"C'mon, girl, get a grip," Kenzie told her pale reflection in the mirror. True, Ross's not-unkindly-meant words had unwittingly awakened memories she preferred to keep buried, but that didn't mean she was going to ruin Angus's birthday by hiding out in the ladies' room. While she had no idea what had triggered her emotional meltdown, she wasn't about to let either Ross or Angus suspect. So when she returned to the table she made sure that her head was held high and that her smile was warm and carefree.

Angus smiled at her just as warmly. "Thanks for the presents, Kenzie. I love them."

"You're very welcome."

"Yes, thank you," Ross said softly, watching her. "Everything okay?"

She nodded.

"You sure?"

"Absolutely."

But he continued to watch her, frowning a little.

"I'm okay," Kenzie said at last. "Really."

And to prove it, she turned her attention to Angus, entertaining him with stories of the many shipwrecks that had earned the Outer Banks the nickname "Graveyard of the Atlantic." When she realized that the mood had grown too subdued—a lot of drowned sailors figured in the tales she told—she taught him some of the ways that American kids misbehaved at the supper table.

One of the tricks she showed him was how to drizzle lemon juice over his clam strips while aiming the wedge so that the seeds shot forward to land in his water glass.

"Bingo!" she exclaimed when he finally managed to get one in on his own.

Ross said nothing, but once or twice Kenzie saw a flash of amusement in his eyes as he watched them. So he *could* let his hair down every now and then, the stodgy old prosecutor. Surely there was hope for him yet!

The waitress appeared to gather up the dishes. "How about dessert?"

Kenzie smacked her forehead with her palm. "Cripes, Angus, I'm sorry! I bought you a birthday cake in Norfolk and left it home in the refrigerator!"

"It's okay," he said, but he looked disappointed.

"I got cupcakes in the kitchen," the waitress offered. "We could put a candle in one of 'em."

Angus brightened. "Oh, yes, please."

"As long as you promise not to serve it with the whole staff singing 'Happy Birthday,'" Ross warned, then raised a brow at his son. "Unless you'd like them to?"

"No, thank you," Angus said quickly. He leaned forward when the waitress left. "Thanks, Dad. That would've been so dumb!"

Kenzie tried to ignore the cramping in her heart at the way Ross smiled back at him almost diffidently. She'd promised herself once before that she wasn't going to feel sorry for Ross Calder. Or get involved emotionally in his relationship with Angus. Or in any way, for that matter. Ross was right: there was no reason to see Angus again after tonight.

She tried not to let the thought depress her.

"Can we walk on the pier?" Angus begged after he'd eaten his cupcake and Ross had paid the bill.

Ross hesitated.

"Please?"

"It's late, son."

"Just for a minute? Please?"

"Well—"

Without another word, Angus bolted for the door.

Ross and Kenzie exchanged a smile.

"Thanks for dinner. It was wonderful," she said, meaning it.

"Actually, I owe you. Angus had a great time, thanks to you."

"Does this mean you don't disapprove of me anymore?"

"Let's just say I've come to realize that you have a lot of redeeming qualities."

He was smiling as he spoke, but his dark, intent gaze held her trapped.

"You're not so bad, either, once you let your hair down," she countered, but she wasn't paying her words any mind. She was watching the way his lips curved when he smiled and thinking what a wonderfully sexy mouth he had.

"Kenzie?"

"Yes?" she breathed.

"Shall we go? Angus is waiting."

"Oh. Oh, right."

Blushing furiously, she hurried out the door. Thank goodness, she wouldn't be seeing either of the Calder men again after tonight! She didn't like the way Ross had started churning up the calm facade she preferred to live behind, one moment reminding her all too awfully of her father, the next moment getting under her skin in a purely sexual way.

The breeze outside was warm, the darkness alive with the rustling of marsh grass. Angus was standing in silvery starlight by the railing at the end of the pier, staring down into the water.

"You can hear fish plopping out there," he whispered when Ross and Kenzie joined him. "What are they doing, Kenzie?"

"Probably hunting insects for their supper."

"I want to go fishing. Can we go tomorrow?"

"I thought you wanted to go treasure hunting on Ocracoke," Ross said.

"How about when we get back?"

"We'll see."

"That means no, doesn't it?"

"We'll see, Angus."

"Okay."

But Angus didn't sound as disappointed as usual or hang his head the way Kenzie had noticed he did whenever he and his father talked. Instead he leaned against the railing, chin in hand.

"Wonder if there's sharks out there."

"Probably," Kenzie said.

"Big enough to eat a person?" the curious boy asked.

"Not in Pamlico Sound," she replied, amused.

"Ever see a killer shark, Kenzie?"

"Not really, no. But I once took care of a baby porpoise that got bitten by a shark."

"In your bird hospital?"

She laughed. "No, honey. We kept it in a tank at the Hatteras marina until the biologists from Virginia Beach came to get it. It's fine, now. Released back into the wild."

"That's good." Angus hid a huge yawn behind his hand.

"Time for bed," Kenzie said automatically.

"But I'm not tired."

"You will be tomorrow. Remember, treasure hunting takes a lot of energy."

"Oh, yeah."

"You always know the right thing to say," Ross said softly as they started walking back along the pier.

She smiled, feeling warm and full and not at all confrontational. "I told you, it all comes from in here." She touched her heart and smiled at him again.

Ross's answering smile surprised her with its sadness. "Sometimes I wonder if I have enough left in mine to share with someone else."

"Oh, Ross! Of course you do!" She grasped his hands impulsively, then lowered her voice even though Angus had wandered out of earshot. "You've got to give it time! Your ex-wife has only been—been gone a few months."

"I'm not grieving for her," Ross said harshly. "It's Angus. Maybe I don't have what he needs right now. Maybe I never will."

"But you do, Ross."

She hadn't let go of his hands yet and now he clasped hers just as tightly. "You think so?"

"Yes. Absolutely."

"Thanks. It means a lot, hearing you say that." His blue eyes held hers as captive as a physical embrace. She felt the heat of it burn slowly through her veins, felt a yearning like nothing she'd ever known rise within her.

Kiss me, Ross, she pleaded with every fiber of her being.

"Kenzie—" he began roughly.

Angus nudged his way between them, yawning. "I'm tired. Can we go home now?" he commanded, taking both their hands.

"Sure, son." Ross's eyes still held hers over the boy's head.

When they got to the car, Angus scrambled into the back seat. Ross held the door for Kenzie, but as she started to get in he stayed her with a gesture. She straightened, looking at him in silence.

"What I said earlier, about not seeing you again after tonight. I hope you understand it isn't just for Angus's sake. I just can't—we can't—"

"I know," Kenzie whispered, and quickly got in the car, pulling the door shut behind her.

Chapter Four

"I am not depressed," Kenzie said aloud. "It's hot, I'm tired and I'm crabby. I am not depressed."

She raked up the last of the old straw bedding and carted it to the compost pile.

"Then why are you talking to yourself?" she demanded on the way back, pulling the cart behind her.

"Because I always talk to myself is why. Got a problem with that?"

Uh-oh. People said it was perfectly normal to talk to yourself. No reason to worry until you started answering back.

On the other hand it was true she *was* hot and tired. She'd gotten up early to feed the birds and clean the aviary, and by the angle of the sun overhead it was getting on to lunchtime. But she still had to check the bait traps to make sure she had enough for the egrets to eat, then drive up to the hardware store for wire to repair one of the cages, then stop at the tackle shop. She might as well wait to eat lunch when she got back.

See there? She had too much to do to feel depressed.

After walking to the end of the dock, she knelt and grabbed the rope to the minnow trap. The water was warm, the sandy bottom dappled with sunlight. Were Ross and Angus out on the same water right now, crossing the sound to Ocracoke on the ferry?

She let the empty trap fall back with a splash.

Okay, so she was depressed. And since she was finally being honest with herself, she might as well admit that she'd secretly been hoping Angus would talk his father into changing his mind about inviting her along.

She would have enjoyed a day on Ocracoke with them. Taking Angus up to the ferryboat's wheelhouse to meet the captain—normally forbidden except for the fact that he happened to be Kenzie's landlord. And stopping at the wild pony pens on the way to Ocracoke Village to show them both the ponies, then setting out to find Blackbeard's buried treasure.

She had always loved doing things with children, especially her nieces and nephews, and sharing new experiences with Angus was equally rewarding. He was so eager to see, to do, to learn. At least with her. And as for spending time with Ross...she knew the thought shouldn't make her feel so giddy, but, hang it all, she couldn't seem to help herself.

Still, Ross had said nothing about the outing when he'd dropped Kenzie off at her house after dinner last night. Remembering the birthday cake, she'd run inside to fetch it.

While she'd been handing it to Ross through the window, Angus had asked innocently, "Why don't you bring it with you when we go to Ocracoke tomorrow? We can have a picnic on the ferry."

Kenzie, seeing Ross's mouth set even though his face was in the dark, knew at once what he was thinking. Yes, he was right, she thought sadly. There shouldn't be any more contact between the three of them. "Oh, Angus, I'm sorry. I can't."

"How come?"

"I've got too much to do. The birds need care and—"

"I can help with that."

"That's sweet of you, but I've got a lot of errands to run, too. You and your dad should be able to find the treasure without my help."

Ross spoke at last, without looking at either of them. "Sure we can."

"I guess so."

Kenzie had already figured out that when Angus hung his head like that he was trying hard to keep his feelings hidden. She bit her lip, tempted to ignore the agreement she and Ross had made by inviting herself along.

But Ross had been right when he'd said that it wouldn't do Angus any good to encourage further contact with her.

He's a kid, Kenzie had thought then, watching the rear lights of the car disappear down the road. He'll be just fine.

She reminded herself of that again now, while putting away the cart and crossing the sandy yard back to the house. No need to worry about Angus. Kids were amazingly resilient.

Like her nieces and nephews. Jamie and Nick, her younger brother's twins, would be Angus's age by now. Zack would be nine. No, ten. He'd had a birthday in June. And Kitty, the tomboy of her older brother's three girls, would be thirteen next month. Baby Elizabeth would be walking and talking by now.

Sighing, Kenzie sank down on the porch steps and tugged off her shoes. More than a year had passed since she'd seen the kids, and she could only hope they remembered her, that someday they'd be able to resume their loving relationship with her at the exact point where they'd left off when she'd been all but cast from the family.

Sometimes Kenzie missed them so much she ached inside. That's when she'd reach for the phone and dial, but always hang up before the first ring. The coldness in her brothers' voices had hurt too much the last time they'd talked.

The helplessness in her sister-in-law's had been just as bad. "I'm so sorry, Kenzie, truly I am. But your father's here right now and I'd rather you didn't speak to the twins. They're sure to blab, and you know Burton's temper..."

All too well. He'd reacted with towering anger when she'd first approached him about her suspicions and accused her of not understanding how Washington's political wheels turned. He had acted in the coldly autocratic way with which Kenzie was familiar, and when she persisted in questioning him, had told her to mind her own business and get back to her graduate school studies like a good little girl. Stung, she'd turned to her brothers, who had dismissed her concerns with a disbelieving shake of the head. But Kenzie's roommate had happened to be engaged to an aide to the governor of the Cayman Islands, and

Kenzie had clearly overheard her father's name mentioned at the engagement party at the British embassy that fateful night. Startled, she'd sidled closer to the hors d'oeurves table where the two strange men were talking and had heard enough to make her heart leap into her throat. She'd asked discreetly who they were and later had done some investigating on her own. Dismayed and disbelieving, she'd gone to her father a second time, hoping he'd explain away her suspicions. Only, he hadn't. So she'd made that awful, difficult decision to draw that cartoon and see if anyone else had suspicions similar to her own...

Through her mother, Kenzie had learned that her father still refused to even acknowledge her existence. Neither his wife nor his sons, daughters-in-law or grandchildren were permitted to mention her name in his presence.

Every now and again she got an e-mail from her middle brother, Stuart, and her youngest brother, Tad, even called on occasion. But her oldest brother, Burt, had all but washed his hands of her, and next-in-line David always did whatever Burt told him to.

Which meant treating their only sister worse than a pariah. At least an outcast's existence was acknowledged. But to the oldest Daniels men, a girl named Kenzie had never even lived.

"It's their loss," she muttered aloud.

And surely her nieces and nephews wouldn't forget her! She had to believe that, if only because she had nothing else to cling to.

Then again, out of sight, out of mind. Her father had warned them not to talk about her in his presence. But did they still talk about her amongst themselves?

Questions like that pained her mother, so Kenzie had quit asking whenever she called. It was all part of learning to live with what she had done.

If she had any regrets at all about publishing that drawing, it was the effect it had had on her mother. Even though Alicia Daniels had stood by her daughter, had assured her time and again that she had done the right thing, Kenzie knew how much her mother had suffered. Both during and after the investigation.

But she had never acknowledged as much to her daughter. "You know Washington," was all she'd say whenever Kenzie screwed up the courage to ask.

Oh, yes, Kenzie did. Although political scandals were a way of life inside the Beltway, they had the longevity of wildfires: erupting quickly and burning fiercely, and then, once extinguished, quickly forgotten.

Except by those who'd gotten burned.

"At least your father didn't get any jail time," Alicia always said.

Gallows humor. It was all she and her mother seemed to share these days.

"I should be glad the two of us still have a relationship," Kenzie muttered aloud. "And here you are talking to yourself again. Cut it out, for cripes' sake!"

Zoom and Jazz were waiting on the porch. Collapsing onto a chair, she thumped their sleek sides, grateful for the companionship. Hanging out with friends was a good way to get rid of one's depression.

"Except that you guys are lousy conversationalists. No offense."

They didn't seem to take any. She ruffled their silky ears.

"Not that I'm in need of anyone to talk to or anything like that."

And she wasn't lonely. Not for Angus, and especially not for Ross.

She tried to push the thought of Ross away. Usually that was easy; all she had to do was think of Angus and tell herself it was Angus she missed.

But where Angus's smiling, freckled face usually came first into her mind's eye, there was now only Ross's, smiling, too, and looking at her the way he had on occasion last night.

True, he was a lawyer, and true, he pushed all the wrong buttons as far as she was concerned, but—

But what?

He was handsome, he was sexy, and when he chose to be charming, she went all soft and stupid inside.

"But I was *not* crying in the ladies' room because he told me to butt out of their lives! And I don't miss him. Why would I miss a guy who puts me on such a roller-coaster ride?"

The dogs whined their sympathy.

Kenzie sprang out of her chair. "Know what? I'm going to

splurge. Eat lunch out. And bring back a doggie bag for each
of you.''

Since that seemed to suit the greyhounds just fine, she showered quickly, changed her clothes and drove the truck into Buxton.

The Red Drum Café wasn't too crowded. Most of the tourists
had already eaten lunch and gone back to the beach. A few
regulars sat at the bar and greeted Kenzie enthusiastically when
she came through the screen door.

Rob Midgett, who ran a local windsurfing shop, patted the
seat beside him. ''Sight for sore eyes is what you are. Where
you been hidin' the last few days?''

''Busy with the birds,'' Kenzie replied. She shifted her gaze
to the bearded man sitting on Rob's other side. ''Going fishing
tomorrow, Earl?''

''Yep.''

''Oh, good. I wonder if you'd mind—''

''I know, I know. Bring you back some bait fish. Honestly,
Kenzie, sometimes I think all you do all day is scrounge food
for them birds of yours.''

''It's an admirable life,'' she protested, grinning.

And a safe one.

Most people who knew her these days considered her a loner.
Which suited Kenzie just fine. Contrary to most small, close-
knit rural communities, the Hatteras Island locals had welcomed
her warmly into their midst. Though a newcomer, she'd made
friends quickly. None of them had seemed aware of her notoriety, or cared. More importantly, none of the single men her
age had taken offense when she'd let them know, politely but
firmly, that she wasn't interested in relationships.

One of the things she loved about living here was that people
understood and respected your wishes to be left alone.

But today she'd come in search of companionship, and the
patrons of the Red Drum Café were just what she needed. While
cars whooshed by outside, they talked about the weather and the
tides, the chances of raising enough money at the next Rescue
Squad barbecue to do some landscaping around the firehouse,
and whether or not Bubber Findlay's wife had really changed
the locks on the doors of her house or if that was just Bubber's
excuse for not going home last night.

Kenzie ordered a hamburger and a milk shake, then threw caution completely to the wind and asked for a piece of pie with her coffee for dessert. Who cared if she spent all her money? And who cared if she got fat?

Certainly not Brent Ellis, who'd dumped her just about a year ago today, nor Ross Calder, who rarely looked at her the way a man would if— —

Whoa! Kenzie's thoughts came screeching to a halt.

Where in heck had *that* come from?

Since when did she care if Ross Calder thought she was gaining weight or not? Since when had *she* ever thought of *him* in a purely physical way like that?

Well, maybe last night, a little. When she'd sat beside him in the car. When he'd smiled at her at dinner and walked with her along the pier. Before he'd made it clear that she wasn't welcome to go to Ocracoke with him and his kid.

Good riddance, she thought, stirring cream into her coffee.

Hopefully she'd seen the last of one Ross Calder, Esquire.

A forlorn hope, it would seem, considering that he was suddenly standing there in the doorway right in front of her.

Kenzie blinked.

No illusion. He and Angus had just stepped inside and were looking around for a place to sit. Father and son were both dressed in shorts and T-shirts. The tip of Angus's freckled nose was sunburned and his dark curls were windblown. He looked adorable, as usual.

As for Ross...he'd always been just a sight too handsome for Kenzie's peace of mind. Maybe that's what made him so unsettling to her. Not just his dour, lawyerly moods, but his dark good looks and those broad, masculine shoulders. She remembered the way she'd felt when he'd touched her last night. The lightning bolt that seemed to slam through her when he'd said in that husky voice, "Kenzie, look at me." The way he'd come so close to opening himself up to her when they'd stood together on the dock before Angus had interrupted them.

Setting down her mug, she slid quietly off her stool.

"Kenzie!"

Too late. Angus had seen her.

"Hi. What are you doing here?"

"Stopped in for ice cream."

Without waiting for an invitation, he scrambled onto the seat Rob Midgett had just vacated. Earl obligingly moved over another seat so that Ross could sit down, too.

Kenzie didn't wait to see the look of annoyance she felt certain was creeping across Ross's face at being stuck with her again. Instead she signaled the waitress to bring Angus a menu. Truth be told, she was delighted to see him, and this time she could enjoy his company without feeling guilty. After all, she hadn't done a thing to initiate this encounter.

She introduced Earl and Carla, the waitress, who was the same age as Kenzie's mother but still couldn't help giving Ross a long, slow, admiring look.

"What'll you have to drink? Coke? Beer?"

"An iced tea would be nice." Ross glanced briefly at Kenzie over Angus's head. "Hello, Kenzie."

"Hi. On your way to Ocracoke?"

"We're on our way back," Angus answered.

"What? You sure didn't stay long!"

Angus looked apologetically at his father. "It was...kind of boring."

"Boring! Ocracoke? What did you do?"

"Drove around. Looked in a couple of stores."

Kenzie wrinkled her nose. "Did you look for Blackbeard's treasure?"

"We didn't know where to start without you."

"Oh. Um, well, did you see the wild ponies?"

"The pen was empty."

"I see."

"The town was pretty enough," Ross conceded. "But crowded."

"And the stores were full of boring clothes and stuff."

Kenzie bit her lip. "Gosh, I can't imagine going to Ocracoke just to shop! Did you at least like the ferry ride?"

"It wasn't fun without you," Angus blurted.

She didn't dare look at Ross. No doubt he was furious about the whole situation. But was it her fault that Angus preferred her company?

No way! She'd never done anything manipulative or underhanded where Angus was concerned! And as for further undermining Ross's relationship with his son, well, she'd leave them to their ice cream and pray she'd not run into them again.

She got to her feet. "Look, I'd better—"

"Here you go." Carla set a tray down on the counter. "Iced tea and a glass of milk. And more coffee for you, Kenzie." She poured it before Kenzie could protest, then allowed herself another worshipful glance at Ross. "How about a piece of key lime pie? Homemade this morning. It's delicious. Just ask Kenzie."

"I'll try some," Angus piped up.

Carla batted her lashes at Ross. "And you?"

He sighed. "I'll have the same."

Carla disappeared into the kitchen. Kenzie had no choice but to sit back down.

"I gotta go to the bathroom," Angus announced.

Kenzie pointed. "It's over there. And don't forget to wash your hands."

"Yes, ma'am," he said in a charmingly authentic Southern drawl, then grinned and scampered away.

Kenzie turned to his father but couldn't bring herself to look at him. Keeping her gaze level with his wide and very masculine chest, she said in a small voice, "I'm truly sorry about your outing. I never should have suggested it. But there's much more to Ocracoke than gift shops and the like."

"I'm sure there is. But please don't feel bad. It wasn't your fault."

She blinked. He sounded as if he meant it. For the first time she lifted her eyes to his face. Good Lord, he was smiling at her!

"And I'm glad we ran into you. Angus has been pouting all morning." Ross slid onto the bar stool Angus had vacated; the one right next to hers. For a big man, he moved extremely gracefully. Kenzie could see Carla making eyes at him through the kitchen door.

Ross looked at her closely. Kenzie gulped. Did he notice the color that had crept to her cheeks? But how could she keep from blushing? He always managed to rattle her whenever he was being nice.

"What's the matter, Kenzie? Have I said something to make you uncomfortable?"

"Darn right you make me uncomfortable," she said in what she hoped was a perfectly calm and in-control sort of tone. "I thought for sure you'd bite my head off for sending you on such a lousy outing. Now you say it isn't my fault. I never know what to expect from you."

Ross gave her a surprisingly rueful smile. "You're right. I owe you an apology for that, too."

Would wonders never cease? Kenzie struggled to gain control of her feelings.

"The trip wasn't a total waste, either," Ross said. "It taught me something important."

"Oh?"

He propped his arm on the counter and looked at her somberly. "It made me realize that I need to try another tactic in winning points with Angus. Obviously being a pal to him isn't the way. Face it, I'm not the spontaneous person you are and I don't have endless insight into what little boys think and like to do. But holding you responsible for my lack of success when you yourself achieve it so effortlessly is unfair."

Kenzie looked at him wonderingly. Just how awful had this outing to Ocracoke been that Ross Calder would be prompted to make such an admission?

Pretty awful, in fact. Even though Ross had made every effort, nothing he had said or done had helped to coax Angus out of his sour mood. It was almost as if the boy had wanted to punish him for banning Kenzie from the trip, although Ross was convinced he hadn't been doing so intentionally. But whatever the reason, Angus had complained all morning long that Kenzie would have known where to go, what to see, what to do. That she always found things to laugh at.

"She knows how to make everything fun," he'd said repeatedly with quiet, almost stubborn conviction.

And damn it, he'd been right. Despite himself Ross couldn't help remembering the way they had all laughed together at dinner last night. The fun they'd had talking about sharks on the Boathouse pier, the easy way the three of them had sauntered back toward the car and how right it had felt to have Kenzie so close to him—until Angus had insinuated himself between them.

Thank God for the kid's timing, Ross thought, remembering with a pang how it had made him feel to look deeply into Kenzie's eyes. There was something about this woman that got under his skin and made him want to be around her, and not only because of the way she charmed his son.

That's why he'd made up his mind last night that he couldn't afford to spend any more time in her company. Not because of Angus, but because of the way she made him feel inside—and the way she'd looked in that clinging blue sundress with her hair flowing about her shoulders and that delicate gold chain nestled in the hollow of her breasts.

He'd done his best last night to ignore her striking looks, but it hadn't been easy what with almost every other man's eyes at the restaurant constantly turning her way. To Ross's astonishment, Kenzie hadn't been aware of them. Unlike Penelope, she seemed not to have a pretentious bone in her body.

But Ross had seen, and for some crazy reason, the admiring looks of other men had aroused a strange sort of jealousy within him. At first he'd tried telling himself his reaction was fueled by resentment at the easy way Kenzie managed to tease Angus until the boy erupted in a fit of giggles. Only, he'd been lying to himself. His reactions were purely instinctive, purely male. The instincts of a man defending from other men what he wanted for himself. Wanted in a way that was one hundred percent, primitively physical.

Lord, even while sitting across from her at the dinner table and telling her this was the last night she and Angus would be together, he was imagining himself sliding the straps of that sexy little dress down off those naked, tanned shoulders. Picturing his hands sliding after them, down to her breasts, her slim waist. Undressing her. Making love to her.

"Here you go, Carla. Keep the change." The man Kenzie had introduced to Ross as Earl slid off his bar stool and laid a few dollars on the counter. "Nice meetin' you, Calder."

Ross forced himself to sound nonchalant. "Likewise."

Earl grinned at Kenzie. "And don't you worry. I'll have Ned bring those mullet around sometime after five."

The warmth of her answering smile touched Ross even though she hadn't aimed it at him. Damn, but it was galling to realize that even now, after his disastrous morning with Angus and the foul mood he was in, he wanted her still.

Even before he'd known who she was! Admittedly he hadn't

recognized her when he'd first stepped into the Red Drum with Angus. Blinded by the glaring sunlight out in the parking lot, he'd stood blinking in the café's dark interior until he'd gradually become aware of the tall, pretty blonde sitting at the counter surrounded by a group of laughing men. She was wearing her hair twisted into a knot and pinned loosely to her head. Denim shorts, sneakers and a white tank top emphasized tanned skin and the easy grace of a serious runner.

Then she'd tipped back her head and laughed along with the others, that warm, sexy chuckle he'd heard so often whenever Angus was around.

He'd reached quickly for Angus's arm, wanting to steer the boy back outside, but by then Angus was calling Kenzie's name and climbing eagerly onto the stool beside her.

The change in his gloom-ridden son had been absolutely astounding and Ross, instead of feeling anger and resentment, had found himself reacting with utter relief.

"I owe you an apology for my behavior last night," he said now, before Angus came back and before he lost his nerve. "You're right. I *was* a little hard on you, telling you to keep away from my kid. Unjustifiably so."

"No problem," she said without looking at him.

He leaned closer. "What's the matter? Not used to getting apologies from a lawyer?"

She smiled at that but still wouldn't look at him. She knew better than that. "I guess I owe you an apology for the lawyer crack."

"It was unfair," he agreed.

"I should have kept my mouth shut. I guess I talk too much." She sounded rueful.

"No. No, you don't. You have a nice, easy way of talking. Angus definitely responds to it. You should have been a teacher."

"Actually I was planning on it. I have a master's in early childhood education."

"So what happened?" he asked, surprised. "I mean, you're not teaching, you're working for a newspaper."

She bit her lip and shrugged. "Politics got in the way, I guess."

Ross frowned. "What does that mean?"

She toyed with her fork. "I—um, it's kind of hard to explain—"

"Hey, that's my seat!"

Ross obligingly made room for Angus. Maybe it was his imagination, but he could have sworn that Kenzie seemed relieved when he moved away. Which was as it should be, he reminded himself sternly.

Thank goodness, Kenzie was thinking, he's finally gone. How much longer could she have tolerated Ross looming over her, large and masculine and much too sexy for her own peace of mind? Bad enough that ever since last night he had somehow started to get under her skin in a more disturbing way than Angus did. How was she supposed to resist that overpowering Calder charm when he was being *nice,* of all things?

As for his seemingly sincere apology, well, she'd heard that one before. A lawyer as shifty and unpredictable as Ross Calder probably wouldn't stick to his word the next time something irked him, and Kenzie knew she irked him plenty.

"When can we come see your birds again, Kenzie? Can I help you feed them?"

She looked a challenge at Ross over the boy's head. Not two minutes ago he'd assured her that he no longer blamed her for his own failures with Angus. Surely that meant he wouldn't object to their spending just a little more time together? "I don't know, honey. That's up to your father."

Angus swiveled in his seat. "Can we?"

Ross ached at the pleading he saw in his son's eyes. He felt torn, helpless. "If Kenzie doesn't mind—"

"Really? When? Can we go right now?"

Ross's and Kenzie's gazes met, held. She hadn't really expected him to agree and now she, too, felt torn. Did she really want to prolong their time together?

It's only for ten more days, her heart cried silently. What harm can it do?

"Hey, Kenzie! How's it going?"

All three of them turned. The booming voice belonged to Gordon Harper, a weather-beaten man in the khaki-colored uniform of a National Park Service ranger. He was Kenzie's closest neighbor and often invited her to eat dinner with his family. The Harpers had four children who served as Kenzie's surrogate nieces and nephews, while Gordon was the one she called whenever her furnace went out or she had to administer care to a bird too big or ornery to handle alone.

She didn't think she'd ever been more relieved to see him. Now she didn't have to steel herself for whatever Ross's answer would have been. "Hi, Gordon. C'mon and join us for lunch."

"Sorry, I'm on my way to Oregon Inlet and I'm running late. I saw your truck outside and stopped in to ask if you wanted to pull hatchling duty with us tonight."

"What's that?" Angus piped up curiously. He was staring at Gordon's uniform with open admiration, and Kenzie had a sudden inspiration.

"Sorry, I'm busy tonight, but why don't you take Ross and Angus? This is Angus Calder, by the way, and his father, Ross. They're visiting from New York."

"Hello, Angus, Ross."

The two men shook hands.

"Gordon's in charge of our loggerhead sea turtle nest monitoring project," Kenzie explained. "When the eggs in the nest get ready to hatch, they need to be watched around the clock so we can be sure the babies reach the water safely."

"And we've got one that looks like it may be popping tonight," Gordon added.

"Baby sea turtles?" Angus asked excitedly. "We can watch them hatch?"

"If we're lucky," Gordon said. "Sometimes we wait for hours and they don't hatch until after we've gone. I'm on duty tonight from eight to midnight and you're welcome to come along. Problem is, I've got room for only one of you in my Jeep, although you can follow behind, Ross, if you've got four-wheel drive."

"Not on my rental car."

"I don't have four-wheel drive either," Kenzie added.

Angus looked glum. "That's okay. I didn't really want to go."

The heck he didn't. Kenzie thought a moment, then had another inspiration. "Hey, Gord, why not take just Angus along?

I've seen three hatches this year so far, and I'm pretty sure Ross will have another chance over the weekend.''

"Got two more nests on the active runway," Gordon agreed.

Kenzie turned to Ross. "Would you mind if Angus went along tonight? The more chances he has of catching a hatch, the better.''

"He's more than welcome," Gordon agreed.

Ross hesitated, unsure of how to respond. While he badly wanted Angus to meet new people and see new things, his inexperience at fatherhood left him incapable of making a decision. He turned to Kenzie, helpless, at the same moment that she laid her hand over his.

"Ross." Her eyes held his. "I've known Gordon for a while. He lives next door to me, and his sons take care of my birds whenever I go out of town. Besides being a terrific father, he's a career ranger. Angus couldn't be in better, safer company.''

He wondered if she knew what those calm words and the warmth of her gentle voice did to him inside. How long since he had met someone he sensed he could trust implicitly? Had he ever?

He looked at his son. "Angus?"

"You'll have a blast," Kenzie said, becoming aware of Angus's expression and remembering how shy he could be around strangers. "Mr. Harper's got two boys your age and they've got extra flashlights you can borrow. The flashlights have red bulbs because you can't shine regular white lights around baby loggerheads. They think it's moonlight reflecting on the sea and get confused and go the wrong way. They've got to reach the ocean fast or they'll die.''

As she'd hoped, Angus was intrigued. Still, he was clearly fighting with himself, so she hurried to press the advantage. "The nests are set back in the dunes above the high-tide mark. If the babies hatch tonight, you'll have to dig a trench to guide them down to the water and then follow along to make sure they get there safely.''

"Really?"

"It's a big nest," Gordon added. "We counted more than a hundred eggs when they were laid.''

It was too much for Angus. "Okay. Are you sure you can't come, Kenzie?"

"Sorry, sport." She wanted very much for him to attempt something new on his own. "But if you go, you'll be able to protect the babies for your father and me and then tell us about it when you get back."

"I could, couldn't I?"

"Where's the nest?" Kenzie asked.

"About a mile past the last Frisco turnout."

"And you've got to be there when? Around eight?" At Gordon's nod she turned to Ross. "Why don't you bring Angus to my place around seven-thirty? Gordon lives next door. It'll save him the trip to Avon."

Mentally she crossed her fingers. How could Ross say no? Angus looked so eager, and Gordon was the kindest, most reassuring-looking man Kenzie knew. Surely she'd made that clear to Ross?

Please say yes, she willed him silently. It would be one way she could help make up for their lousy morning. And of course divert Angus's attention from his request to come home with her. No more roller-coaster rides for her, she'd decided. The less that Angus—and Ross—disrupted her calm and uncommitted life the better off she'd be.

But it seemed Ross had already made up his mind. "Thanks," he said, looking at Kenzie as though he were seeing her for the first time. "We'll be there."

Chapter Five

Kenzie was on the porch untangling a cast net when Ross and Angus pulled up to her house that evening. Jumping out of the car, Angus came clattering up the steps, letting himself through the gate without a trace of the shyness he had shown the first time he'd visited. He was wearing a baseball cap and had a disposable camera in his pocket. A gap-toothed grin lit his freckled face.

"We've been reading up on loggerhead turtles, Kenzie! Did you know when they hatch it's called a boil? And crabs can eat them on their way to the water or they can get stuck in tire tracks. That's why we have to watch them. They're en-endangered...is that the right word? So every one that makes it to the ocean is important."

Kenzie looked over his head at Ross, who was coming up the steps behind him. "He's been talking nonstop since we left the café," Ross said, smiling.

Despite herself, her cheeks warmed. His smile definitely did funny things to her insides. Quickly she rolled up the net and draped it over the railing. "I'm glad you did some research,

Angus. This way you'll know how important your job is tonight. How about something to drink? Or are you hungry?''

"We had pizza on the way over.''

"Then let me pack you some juice, in case you get thirsty while you're at the beach. And a towel. I'm making a snack for all of you. Oh, there's the timer now. Come on in.''

The kitchen smelled deliciously of baking brownies. Switching off the timer, Kenzie pulled them from the oven. "I know they're not very nutritious, but turtle-nest watching requires some heavy power snacking.''

She set the pan on a rack to cool. Turning, she found Ross's eyes upon her. She tended to forget just how wide shouldered and tall he was until he set foot in her tiny kitchen.

"You're much too kind to Angus.''

"I'm more than happy to do it,'' she mumbled, more aware of him than she wanted to be.

"Can I have a brownie now, Kenzie?''

Thank goodness for Angus. Smiling, she slapped his hand away. "Let them cool first or you'll fry your fingers. Here. Feed Zoom and Jazz a snack in the meantime.''

She handed him a box of doggie treats, then bustled around the kitchen cleaning up.

Folding his arms across his chest, Ross leaned against the refrigerator door, watching. "You look very domestic.''

Kenzie laughed. "You make it sound like seeing a woman in the kitchen is a novelty.''

"It is, for me. Penelope didn't cook.''

"So who did?''

"We had a housekeeper.''

"Oh.'' She'd almost forgotten there were people who lived like that. Like her parents in their spacious Georgetown home, surrounded by the genteel trappings of the upper class: priceless works of art, French antiques and rugs from the Orient that had cost more than her little cottage here in Buxton was worth. Once, she'd lived that way, too. Couldn't imagine another way of life, but she wouldn't trade this moment with Angus and Ross in her tiny little cottage for all the money in the Philadelphia mint.

"Do you have a housekeeper now?''

"No, but I think we're going to need one when Angus starts school.''

Through the doorway she saw Angus's happy smile fade. The hand that had been stroking Zoom dropped to his side. "Hey, sport, the brownies are ready."

Angus helped her to cut and seal them in plastic baggies. "They're still a little warm so they may get gooey," Kenzie said, "but at least it'll keep the sand off them."

Angus nibbled one experimentally, then closed his eyes in bliss, his fear of school forgotten. "Mmm. Can you show me how to make brownies sometime, Kenzie?"

"It's easy," Ross answered for her. "Open the box, add water and put them in the oven."

Kenzie regarded him archly. "I'll have you know these brownies are made from scratch. We don't use mixes here."

"Oh, pardon me." He looked hopefully at the few left in the pan. How long since he'd eaten homemade brownies warm from the oven? Not since his mother had died, he realized. A dozen years ago or more. After their father had walked out on them, she had done her best to make life for Ross and his brother as normal as possible. Cooked supper for them when she came home from work. Baked brownies and birthday cakes. Attended all of their school functions and helped them with their homework. But the strain of it all must have worn her down and Ross had often wondered if it had somehow made her more susceptible to the cancer that had cut short her life.

There was a knock on the screen door. A redheaded boy of twelve or thirteen with freckles on his nose just like Angus peered inside. "All right! I smell brownies!"

"Hey, Dan. C'mon in. Have you come to fetch Angus?"

"Uh-huh. Dad's ready to go. Hi, Angus. I'm Dan."

"And we're Chris and Tommy," chorused two younger voices from the porch. Angus's eyes lit when he saw that one of the boys was carrying a soccer ball.

"Football!" he exclaimed excitedly.

"Soccer." Tommy, the youngest at nine, rolled his eyes at the English boy's ignorance.

"It's called football in Europe, you loser," Dan informed his brother, punching his arm. "You play, Angus?"

Angus's face fell. "No. I wasn't allowed at home."

"No problem. We'll play while we're waiting for the boil to start. Show you the ropes."

Angus was so excited that he would have followed them without the brownies, the drinks or his towel. Kenzie managed to shove the bag into his hands before he took off down the steps after them.

"I've never seen him so worked up," Ross said, watching them vanish down the driveway. Turning, he caught sight of Kenzie's face. "What? What did I do now?"

"Why on earth don't you let him play soccer at home?" she demanded heatedly. "He's old enough to join a team! There's no better way to make friends or build—"

"He meant at his grandparents' house. That's where he was raised."

"Oh." She turned to face him, waiting.

Ross took a deep breath. "Angus grew up in a town house in London. His mother had custody of him until she died. I had no influence over what he was or wasn't allowed to play."

"But surely during your visits—"

"There were no visits," he interrupted, raw pain in his words.

His voice, the expression on his face, made her stare at him, aghast, as slowly, understanding blossomed inside her, and grew and grew until she grasped the full import of what he had said.

He stood waiting almost defensively for her to speak, but she knew better than to respond. The admission had been painful enough. She was not about to make matters worse by probing.

Turning, she took two plates from the cabinet. With the spatula she lifted a brownie onto each, then went to the refrigerator. "Coffee would be more appropriate, but nothing beats a cold glass of milk when you're eating warm brownies."

Almost numbly Ross accepted the plate and glass she offered, then followed her into the living room. He sat down on the plush white sofa while she curled up in an armchair across from him.

His first bite almost made him forget the ache of his admission. After two more, the whole brownie was gone. Kenzie brought him another without asking.

He was intensely grateful for her silence. Another woman would have demanded to know more, but Kenzie asked no questions. Instead she sat with her bare feet tucked beneath her, eating without a word.

When they were done, she collected their plates and headed

for the kitchen. "Why don't I make some coffee anyway? It'll be midnight before Angus gets back."

"No, thanks. I'm fine."

"We forgot to figure out how he's going to get home. Do you want me to bring him to Avon when the Harpers drop him off? That way you won't have to make the trip twice."

"No need for that. I'd planned all along to pick him up."

"Okay."

Ross knew he should leave. They'd eaten their brownies and there wasn't any reason to stick around until Angus returned. But the words he'd uttered earlier still hung like an unanswered question between them.

He looked down at his hands. Without Kenzie in the room, he found it easier to speak. "Penelope and I were married three, maybe four years. At least, that's how long we managed to stretch out the relationship. But by our third anniversary she was already living with her parents in London while I stayed in our apartment in New York."

"Was that a mutual decision?"

His mouth thinned. "You bet."

"Did you already have Angus then?"

"No. He was—I have to give my father-in-law credit for that. He's the one who insisted Penelope and I try to reconcile rather than filing for divorce. To help our relationship get back on its feet, he sent us on a cruise. Purchased the tickets without consulting me."

Kenzie was still bustling around in the kitchen. "That was kind of him."

"You don't know Sir Edward Archer."

"He's knighted?"

"As well as distantly related to an earl. A bloodline and a name he badly wanted to keep unsullied by scandal, like a divorce in the family."

Kenzie's voice from the kitchen was indignant. "What does that matter in this day and age?"

"To him, a lot. Definitely a man of the old school. He took the failure of his daughter's marriage very seriously. And I've always wondered if maybe he wasn't driven a little by desperation at the thought of having both Penelope and her mother hanging around his neck for the rest of his life, or until Pen chose to get married again. But I'm not sure if that was true or if I was just being ugly about it.''

Kenzie offered no opinion and again he was grateful for her silence. "Looking back, I was crazy to agree. But I was young and stupid and, I admit, not really thrilled with gaining an ex-wife and alimony payments. I was also something of a snob, much like my esteemed father-in-law, and didn't want to admit I'd failed at anything, especially a marriage.''

A blender whirled noisily, startling him. Kenzie came around the door with two margarita glasses garnished with limes. "I thought the salt would make a good contrast to the brownies.''

She sat down across from him again and looked him straight in the eye. "You may be a snob, Ross Calder, but you're also full of bull. You never would have agreed to that cruise if you hadn't still been a little bit in love with her.''

"Wrong. I felt a certain duty—''

"Oh, come on! You don't strike me as the kind of guy who'd put his soon-to-be ex-father-in-law's wishes before his own. If you were totally through with that marriage you would have returned those tickets no matter what.''

"Still wrong. As you said when we first met, quite correctly, I'm a heartless son of a bitch who doesn't care for anyone or anything.''

"Those were not the words I used.''

"But that's what you meant. Not only am I a lawyer, but a callous and conniving one, right?''

"You are not. Like I said, if you were, you would have given those tickets back. Instead you chose to give the marriage another try.''

He could feel himself relaxing, even smiling a little. It felt good to hear tough-as-nails political cartoonist MacKenzie Daniels saying something nice about him, whether it was true or not.

He took a sip of his drink. She'd been right about the salt. "Does this mean I've gotten an upgrade in your eyes?''

"Possibly.''

"Ah. So I've gone from a bottom feeder to what? Mud minnow?''

"Maybe a little higher than that. A trolling feeder.''

"Like a shark or barracuda?''

It seemed so apt a description they both had to laugh.

God, she was easy to talk to, Ross thought. And it felt so damned good to talk after all this time, all the bitterness. Only Delia knew something of the tale, and most of it she'd had to surmise.

"So what happened next?"

He leaned his head back, remembering. "The cruise was an unqualified disaster." Now that he'd let his defenses down, the words were coming more easily than he'd imagined. "We hadn't been under way for a day or two before I realized that nothing had changed between us, nothing. Penelope was just as self-centered, cold and demanding as ever. And she accused me of being the same. Still, to give credit where it's due, we both tried hard to make it work. We danced at the captain's dinner, made an appearance in the casino, sat and watched the stars from the observation deck. But Penelope ended up flying home to Mummy and Daddy from Madeira, our first port of call, and I was damned happy to see her go."

"Were you really?"

"By then," he said quietly, "yes."

Kenzie's heart ached. She'd warned herself not to ever feel sorry for this man, but how could she ignore the pain that darkened his eyes? It made him seem so vulnerable, as if the coldness that always surrounded him really was just an act. Lord, if it were true, she had misjudged him badly.

"I suppose you're wondering where Angus fits into this."

In truth, she'd forgotten, wrapped up in the wonderment over her reaction to Ross's pain.

He took her silence for agreement. "Angus was conceived on that very voyage. As I said, we really did give it a hell of a try. Not that I intended to get her pregnant or anything. But I was hoping we might rekindle some of the...you know, some of the passion we'd shared in the past."

Now it was Kenzie who wished she were still in the kitchen. Earlier, she'd given Ross a sense of privacy by deliberately leaving the room while he talked, but now there was no one to run interference for her while she found herself blushing furiously at such an intimate confession. At the thought of Ross Calder making love to someone, lying naked on a bed, touching a woman's skin with his strong, sure hands. Pleasuring her with kisses from that hard, full mouth.

Oh, Lord.

"Do you always drink your margaritas so fast?"

She forced a smile. "Doesn't everybody?"

"Yeah, maybe so." But Ross was thinking that even if Kenzie was right and he had still felt something for Penelope at the beginning of the cruise, the feeling had died a quick death in the few days that followed. Thrown together by the narrow confines of their shipboard life, he'd instantly come to realize how far apart they'd grown during their separation. How indifferent he'd become to the things that were so important to her, how intolerant of the spotlight of attention she craved.

To be honest, it had been damned easy to let her go.

Furthermore, Penelope's lies and deception had taught him that where women were concerned, it was best to maintain only the most casual contact with women, and so far that part of his life had been working out darned well. If only he and Angus were on better terms. If only Angus cared for him, even a little. Welcomed his attention...

Don't even go there, old boy, Ross told himself quickly. Easy as Kenzie was to talk to, he was not about to risk losing control over his emotions, the way he had when he'd talked to Delia the other night. Angus was a taboo subject, and he wasn't about to let Kenzie suspect how much his chest hurt and his throat closed up whenever he tried to talk about his feelings for his son.

"All in all," he said lightly, "I came out of the whole thing unscathed."

"Did you really?"

He looked up. "You sound skeptical."

Kenzie took a deep breath. If he could be honest about painful things then so could she. "I think you're hurting about Angus a lot more than you care to admit. Or—or is it his mother you miss?"

He got up to roam the room, suddenly as tense as a crouching tiger. "Penelope? No. I didn't speak to her, or hear from her, for years following that cruise. And we were estranged until the day she died."

Kenzie didn't pause to analyze the relief she felt. "But you said Angus was—"

"That's right. She was pregnant when she flew home from

Madeira. Neither of us knew, of course, and afterward Penelope didn't see fit to tell me.''

Kenzie caught her breath. ''Do you mean—are you saying she hid his existence from you?''

''Yes, indeed. Even though she'd listed me as the father on his birth certificate and chosen to give him my name rather than calling him Archer. But that was greed on her part. She wanted Angus to have dual citizenship, in the event she returned to the States to live. She had a fondness for New York and Palm Beach.''

Kenzie felt her heart break at the bitterness in his tone. ''Oh, Ross, I can't believe that she—that anyone—my God. How did you find out?''

Ross resumed his pacing. ''By accident. I was in Italy researching a case and somehow ended up with a ticket to La Scala. An English production of *Turandot* or *La Bohème* or something, I don't remember now. But an acquaintance of Angus's grandparents was a member of the touring company and I ran into her the following day. She told me, quite casually, that Penelope was living in London with a young son. It wasn't too hard to find out the rest.''

''You said you never visited him.''

''Believe me, it wasn't because I didn't want to. I tried.'' He stared down into his glass, not knowing how to continue. He only knew that, unpleasant or not, he had to finish what he'd started. He had to tell someone—tell *her*—the things he'd hidden away for so long. The terrible things that had happened after.

He cleared his throat.

''The very same day I found out about Angus I flew to London to see him. But he wasn't there. And not only did Penelope refuse to tell me where he was, she refused at first to even acknowledge I had a son.''

''But why?'' Kenzie asked in disbelief.

Ross shrugged with feigned indifference. ''Typical selfish behavior on her part. She loathed me thoroughly by then.''

''But she finally told you where Angus was?''

''Oh, yes, she did. Though she refused to allow me to see him. In order for me to do so I had to resort to legal intervention.''

"Oh, Ross, it doesn't seem possible!"

He uttered a harsh laugh. "It gets worse. Angus was spending most of his time in Norfolk, at the Archers' cold, gloomy estate in the middle of nowhere. Most of the time he had only a housekeeper looking after him because Penelope traveled frequently. And whenever she was gone his grandparents simply sent him away. They preferred living in London, and I imagine he was too rambunctious and noisy for them. I also learned that he was being homeschooled by the housekeeper or the groundskeeper or some other servant in Norfolk and not attending school with kids his own age. So you can see why I came to the decision that he'd be better off with me."

"Of course! How can you doubt that?" Kenzie demanded passionately. She took a deep breath to steady her emotions. "So you began custody proceedings. Penelope didn't take that well, I assume."

"No." Ross ran a hand through his hair. "Around that time the press caught wind of what was going on, or maybe the Archers tipped them off, I don't know. Either way, with the family being the well-known scions of society they were, naturally the tabloids took that juicy bit of news and ran."

"A media circus," Kenzie said flatly. Oh, Lord, how well she knew about that! "When did this happen?" she asked more gently.

"Last winter."

"Last winter! But Ross! Isn't—isn't that when Penelope died?"

Ross clenched his hands as he nodded.

"What happened?"

"Just when the proceedings were heating up and the press was having their field day, Pen left for a long weekend in Naples to get away from everything, especially from me. She left with a lot of fanfare, probably wanting to make sure the press and the attorneys saw how all the stress, all my evil machinations to snatch her son from her, were wearing her down. Two days later she was killed when her sight-seeing plane crashed on takeoff."

Kenzie didn't know what to say. She could only look at Ross in numbed disbelief.

"I myself wasn't in London at the time," Ross went on heavily. "I'd flown back to New York for a day or two to take care of business. I was trying to establish a new practice in Queens after my old law firm and I parted ways.''

"Parted ways? I don't understand.''

"My old firm had offices in Manhattan and London,'' Ross explained. "That's how I met Penelope in the first place, by the way, when I spent a few months there filling in for someone on sabbatical. Anyway, because Pen had been something of a media darling when we lived in New York, the local tabloids picked up on the story, as well. Oh, not with the same vengeance as the London papers, but it did garner a few breathless mentions in the society pages. That, and the fact that I'm convinced Penelope put a few poisonous words in our senior partner's ear, made my colleagues decide I was a liability to the firm's good name.''

"So they asked you to leave.'' Kenzie's voice shook with outrage.

"Put down your dukes,'' Ross said with a faint smile. "Though I appreciate your support, I'll have you know it was a mutual decision. I'd been growing somewhat disillusioned with the high-profile cases I'd been taking on and the direction in which the firm was headed. At the time it didn't seem like such a sacrifice to—''

"Woof!''

Zoom and Jazz were on their feet barking, the sound drowning out his words. From the aviary came a muffled thump and then the shrill screaming of awakened birds.

"Oh, no!'' Kenzie was already heading for the door. "Something's gotten into the aviary! Grab the flashlight and come on!''

"Where is it?''

"In the drawer next to the stove. Hurry!''

Out in the aviary the birds were still shrieking. Flipping on the light, Kenzie saw several dark shadows slip over the top of the nearest cage.

"Son of a—! Raccoons! I know I should've fixed that wire this afternoon!''

Ross aimed the flashlight at an overturned feed barrel in the next room. "Looks like they were after an easy meal.''

"I must've been nuts to let those repairs go,'' Kenzie fumed.

She knew exactly how the raccoons had gotten in, and what she should have done to prevent it. If any of the birds had been hurt because she'd spent the afternoon at the Red Drum Café instead of fixing that hole in the fence...

She took a quick tour past the cages. Though alarmed, the birds seemed to be okay. With the flashlight she inspected the outside aviaries. Everyone was accounted for, which was a huge relief, because raccoons were extremely adept at opening latches.

Everyone was there, she suddenly realized, except for the occupant of the last fenced-in run. The raccoons must have opened the chain-link gate to the run, eaten the rest of the fish she'd put out just before dark, then moved on to the feed barrel in the other room only to end up overturning it. Kenzie, her heartbeat accelerating, swept the run with her flashlight.

Empty.

"Oh, hell." She hurried toward the front room. "Ross, we've got trouble. The raccoons pried opened Smarty's cage and now he's gone!"

"Smarty? Who's Smarty?"

Kenzie was already searching every darkened corner of the storage room with her flashlight. "I'll explain in a minute. Just get away from that feed! Quick!"

Ross had been using a bucket to scoop up the spilled corn and put it back in the barrel. To Kenzie's horror, he didn't obey. Instead he propped his hands on his hips and gave her a mocking glance. "Mind telling me what's gotten your goat? No need to look so scared. The raccoons're gone and there's nothing—"

"Ross, please!"

Too late. At that very moment a huge brown pelican came charging at Ross from out of the shadows. Giant bill agape, it lunged, and Ross, reacting quickly, leaped out of the way.

But not fast enough. In a flash the pelican had latched onto the seat of his khaki shorts with his huge, clacking bill.

"What the—Kenzie! Get this thing off of me!"

Kenzie grabbed a towel and waved it threateningly in front of the pelican. Smarty paid no attention.

"Kenzie! Ow! Will you *please* get him off?"

"I'm trying!"

"Not hard enough! Ow!"

"Ross—"

"Hurry, will you!"

She had no choice but to twist up the towel and rat-tail Smarty good with the end of it. Having been raised with four brothers whose locker-room behavior was legendary helped enormously with the accuracy of her aim and the loudness of the snap. Smarty gave an indignant scream and backed off.

Instantly Kenzie moved in, using the towel like a bullfighter's cape to herd him down the aisle. "Ross," she panted, "open the gate and don't let him past you."

"Trust me, I'll tackle him if I have to."

"Watch out for his—"

"Hey! Stop it! Kenzie, whack him again! Hurry! He's got my sleeve!"

Together they finally managed to get the pelican back in the cage, although it wasn't easy. Smarty fought them every step of the way, and managed to get in a painful nip here and there not only on Ross's arms and backside but Kenzie's, as well.

When Ross finally slammed the gate behind him, the pelican flew at the wire, hissing and glaring at them with his unnerving yellow eyes.

"Oh, man!" Exhausted, Ross collapsed against the wall.

"Whew!" Kenzie agreed, slumping onto a nearby crate.

They looked at each other, neither speaking, both trying to catch their breath.

"You okay?" Ross asked at last.

"Uh-huh. How about you?"

He rubbed his backside ruefully. "Can't figure out what hurts worse. This or my pride."

Kenzie opened her mouth to speak, then uttered a strangled gasp of laughter.

Ross glared. His dark hair was tousled, his shirt tail pulled out. "What's so funny?"

"Y-you!" she gasped, giggling. "Being attacked by a p-pelican!"

"Hey, come on! I had no idea he'd go for my—my rear!"

But his lips twitched and then he was laughing, too.

"I—I tried to warn you!" Kenzie choked. "He'd just about k-kill for food!"

She couldn't remember laughing this hard since...since she'd

lost her family. Great peals of laughter that made her eyes water
and her stomach hurt and felt so good after all the pain.

By the time her fits had given way to an occasional snicker,
Ross, too, had regained his calm. Reaching down, he hauled her
easily to her feet and stood looking at her with his dark eyes
dancing.

"Lord, I needed that."

She wiped her eyes, smiling back at him. "So did I."

"I don't think I've laughed like that in years."

"Me, neither. Must've been the margaritas."

"Maybe so. But I'm grateful to you."

"For the drinks?"

"For the laugh."

"I'm the one who should thank you for that." Her eyes
danced back to his. "I've never had a guy sacrifice his butt like
that for my amusement."

"You think I did that just for you?" he growled.

"I can't imagine you doing it for another girl."

"Neither can I," he said, and even though he was still growling, his voice had suddenly changed.

Kenzie looked up quickly to find the laughter gone from his
eyes, replaced by something—something that made her breath
hitch and her heart skip a beat.

"What am I going to do with a woman like you?" he asked
roughly.

"Do you—do you need to do something with me?" she
breathed.

"Hell, yes."

"What?"

Instead of answering, he cupped her face with his hands and
lowered his head to her trembling, upturned mouth.

Oh, my.

No matter how innocent, no matter how lighthearted the gesture, the kiss rocked her to the soul. Ignited a spark that flared
into fire, racing through her veins.

Ross was still holding her face in his hands while his lips
moved over hers, and she reached up to clasp his wrists, not
sure if she intended to draw him closer or if she only wanted to
hold on. She could feel the fierce thrumming of his pulse be-

neath her fingertips, and desire, like honeyed liquid, poured through her.

She couldn't remember if she'd ever reacted this quickly to a kiss before. If she'd ever reacted this way at all.

"Ross—"

A plea. For him to release her? Or never stop?

She made a sound low in her throat as Ross's lips trailed over hers without pause, parting them, deepening the kiss so that there was no longer anything innocent about it. She ached to slide her arms around his neck, draw him closer until his big body was pressed against the heated length of hers.

But then, abruptly he let her go. "Oh, man," he said raggedly.

She couldn't look at him. A moment ago she'd been panting with laughter. Now she was breathless with desire, with confusion, with shame. This man had made it clear from the start that he didn't care for her company, that he considered her a threat to his shaky relationship with his son. And here she had gone all weak in the knees the moment he'd kissed her. Had kissed him back. And wanted more.

Scarlet faced, she moved away from him and checked the locks on the cages one more time. Then she switched off the lights and, without waiting for Ross, went back up to the house.

He was right behind her when she entered the kitchen. Ignoring him, she piled the dishes into the sink. Turning, she reached for the soap dispenser but Ross blocked her way, trapping her against the counter with one of his arms propped against the cabinet above. When she started to duck beneath it, he chuckled softly and refused to budge.

"What?" she demanded, glaring at the middle of his chest. She couldn't bring herself to look into his eyes.

"No need to be so mad. Kissing a lawyer isn't going to kill you."

Good. Let him think she was mad. Better than letting him suspect the truth.

She scowled at him, wishing she really was mad, but it was impossible to pretend when he was standing so close and smiling at her with that lethal Calder charm. "You could at least pretend it wasn't so funny."

"Funny? You think I think kissing you is funny?"

"Well, you're smiling, aren't you?"

"That's because you're so adorable when you get flustered."

Flustered! She wasn't flustered! She was...was...shaken and bewildered, that was all. By the unexpected kiss out in the aviary. By her unexpected reaction to it.

"Kenzie, what is it?"

She couldn't lie. Not when he was looking at her like that. "You kissed me. And then you said—you said I was adorable."

"Well, you are."

"But I didn't—didn't think you could stand me," she whispered.

His expression changed and he thrust his hands into his pockets, quickly, as if to prevent himself from touching her again. "For God's sake. How can you think that? Have I really been so awful to you?"

"In the beginning, yes."

"And now?"

"Nothing's really changed."

"Damn it, Kenzie, it has."

"No, Ross, it hasn't."

His expression was thunderous. "How can you say that?"

"Because you're so scared of being hurt you keep everyone at arm's length, especially me."

"I do not."

"Yes, you do. That's why you're always telling me to stay out of Angus's life—and yours."

"Aw, Kenz—" Raw pain was in his voice, in his eyes, as he looked at her.

"I'll tell you what else I think," she added, taking a deep breath.

"What?"

"I think there isn't any need to keep *me* at arm's length. I'm not Penelope, Ross, nor am I a threat. I am not going to take your son away from you."

"Is that so?" He sounded very casual, but Kenzie saw that he didn't look at all angry anymore. In fact, there was a dawning wonder in his eyes that made her breath catch in her throat.

"So you're saying I shouldn't keep you at arm's length," he went on slowly, without waiting for her to answer, and before she could think of a suitable retort he slid his hands over her hips. "Know what?"

"What?"

"You're right. That's much too far away."

"Ross," she breathed as he brought their bodies, oh, so close.

"Know what else I think?" he added, his lips hovering barely an inch above hers.

"W-what?"

"That you are a threat."

"A threat?"

"Damned right. To *my* peace of mind. To my sanity."

"Really?"

"Let me show you what I mean."

And his mouth took hold of hers again, hot and demanding. Tightening his arms about her waist, he brought her closer so that she could feel the extent of his desire for her. She moaned low in her throat as her knees went weak.

"See?" he asked breathlessly.

Feeling breathless herself, she pushed away from the counter and linked her arms around his neck. "I see what you mean," she whispered against his lips. "But there's a cure for this kind of insanity."

"Is there?" His eyes smoldered with desire.

"Oh, yes."

"Can you give me a demonstration?" he asked, cupping her buttocks with his big hands and fitting her even more tightly against him.

"I think you've already got the idea," Kenzie replied, leaning into him, loving the feel of his hard male body meshing with the soft curves of hers.

"That and more, sweethcart," he whispered, his mouth hovering over hers. "Shall I show you?"

Without giving her time to answer, he lifted her against him. In two short strides he had carried her into the bedroom and laid her down on the coverlet amid a tangle of limbs, his mouth on hers.

Desire poured through her as his kiss became more searing. He pulled off her shirt and his sure, strong fingers unclasped her bra, making her moan and arch against him as he caressed her breasts. She helped him take off her shorts, her panties, writhing beneath him as his lips continued the magic his hands had begun.

Turning toward him, she slipped her own hands beneath his T-shirt, skimming her palms across the ridges of his wide chest. Only now did she realize how much she had ached to touch him like this, to feel the rock-hard muscles beneath her fingers and hear his responding groan.

"So good," he murmured. "I never dreamed it could feel so good to have you touch me."

Then he took her by the hips and turned her to him, the pressure of his man's body hard against hers. Kenzie pulled him closer and arched her hips as he positioned himself above her.

"You're beautiful," he breathed, looking down at her in the moonlight. "More beautiful than I ever imagined."

"Have you been imagining me naked?" she teased, struggling to retain the last shred of sanity before passion swept her over the edge.

"Ever since you wore that tight little dress to the Boathouse."

Her eyes widened. "But you didn't—you never—"

"Let you know what I was thinking? Showed you the way I felt? Well, that was stupid of me. Let me make up for it now."

She waited, shivering with impatience, while he fumbled in his wallet, then took care of the protection that told her how important her well-being was to him.

A ruptured sigh escaped her as he finally slipped between her legs. Whispering her name, he caught her to him, moving in and out in a rhythm that was as natural to both of them as breathing.

There was no need to speak. No need for anything but the total surrender to something they had denied since their first meeting—that neither had acknowledged until this moment had even existed.

The sensation was pure magic, the intimacy beyond bearing. With every thrust Ross took possession of her anew, and she clung to him, moving with him until a shimmering, shuddering moment of piercing ecstasy swept both of them away.

Kenzie wasn't even aware that her eyes were still closed until Ross trailed feathery kisses across her lids. She shivered with sated delight to find him still a part of her.

"Kenzie," he whispered.

Their eyes met. She knew she had to say something. But she was still too filled with the wonder of what had just happened.

"Wow," Ross whispered at last. "I never knew it could be this good."

"Neither did I," she whispered back.

He trailed a finger lightly across her cheek. She shivered at the gentleness of his touch. "Kenzie, there's something you should know. I never —"

Headlights splashed across the far wall, accompanied by the crunch of gravel as a car turned up the driveway.

"Gordon!" In a panic Kenzie whipped back the covers while Ross scooped up his clothes and retreated into the bathroom. Footsteps sounded across the front deck, followed by the thumping of the dogs' tails as the screen door opened.

"Hello? Anybody here?" Gordon's voice was barely above a whisper. "I've got a sleeping boy with me. Where should I put him?"

"On the sofa," Kenzie whispered back through the bedroom door. "Be right out."

By the time she was dressed, she found Ross and Gordon in the kitchen, Ross looking perfectly calm and in control. She was grateful for that, because it helped her sound calm herself as she greeted the ranger and glanced at the clock. "You're back earlier than I expected."

"The boil started right when we got there. Good thing, too. Any later and Angus would've slept right through it." Gordon smiled. "He told me you took the early ferry to Ocracoke this morning, Ross. Once the turtles hit the water he sort of hit the wall. Fell asleep in the Jeep on the way home."

"Was it a good hatch?" Kenzie asked.

"Man, was it ever. A hundred and twelve baby loggerheads, to be exact. Angus was so excited even my kids got caught up in it, and they were starting to get jaded. This is their eighth nest so far this season. Like I said, I put him on your couch, Kenz. He's all tuckered out."

"Thanks, Gordon. Care for a drink before you go?"

"No, thanks. Got to get my own kids to bed."

"I really appreciate this," Ross said, offering his hand.

"My pleasure." Gordon sounded as if he meant it. "See you later."

After letting him out the back door, Kenzie went with Ross into the living room where Angus was curled up on the sofa. Gordon had taken the trouble to remove the boy's sneakers and tuck a knitted throw around him.

"You can tell he has four kids of his own," Kenzie whispered, smiling.

Ross smiled back. "Yeah."

They looked at each other across the darkened room, then Ross sighed. "I'm sorry, Kenzie, but I've got to get him to bed."

"Of course you do." She was sorry, too.

"We can talk tomorrow."

"Okay."

Ross leaned over the sleeping boy. "Angus, wake up. Time to go home."

"Hmm?"

"I said, it's time to go back to the beach house. You need to be in bed."

"Why can't I sleep here?" Angus's voice was groggy.

"Because this is Kenzie's couch."

"It's comfortable. Can I stay?"

Ross gave Kenzie a helpless glance.

"Angus." She knelt beside him and gently tousled his hair. "Angus?"

He stirred, then sighed. "What?"

"You need to get up, sweetheart."

"I don't want to."

Kenzie sat down beside him. Still stroking his hair she looked up at Ross. "You'll have to carry him out to the car. I can't even get him to open his eyes."

"Kenzie?" Angus whispered.

"Yes, honey."

"Can you sit with me like this for a while? It feels nice."

"Sure."

He sighed contentedly. "Nobody's ever sat with me before."

"You mean at night, while you tried to fall asleep?"

"Mmm-hmm. Sometimes I was scared and Mummy would come in. But she told me big boys weren't afraid of the dark."

Ross, who had been reaching down to pick up his son, went still. In the dim light from the hall, his eyes nailed Kenzie's.

"Just go to sleep, honey," Kenzie said in the same soft tone, continuing to caress him. "Everything's fine."

When his breathing was deep and even again, she got up quietly and followed Ross onto the porch.

"Do you mind if he stays?" Ross whispered, not looking at her.

"Not at all. He's all done in."

"Thanks. I really appreciate it."

"No problem."

She waited, but he said nothing about staying, too. She ached to tell him that he was welcome, but knew better than to speak.

"What time do you want me to come for him in the morning?"

"He can call you when he wakes up."

"Thanks," Ross said again. Thrusting his hands deep into his pockets, he looked up at the black sky. Kenzie's heart wrenched at the hurt she knew he was feeling.

"Kenzie?"

"Hmm?"

"What sort of childhood do you think Angus had? Before he came to stay with me, I mean?"

"I wish I knew," she whispered.

He scrubbed his hand wearily across his eyes. "Lord, so do I. But I haven't a clue. I wasn't there. Still, ever since he's met you, he's started revealing things that make me wonder." His voice roughened. "That's why I wanted to be a part of his life as soon as I found out about him. It wasn't just Penelope, who never had room in her heart for anyone save herself. I was worried about her parents, their cold, rigid ways, their unloving household. Not that I've been doing a better job of parenting now that I do have him."

"Oh, Ross—"

He shook his head, causing the hand Kenzie had reached out to him to fall back to her side. "Oh God." His voice was raw. "I've always known that I've failed him, but now it looks like everybody else did, too."

"Ross, you don't honestly believe that, do you?"

But he still refused to look at her, to let her in. "Sorry, Kenzie. I've got to go. Are you sure you don't mind keeping him here?"

''Not at all. He'll be fine. Would you like to—''

She was going to invite him to stay, as well, but Ross had already walked away from her, down the porch steps and into the night. The car engine cranked and taillights glowed. A moment later he was gone.

Alone in the darkness, Kenzie listened to the crickets shrilling. Tree frogs answered from the marsh. Slowly she went back inside. After locking the door, she began switching off the lights, although she left a single lamp burning in the kitchen in case Angus woke up and didn't know where he was.

Zoom and Jazz had taken the loss of their couch in stride and were splashed out on the hall rug. She fondled their ears, then stepped over them and went into the bedroom. In the darkness she undressed for the second time that night and slipped on the oversize T-shirt she used for a nightshirt. Although there was work to do at her drawing board she ignored it. After brushing her teeth and washing her face, she crawled into bed.

Her heart felt heavier than a boat anchor. Normally she would have been thrilled to have an overnight guest like Angus, as she had always loved sleepovers with her nieces and nephews.

But all she could think of was Ross.

The stunned way he had looked at her when Angus had asked her to sit by him.

The way he had stood there on the porch with his shoulders bowed, so utterly defeated.

The way his voice had sounded when he'd bade her goodnight and stumbled down the steps to his car.

She could feel her heart swelling with aching emotion for him. Only a few days ago she had warned herself not to feel sorry for this man. But now it was too late.

Worse, she knew that she didn't really feel sorry for him. Ross Calder was not a man to be pitied. What she felt for Ross right now was more complex—and a lot more dangerous. So was what had happened between them before Gordon Harper brought Angus home.

Kenzie sighed and covered her eyes with her hand. There was no denying that she'd fallen in love with Angus from the very first moment he'd crash-landed his kite on her. That's why, despite Ross's objections, she'd taken it upon herself to get involved, to defend the boy from hurt and loneliness, to shield him from the unfeeling ogre she had come to believe was his father.

Only, she knew now—had sensed for some time—that Ross wasn't an ogre. That he loved his son deeply and was desperate to do right by him. She had seen him agonizing over Angus tonight in a way she knew her own father never had over her. No, Ross was nothing like her father. He was good and kind and sweet and didn't deserve the hurt he had suffered. Not to mention that he was wonderful beyond words in bed.

Kenzie sat up, hugging her knees with her arms. If her heart had been heavy before, it was at critical mass now. She didn't want to feel this way, didn't want to continue down the path that seemed to have opened before her. There was no doubt that she already loved the son. If she wasn't careful, she'd end up falling in love with the father, too.

Chapter Six

"Kenzie?"

Yawning, she pried open an eye to see Angus standing in her bedroom doorway. "Hmm?"

"What am I doing at your house?"

She opened the other eye and lifted her head from the pillow. "Oh, good morning, Angus. You fell asleep on the couch last night."

"I did? I don't remember." He looked expectantly toward her bed. "Where's my dad?"

The assumption that Ross had spent the night here, too, was an innocent one for an eight-year-old to make, but still Kenzie blushed. "He went home. You're supposed to call him when you're ready to go."

Pushing the hair out of her eyes, she glanced at the alarm clock. Seven-thirty. "Maybe you'd better wait a little while. Do you mind?"

He shook his head, smiling and shifting from one bare foot to the other. Feeling shy, Kenzie realized. She knew how to remedy that.

"Give me a minute to jump in the shower. Then let's have

some breakfast and you can tell me about the sea turtle boil. Would you mind feeding the dogs in the meantime?''

''Could I really?''

''Sure.''

Later, while she fried bacon and eggs and mixed up pancake batter, Angus told her about the turtles. Overcome with enthusiasm, he barely stopped long enough to take a breath.

''They were so cute, Kenzie. Not much bigger than my hand, but Mr. Harper wouldn't let us touch them. They were real slow and clumsy, too, till they got in the water.'' His smile faded. ''Mr. Harper says not many of them will come back to the beach to lay eggs when they're grown-up. He says lots of them get eaten out in the ocean.''

''That's why they're endangered,'' Kenzie agreed. ''Nobody knows for sure, but they say fewer than one in a thousand makes it to adulthood.''

Angus scowled. ''Not the ones in *my* nest!''

''You could be right,'' she said lightly. ''How about another pancake?''

''Yes, please. And some of that topping. What's it called?''

''Maple syrup. Never had it before?''

''I never had breakfast this good before. At least, not since we came here.''

''To the Outer Banks?''

''My dad doesn't cook too good,'' Angus said gloomily.

''Oh?''

''You won't tell him, will you?''

Kenzie propped her elbows on the table and smiled at him, her heart warm as she thought of Ross. ''Of course not. So what does he feed you for breakfast?''

''Lots of different things. He burns them mostly. I had cereal yesterday. That was good.''

''Hard to burn that,'' she agreed. ''What kind of breakfast did you eat in England?''

''Sausages, eggs, sometimes porridge. My grandparents had a cook.''

''So did my parents. Was yours nice or mean?''

Angus shrugged.

''Ours was mean. We were never allowed to have snacks,

even when we were starving. And once she spanked my brother Stuart for licking cake dough from a spoon.''

The corners of Angus's mouth turned up.

"Did that ever happen to you?" she pressed.

He shrugged again.

Kenzie helped herself to another pancake. "Do you miss England?"

"I like being here."

"How about your grandparents?"

Another shrug.

"What about your mother, honey? Do you miss her?"

He stared down at his plate. "I guess."

Kenzie got up to clear away the dishes. She knew better than to press him further. Clearly he wasn't ready to open up yet. "I've got to take care of the birds now. Feed them, clean their cages, give some of them medicine. Would you like to help me until it's time to call your father?"

He looked as though he'd just been promised a fabulous present. "Could I really?"

"Angus—" she hugged him tight "—I'd be honored to have your help."

"What do we do first?"

"We'll need—"

They were both startled by the slamming of a car door.

Angus peered out the window. "It's my dad."

Ross's bulk filled the kitchen doorway. "Hi. May I come in?"

Kenzie eyed him warily, not sure of his mood. "Please do."

"I had a feeling I should come by early. Angus is usually up before the sun. I hope he didn't wake you, Kenzie?"

He was wearing the lawyer's look again. With his handsome face expressionless and his eyes not meeting hers, Kenzie couldn't hope to guess at his thoughts. She forced herself to smile. "Not at all. We were just finishing breakfast."

"I'm going to help Kenzie with her birds."

"Some other time, son. You've been here long enough."

"But I just woke up!"

His logic was adorable, but Ross didn't smile. "Kenzie's got a lot to do today, and so do we."

"But—"

"No buts. Get your shoes and socks and tell Kenzie thank you for having you over."

Kenzie turned back to the sink as Angus left the room, determined not to interfere. Her heart had turned a crazy somersault when she'd first seen Ross outside the screen door, but now it lay heavy inside her. If he felt the need to put up that impenetrable wall again after letting his guard down so completely with her last night, she couldn't exactly protest. But, oh, it was hard.

Angus appeared in the doorway. "Thanks, Kenzie," he mumbled.

"You're welcome, sweetie."

Say something, his eyes pleaded with her.

I wish I could, her heart cried. Not just for Angus's sake, but for his father's.

She went with them onto the deck.

"I really appreciate your letting Angus spend the night, Kenzie." Ross seemed to be avoiding her gaze deliberately. God knows he had to. For Angus's sake, as well as his own. Kenzie could understand his fear of letting her mean more to his son than she already did. But what did she mean to him. Did he think last night had been a mistake? Granted, a piercingly beautiful mistake, but a mistake nonetheless? No doubt he couldn't afford to have a relationship cluttering up his life when he had such a difficult task as befriending Angus on his hands.

Ross took Angus by the hand and led him down the steps. "Thanks again, Kenzie."

"Anytime." She wished she had the nerve to confront him, to ask him what had happened to the man who had loved her last night until her knees went weak. Who had made her feel as though she was actually beginning to matter to him.

Instead she watched them drive away and wondered if this time it was for good. She counted the days in her head. In little more than a week they'd be on their way back to New York. A troubled boy and a lonely man, and no way for her to help either of them.

"It's none of your business, MacKenzie Daniels. And you're not in the child-psychology field anymore. You're a cartoonist now, remember?"

And still talking aloud to herself like a lonely old lady.

She went back inside. Finished washing the dishes and debated calling her mother, then realized her father wouldn't have left for work yet.

"I'll do it later," she mumbled. "And stop talking to yourself!"

But later she sat at her drawing board waiting for the muse to hit, the need to hear her mother's voice forgotten. Sometimes, while reading the newspaper or watching TV, the absurdity of what some self-serving politician was saying would strike her like a lightning bolt and she would have no trouble drawing a cartoon to express how she felt. Usually those were her best drawings, and more often than not they'd be picked up by other publications across the country.

But today was not one of those times. By two o'clock she had nothing to show for her efforts but balled-up pieces of paper and a badly chewed pencil nub.

On top of that, it started to rain.

"Oh, great," she muttered, looking up as the first big drops plopped against the window. So much for an evening run on the beach. Had the rain ruined Angus and Ross's plans, as well?

"It's none of my business."

She reached for the remote and switched on the TV. Surfed through the channels until suddenly a familiar face, a familiar voice, made her backtrack in a hurry.

"...the subcommittee made clear recommendations on that issue. And I intend to see they're carried out."

Brent Ellis. Being interviewed on a business segment of CNN. Looking tanned and fit and dressed to kill in a Hugo Boss suit and striped silk tie. Unlike Ross Calder's rugged features, Brent's were refined, almost elegant. Once, she'd thought him the handsomest man in the world. She closed her eyes and let his voice wash over her, remembering how the sound of it used to make her feel inside.

She'd been madly in love with Brent Ellis ever since her freshman year of college. Yes, she'd wanted to marry him and have a family and live happily ever after. She'd been badly hurt when he chose to side with her father by breaking off their engagement. More hurt than she'd ever let on.

But now, studying his familiar, once-loved face, she felt nothing but a vague contempt. He'd not hesitated to sell her out and discard their dreams for the sake of ambition. Was that really the kind of man she'd wanted?

"But I don't want him," she said aloud. Not anymore. And it suddenly struck her that even when she'd been in love with him she'd never wanted him as badly as she did Ross Calder.

Oh, Lord, Kenzie!

Unfortunately, it was true. Looking at Brent's handsome, animated face on the screen, she remembered how it had felt when he kissed her, held her in his arms and whispered sexy words in her ear. But like a fist in the gut came the realization that last night Ross Calder's kisses and gentle touch had aroused in her more need and passion, more *lust,* than her fiancé's ever had.

So that was it.

Relief washed over her like rain. She wasn't falling in love with Ross. She'd just wanted to go to bed with him. Nothing shameful about that admission—or the fact that they had. She was a healthy young woman and he was a virile man. And it had been nearly a year since Brent had dumped her.

"You're not falling in love with him. That ought to make you feel a heck of a lot better," Kenzie said aloud.

Somehow, it didn't.

Sighing, she reached for the remote. On the screen the perky reporter was wrapping up the interview. "Good luck in your bid for the Senate," she chirped. "And congratulations again on your upcoming marriage. When's the big date?"

Brent looked charmingly bashful. The faker. "Probably not until after the elections, Paula."

So he'd have time to dump his latest fiancée if she did anything to jeopardize his political ambitions, Kenzie thought cattily.

Her bad mood lingered throughout the day and into the evening, just like the rain. And both were there to welcome her when she got up the next morning and went into the aviary where Smarty, sensing her distraction, managed to sneak in a savage nip at her ankle as she put food in his pen.

"Better watch it," she warned, rubbing the injured spot. "The barbecue spit's waiting out back."

The absurd image of roasting pelican made her smile. "Actually, I owe you one." If Smarty hadn't escaped the night before last, Ross would never have kissed her.

On the other hand, if he'd never kissed her, one thing wouldn't have led to another and she wouldn't be pining for him right now.

Not that she was pining. Still, she couldn't help heading straight for the bedroom when she returned to the house. But there was no message on the answering machine. She eyed the clock. Nearly noon. What were Ross and Angus doing on a rainy day like this?

Why should she care? Or expect them to call her?

She was heading back to the kitchen when the phone rang. "Hello?" she said eagerly.

"Hi, Kenz."

"Tad!" She was genuinely glad to hear her youngest brother's voice. "How's everything?"

"Not bad. How about you? The summer tolerable so far?"

"So far, so good."

Usually they limited their conversations to small talk like this while skirting the more painful issues, but Kenzie was in a confrontational mood today. "How's Dad? Come to his senses yet?"

There was a moment of silence. Then Tad sighed. "You know he hasn't."

"So what's he up to? How's Mom?"

"Planning Labor Day weekend at The Farm."

The Farm was what everybody called the family's property on the Eastern Shore of Maryland. At present nearly two hundred acres were under cultivation, the land rented out to a neighboring farmer while the Daniels family used the sprawling brick mansion that stood on the shores of the Chesapeake Bay as a retreat from the sweltering Washington summers. As children, Kenzie and her brothers had kept ponies stabled in the barn and learned to hunt deer and waterfowl from the caretaker who lived there year-round. The family's annual Labor Day barbecue was renowned throughout Washington, and several past presidents had preferred to spend the long weekend there rather than at Camp David.

Kenzie had been explicitly asked not to attend last year.

"Mom's planning all kinds of stuff. Libby'll be starting first grade and Justin's turning ten. She wants to celebrate both while we're there."

"You're there, you mean. I'm not invited."

Another painful pause.

"Maybe I should show up anyway."

"Aw, Kenz—"

"I know, I know, Mom's heart wouldn't take it."

She was sorry now that she'd even asked about her parents. "I saw Brent yesterday on *Washington Week*. So he's getting married, huh?"

"Um, yeah."

"Anyone I know?"

"I don't think so. She's from Baltimore. An interior designer."

"Isn't that interesting. Brent's probably planning to have her redecorate the White House when both of them move in."

"I'm sorry, Kenzie."

She realized she was making Tad uncomfortable. "No problem. And you know what? I'm not sorry."

"Really?"

"Nope." She was over Brent Ellis. Completely.

But her heart still hurt over her family. After she and Tad had hung up, she brooded for a minute with the phone in her hand, tempted to call her mother and say she was coming to The Farm on Labor Day weekend no matter what her father or Burt, Stuart or David had to say about that.

Yeah, right.

The moment she cradled the phone it rang again.

Probably Tad, forgetting to tell her something. "What?"

"Kenzie?"

Ross's voice. She felt happiness pour through her like sunshine.

"Kenzie, are you there?"

"Oh, hello, Ross. I'm sorry. I thought you were somebody else."

"Should I call back later?"

"No, it's okay." But it wasn't. Her stomach was all fluttery just because he was on the line. "What's up?"

She could hear him hesitate. "I wonder if you could do me a really big favor."

Her heart soared. "Sure."

"Would you mind watching Angus for a few hours tomorrow? I've got to interview a client who's visiting family in Virginia Beach. From the map, it looks like a two-hour drive or so. Angus would be bored out of his mind if I took him along.''

''No, he wouldn't. Virginia Beach is a blast for kids his age. They've got an aquarium and a wax museum, go-carts—''

Now why was she shooting herself in the foot this way?

''I wouldn't have time to take him any of those places.''

''You're right. I forgot.''

''But you could.''

''Excuse me?''

''Why don't you come along? Make a day of it? And I'll take the two of you out to dinner before we drive back.''

No, no, no, her coldly reasoning brain insisted.

Yes, yes, yes, her heart cried out.

''Or is that too much to ask, Kenzie?''

To see Ross, to ride with him in his car, to eat dinner with him afterward? Not to mention spend the day having fun with Angus as opposed to staring bleakly at her sketch pad? Wondering gloomily if anyone beside Tad and her mother cared that she wouldn't be coming to The Farm this year?

''You wouldn't mind having me along?''

''Angus would love the company.''

And you? she wondered, but didn't quite have the nerve to ask.

''We'd have to leave at seven. Is that too early?''

''No. Should I meet you at your place?''

''That'd be great.'' He gave her the address, thanked her and hung up.

She went back to her desk. Looked at the sketches she'd not been able to complete the day before. Picking up her pencil, she sat down and began humming softly to herself.

The sun was up and a soft wind was blowing when Kenzie pulled into the driveway of Ross and Angus's rental house. The house stood high on pilings just behind the dunes. An oyster-shell walk led to the stairs. She climbed two flights to a spacious deck and knocked on the glass door.

''Kenzie!''

Angus launched himself at her. "Are you really taking me to a wax museum? And for a ride on the go-carts?"

"Steady, sport. You've got too much energy this time of morning. But if your dad says okay, I am."

His toothy grin reminded her of how much she'd missed him. "He said he didn't mind at all. C'mon in. I'm just finishing my breakfast."

He scrambled back onto the stool at the counter while Kenzie stepped wonderingly inside the house. "Wow."

The kitchen was nearly three times as large as hers, with a huge center island and counters topped with hand-painted tiles. It was equipped with every gadget imaginable, from a microwave and food processor to an espresso machine and bread maker. That, and the gorgeous view of the ocean, was enough to make Kenzie stop in her tracks.

"This place is unbelievable!"

"Think so?" Ross stepped around the corner. Kenzie's heart skidded to a halt at the sight of him. He was wearing a light gray shirt, dark pants and a knitted tie. Casual but impressive. And as usual, exuding that magnetism she could never seem to ignore. All of the feelings she'd been denying for him came crashing back in a rush of bittersweet longing. When was she going to admit to herself it wasn't just Angus she'd missed?

"I've never set foot in one of these houses before," she said, turning away before he could see the truth in her eyes. "I had no idea they were so luxurious. They look so—homely from the outside."

"It's a lot of room for just the two of us," Ross agreed. "The place sleeps ten. But it was the only house available for two weeks. The rest were booked." He cleared his throat. "I appreciate your coming."

"Glad to help."

Kenzie wandered back onto the deck. She needed a moment to collect herself. Not only because she wasn't used to seeing Ross in a tie, but because he looked so...so awe inspiring in this elegant setting: competent, powerful and perfectly at home. Her heart ached in a strange way when she recalled how out of place he looked in her tiny, cluttered kitchen.

"Get a grip, Kenzie," she whispered aloud. "He's handling our postlovemaking relationship a lot better than you are."

"Can we go now?" Angus asked when she came back inside.

"Are you done with your breakfast?" Kenzie countered automatically. Then she blushed. She was here as a guest. It wasn't her job to look after Angus. Not until they reached Virginia Beach, anyway.

She insisted that Angus ride in the front seat with his father. That way she'd be spared sitting next to Ross herself. She knew his closeness would have too disturbing an effect on her. Besides, from the back seat she had a nice view of his broad shoulders and the dark, curly hair that was so like his son's. If she moved her head just a little she could watch his hands on the steering wheel: big, competent hands that just the other night had caressed her body and aroused such heated longing within her.

Surely he had thought about that night since then?

"Where's your meeting?" she asked quickly.

Ross handed her a map, his cell phone and a paper with scrawled directions. "See if you can find out how far away that address is from where you plan to take Angus. I'm going to have to drop you off since you're not authorized to drive the car. I shouldn't be but two, three hours at most. I'll call you on the cell phone when I'm on my way back."

Kenzie dropped the phone into her backpack. To her delight, Ross's appointment wasn't too far away from the beachfront area. "You can drop us off at Twenty-second and Atlantic. We'll rent bikes and cruise the boardwalk."

Angus frowned. "I don't know how to ride a bike."

"You don't have to. These are special ones that have bench seats and look like golf carts, only you have to pedal them."

Angus perked up instantly. "How long before we get there?"

"A couple hours, I'm afraid." She rummaged in her backpack. "Fortunately, I know just how to keep you from getting bored. Here, put these earphones on. I brought you a book on tape."

"What's that?"

"It's a read-aloud book you listen to. This one's called *The Hobbit*. Have you read it before?"

Angus shook his head.

"Isn't that a little advanced for him?" Ross asked.

"You can never be too young for Tolkien. And this one's a

classic. Besides," she added, sliding the first tape into the player, "it's three and a half hours long."

Ross watched Angus settle back in his seat, headphones on, a rapt look on his face. "I'd never have thought of that."

"Trust me. A few hours in the car with a restless kid and you'll never forget again."

"Is that the voice of experience speaking?"

"Definitely."

"How many siblings do you have, Kenzie?"

"Four brothers."

"You were the only girl?"

"Sure was." She kept her voice light even though talking about her family always made her uncomfortable, especially with him. "How about you?"

"An older brother."

"Is he a lawyer, too?"

His eyes met hers in the rearview mirror. "Actually, he's a police chief in a little town in upstate New York. Do you disapprove of that career?"

But his eyes were twinkling and Kenzie felt the tension drain out of her. "It's a very noble profession, actually."

"So is upholding the law and preventing miscarriages of justice."

"Touché."

She settled back in her seat, her heart light, almost airy. This was the first time the mention of Ross being an attorney hadn't turned their conversation into a confrontation.

No, unfortunately that confrontation came later, when Ross pulled up to the curb on Atlantic Avenue and took out his wallet. "How much money do you think you'll need, Kenzie?"

"For what?"

"The aquarium, bicycle rental, lunch. Whatever."

"Oh, thanks, but we're fine."

He was already peeling off a number of twenty-dollar bills. "You're going to need cash. It sounds like an expensive day."

"No problem. I brought plenty of my own," she lied.

"But you're watching Angus."

Kenzie got out of the car and shouldered her backpack. "I know. See you later."

Ross frowned at her. "Kenzie, he's my son. You're not responsible for paying his way."

"I'd like to consider him my guest today."

"But you came along at my request. That means you—"

That she was supposed to be a paid baby-sitter? No way was she going to stoop to that role! Her chin tipped. "Ross, it isn't necessary."

"And I say it is."

"Don't be silly."

"Good Lord, Kenzie, will you just let me pay?"

"No."

He glared at her out of the car window. "Quit being so darned stubborn."

"You're the one who's being stubborn!"

"*I* asked you to come along today, so *I* want to foot the bill."

"Hey!" Angus popped up between them. "Can you quit fighting now and take me to the aquarium, please?"

"We aren't fighting," Ross said tightly.

"Yes, we are," Kenzie countered, glaring.

Noticing the suddenly anxious look on Angus's face, she softened. "Okay, tell you what. I'll pay for lunch and the aquarium. Ross, you foot the rest of the bill."

"Deal."

He grinned as he handed her the money. "Excellent mediation, Ms. Daniels."

She'd never been able to resist his smile. A minute ago she'd wanted to smack him on that square, masculine chin. Now she felt the warmth of his smile tingle right down to her toes. "C'mon, Angus. Let's roll."

Ross watched them walk away, Angus skipping along at Kenzie's side. There was no sign of the silent, unhappy boy Ross had first brought to Cape Hatteras more than a week ago. It did his heart good to see Angus act that way, and to find himself free for once of the sense of failure he always felt because he wasn't any good at making his son smile. Blaming himself because he'd never gotten the hang of that touchy-feely stuff—the way Kenzie obviously had.

Ross angled around to watch as she and Angus crossed the street toward the boardwalk. His heart sank and he sighed.

What to do about Kenzie? How long could he go on pretending indifference? It had been hard enough when he'd first seen her this morning to hide the fact that he found her irresistibly attractive dressed in jeans that rode low on her rounded hips and a boat-necked T-shirt in soft lavender, wearing her hair in a French braid. She'd looked wholesome and beautiful and totally without guile—the way she'd looked the other night in the aviary after they'd managed to trap Smarty in his pen. Charmed by her dancing eyes and laughing mouth, he'd given in to a weak moment and kissed her.

Not a smart thing to do as it had turned out, because that impulsive gesture had quickly exploded into a not-so-harmless one. The moment she'd clasped his wrists with her hands, he'd known that she wanted him. And the moment her lips had parted beneath his, he'd realized how much he wanted her.

It was like stepping in front of a roaring fire. All of the emotions that had roiled in him since meeting MacKenzie Daniels for the first time had electrified into a single blaze of passion. Lord, he'd wanted her, and making love to her had been sweeter and more satisfying than anything he'd ever known. He'd not been able to think of anything else but her ever since.

Save for Angus. And that's why he knew he had to keep his feelings under control. No way could he concentrate on his relationship with Angus if he was blinded by lust for a woman like Kenzie. And that's all it was, really. Lust.

It had to be, didn't it? Just think how easy it had been to put Kenzie out of his mind the moment his passion was sated and Angus had provided the painful distraction of revealing those things about his past. And look how easy it had been to push Kenzie from his thoughts for the past two days while he kept Angus busy on the beach and buried himself in work after the boy had gone to bed.

In fact, Ross had to congratulate himself on finishing several projects, including an appellate brief for a client doing a lengthy prison term, by the time Delia called him yesterday to inform him about Matt Klausner's visit to his mother in Virginia Beach.

The Klausner case was one of two major criminal cases Ross was juggling at the moment and he'd not wanted to pass on the opportunity of meeting with Matt during these two idle weeks away from the office. The problem of what to do with Angus had been solved by Angus himself.

"Why can't I stay with Kenzie?"

Ross hadn't been prepared for the rush of relief that had swept over him at the thought. Calm, capable Kenzie. If he trusted anyone who lived on the Outer Banks to watch his son for the few hours he'd be gone it was Kenzie.

And, no, he hadn't latched onto the idea because he needed an excuse to see her again. Nor was he sitting here in the car right now wishing he didn't have a client meeting but could instead spend the day with Kenzie and his son riding bikes on a boardwalk.

Ridiculous.

And to prove it, he put the car in gear and drove away from the curb without another backward glance.

In the meantime Kenzie and Angus had crossed the paved bicycle path running parallel to the street and climbed onto the boardwalk.

Angus pointed at the four-seater bicycles with striped red awnings that rolled along the walk below. "Wow! Are those the kind we're going to rent?"

"Yep. What do you say we visit the aquarium first? It's early, so it won't be crowded. Then we can pedal along the beachfront until we find a restaurant we like and eat lunch."

Angus's freckled face glowed. "Super!"

As they started down the boardwalk the cell phone in Kenzie's backpack jangled. "Your dad must've forgotten something. Hello?"

"Oh, excuse me," said a female voice. "I must have dialed the wrong number."

"Were you looking for Ross Calder?"

"I was. Who is this?"

"MacKenzie Daniels. I'm using his cell phone this morning."

"Oh, Ms. Daniels! How nice to meet you—at least over the phone." The woman's voice had grown noticeably warmer. "I'm Delia Armstrong, Mr. Calder's business manager. Is he there?"

"He's gone to a meeting. Angus and I are visiting the boardwalk at Virginia Beach."

"Oh, how lovely. I'm glad. But I had wanted to catch Mr. Calder before he went into that meeting."

"He gave me the number—"

"I have it, too. Thank you so much, dear. And give my love to Angus. I'm sure you'll have a wonderful time together."

Kenzie put the phone back, a puzzled frown on her face. "That was Delia Armstrong. She said to tell you hello."

Angus looked shyly pleased. "She's nice."

"And she seemed to know who I was. Now, why is that? Has your father mentioned me to her?"

Angus shrugged, then pointed to an arcade farther down the boardwalk. "Oh, Kenzie! Can we go in there?"

"Why not?"

Watching Angus play games would give her time to mull over Delia Armstrong's apparent knowledge of her existence. Now, why on earth would Ross mention her to his business manager?

Chapter Seven

The cell phone rang again as Kenzie and Angus were pedaling away from the restaurant where they'd just eaten lunch.

"Hello?"

This time it was Ross. "I'm through with my meeting and on the way back. How's it going?"

"Super." She couldn't keep the smile out of her voice—just hearing his was enough to lift her spirits.

"Great. Where should we meet?"

"Same place you dropped us off. About two o'clock? We've got to return the bike."

"No problem."

Kenzie switched off the phone. "That was your dad. He's meeting us in about forty-five minutes."

"Is that enough time to visit the kite store?"

"You betcha."

Angus had been awed by the many kites flying over the beach in exotic shapes like whales, airplanes, even a pair of dice. The store itself was a delight even to Kenzie. Hundreds of nylon kites hung from the rafters in a riot of colors, from rainbow hues to pastels to hot pink, lime and orange.

Angus's eyes were huge. "Ooh, Kenzie! They're all so grand!"

"Then pick one out, sport."

He gaped at her. "You mean—you mean I can have one?"

"I'd like to give you one to take home to New York. After all, we first met because of a kite."

And they'd be saying goodbye with a kite, too, Kenzie thought with a pang.

Angus had a tough time making up his mind. Some of the kites he considered were pretty expensive, and Kenzie quailed inside when she saw the price tags, although she said nothing aloud. Not that she was short of money or anything. Her rent was low and she didn't spend a lot on herself, but fending on her own on a cartoonist's pay wasn't exactly a lucrative situation. Not to mention that she spent hundreds of dollars a month buying food and supplies for her birds.

But she was going to get Angus the kite he wanted no matter the cost. Only, it would've been easier to afford it if she had agreed to accept the money her mother had offered her the last time they had spoken. Not that she ever would, no matter how welcome it would be. When times were lean, Kenzie waited tables at a friend's restaurant down in Hatteras Village. If Angus picked out an expensive kite, she'd simply work off the bill there.

But in the end he chose one that was modestly priced: a blue-and-green sphere with flowing yellow and purple streamers that turned and bounced as it flew in the wind.

"Pretty cool," said Ross when he saw it.

"Can we fly it when we get home?"

"Sure. Are you hungry? How about some ice cream?"

"No, thanks," said Kenzie, opening the car door. "We just ate."

"I want to sit in the back," Angus announced. "That way I can play with my kite while I listen to the tape."

Kenzie slid into the front seat, grateful for the air-conditioning.

"Your nose is sunburned."

"We spent a lot of time on the beach."

Ross shifted gears and pulled out into the street. She had a cute nose, but he wasn't about to tell her that. "How was the aquarium?"

Angus eagerly related what they'd seen, then recounted his victories in the video arcade and described the sights along the boardwalk. When he finally put on his headphones and fell silent, Ross smiled at Kenzie.

"Happens every time."

"What?"

"He talks his head off whenever you're around."

"Ross—"

"Wait, I'm not mad about it. I'm grateful."

She studied him wonderingly. "You *have* changed, haven't you?"

"I just finally accepted that I'm not—not good at those things." He cleared his throat. "I suppose it's because I never had a proper role model."

Kenzie frowned. "Meaning your father?"

"Yeah."

"What happened?"

Ross shrugged. "He left the family when I was three."

"Left the family?"

"You know, walked out on us. Left my mother to raise me and Alex."

"Your older brother."

Ross nodded.

"I'm sorry," Kenzie whispered, meaning it.

"Oh, I don't feel sorry for myself," he said uncaringly. "I just wish I had more experience to go on when it comes to raising Angus."

But even though his lean profile was turned to her, Kenzie saw the tightening of his jaw and the way his hands gripped the wheel. A fierce protectiveness suddenly flared inside her. She wanted to wrap her arms around him and lay her head against his heart and assure him it didn't matter. That he and Angus had made a lot of progress since the first time she'd met them on the beach in Avon.

Instead she looked out the window until the urge passed.

"We never found out what happened to him," Ross said after a moment. "My mother heard from someone that he'd gone out West. Wyoming or Idaho, I don't know. After she died, Alex tried to find him and finally discovered that a death certificate had been filed in British Columbia. Natural causes. Neither of us cared to find out more.''

Now why in hell was he telling her this? He'd never discussed his father's abandonment with anyone. He'd always been more ashamed than sorry—which was probably why he was so good at trying domestic cases. Bringing deadbeat dads to justice took away some of the sting. Never mind that nowadays most of his clients were women who couldn't afford to pay their legal bills. It made no difference to Ross. All too well did he know how hard a single mother had to struggle to keep a roof over her children's heads and enough food on the table.

At least his mother had been alive long enough to enjoy his success in the Manhattan law firm of Cavanaugh, Masters and Poole. He'd been able to pay off her mortgage, remodel her house, send her on a number of trips with a friend before she'd passed on. Which thankfully had happened long before the demise of his marriage. He winced as he thought of how much it would have hurt her to discover she'd been grandmother to a grandson she'd never known existed.

No one should have to live through pain like that. He should know.

''Ross?''

He felt Kenzie's hand on his arm. Her touch was gentle, like her tone.

He didn't take his eyes off the road, knowing better than to look at her. ''Hmm?''

''Are you okay?''

''What makes you think something's wrong?''

''You're so preoccupied. And you're...um...driving a little fast.''

''Sorry.'' He eased off the accelerator.

Silence. In the back seat, Angus switched cassettes.

Ross took a deep breath, struggling to regain his composure. If he didn't erect a wall between himself and this caring, sensitive woman immediately, he was going to break down completely and make an utter fool of himself. He was going to admit things he had no right to be saying to someone he'd known for such a short time, even though they'd been intimate, even though he'd make love to her again—and again—if given half the chance.

Ross, forget her. You're going back to New York in a few days and she's a woman who dislikes lawyers, distrusts you and probably thinks you're as lousy a father as Alex does.

He clenched his teeth. "Kenzie, I know I promised to take you and Angus out to dinner, but would you mind if we called it a day? I've got a lot of work to do on this case."

"No problem."

"Thanks."

He retreated into his thoughts and Kenzie, though her heart ached, knew better than to disturb him. She had learned a lot about Ross Calder in the past few days—probably more than she ought to know. Problem was, the more she found out about him the harder it was not to care.

Like this latest piece of news. How could she possibly pretend to go on disliking him for being a coldhearted lawyer when she now knew him to be a man who had grown up without a father? Who had fathered a son of his own and not even known for almost the boy's entire life that he existed? A man who had been badly hurt on the inside no matter how convincing the tough-guy act on the outside?

Then again, what did it matter that she no longer disliked this man? That she was falling in love with him? Once he returned to New York she'd never see him again.

She quickly turned her attention back to the scenery. The sun was still high in the sky, turning the water of Oregon Inlet turquoise. Cars were still parked in the turnouts along the two-lane highway; the beaches were still filled with people enjoying the fine weather.

I love this place, Kenzie thought suddenly. Surely she'd regain her sense of peace, of happiness, here after Ross and Angus left?

"Can you help me fly my kite tomorrow, Kenzie?" Angus asked as he put in the last cassette.

"We're going kayaking tomorrow," Ross reminded him.

Kenzie looked up. "On the sound?"

Ross nodded. "It's a nature tour. We're hoping to see dolphins."

"I don't want to paddle an old kayak," Angus said from the back seat.

Kenzie shook her head. "It's really cool, Angus. Trust me, you'll have a blast. Just remember to wear sunscreen, and bring mosquito repellent and bottled water."

"The day after we're going deep-sea fishing," Ross said, grinning. "What should we take then?"

"Dramamine."

"Is that all?"

"Trust me, it's all you'll want once you get a few miles offshore."

"Ever thought about writing an advice column for the local paper? Telling city folk how to survive the Outer Banks?"

Kenzie laughed. "Not everyone's as inept as you."

He chuckled. "I've been called plenty of things in my day, but never inept."

"That's not what I heard."

"Oh?"

Kenzie glanced into the back seat to make sure Angus had his headphones on. She lowered her voice. "I have it on good authority that you're hopelessly inept in the kitchen."

"Okay, you got me there."

"You should be ashamed of yourself, making cold cereal for Angus when you've got that wonderful kitchen at your beach house to cook in."

"It did occur to me that the owners must be pretty serious cooks. I don't know what half those appliances or utensils are for."

"Shame on you."

"You make a pretty mean brownie," Ross remembered. "And Angus was crazy about your pancakes."

"Was he?" she asked, pleased.

"Where'd you learn to cook?"

"At home."

She didn't elaborate, not wanting Ross to know that she'd practically grown up in the kitchen under the tutelage of Alida, her parents' Filipino housekeeper. Much as she and her brothers had driven the poor woman mad, Alida had insisted that they all learn to cook, and from her Kenzie had developed a passion for it.

Alida's cooking was legendary in a town of legendary chefs, and from the time she'd been a little girl, Kenzie had helped prepare meals for the likes of senators, visiting ambassadors and one or two sitting presidents. She had loved nothing better than to accompany Alida to the Asian markets far from home on quests for the freshest seafood, range-fed chickens and just-picked produce before going back to Alida's kitchen to work magic on them.

But revealing to Ross where she'd learned to cook would only open up the floor for questions about her life, and Kenzie wasn't about to discuss her family with him. The topics of fatherhood and lawyers alone were too explosive for either of them.

It didn't matter anyway. Ross and Angus would be busy tomorrow and the day after with plans that didn't include her. Only a few more days remained after that until they went home. She'd probably not be seeing them again.

"Here we are." Ross turned the car into the driveway.

Angus took off his headphones. "That was a really super story!"

"Did you like it?" Kenzie asked warmly.

"Uh-huh." He handed her the tapes and scooped up his kite. "Can we go swimming now and then fly my kite?"

Ross pocketed the keys. "Sure."

"Oh, good. Can you come, Kenzie?"

"Sorry, kid. The birds'll be hungry and Zoom and Jazz probably need to use the bathroom."

She gathered up her backpack as she spoke and slid out of the car. Angus was already heading for the stairs clutching his kite. "See you later, sport."

He grinned at her. "I had fun. Thanks for the kite!"

She turned to Ross, keeping her eyes downcast while fumbling for her keys. "I had fun, too. Thanks for asking me along."

"I'm the one who's grateful. It would've been impossible without you. About the kite. How much—"

"It's a present for Angus."

He followed her to the cab of her truck and stood leaning against the door as she got in. "He just had a birthday. Let me pay for it."

"Absolutely not."

She put the key in the ignition. Ross made no move to shut the door, just stood there peering in at her, clearly frustrated. "Kenzie, I wish you wouldn't."

"Why not? You're leaving in a few days. He can keep it as a souvenir."

Ross propped one foot on the running board and stared down at it as though lost in thought. "A goodbye present," he said at last.

"Something like that." The words came out roughly.

"Okay."

He straightened. She could feel his gaze on her, searing, compelling, but she kept her eyes glued to the ignition.

"Okay," he repeated.

She put the truck in Reverse. Ross stepped back.

"Thanks again, Kenzie."

"My pleasure. See you around."

She didn't look back as she drove off, because tears were stinging her eyes. You didn't have to be a genius to realize that this was goodbye.

Ross watched the truck until it disappeared around the corner. Inwardly he struggled to squelch the emptiness and uncertainty that was the pain of Kenzie's leaving. He wasn't an idiot. Nobody had to tell him that this was goodbye.

"Man!" Ross dropped the cooler on the kitchen counter with a thump. "That was some outing!"

Taking off his sunglasses, he stretched his aching shoulders. "I forgot how many muscles you use fishing. My arms feel like rubber. How about you, son? You okay? Want something to drink?"

Angus nodded and flopped down on the sofa. He was sunburned and tousled and very sleepy looking.

"Maybe you should take a nap."

"I'm too old for naps."

"A rest, then. You've had too much sun. And I'll bet you're tired."

"Kind of."

"Good. Then go lie down for a bit. I'll take care of the fish in the meantime."

Angus climbed onto the bar stool to look into the cooler. "It's pretty, isn't it?"

Ross didn't think so, but he knew better by now than to say as much. "The prettiest one I've ever seen."

"And it's going to taste delicious, isn't it?"

"Sure." Another lie.

Angus frowned. "You know how to cook it, don't you?"

"Um, yeah."

The boy chewed his lip, then brightened. "I bet Kenzie'd know what to do with it. Can we ask her to cook it for us? I'll take a bath and a nap before she comes, I promise."

Kenzie. Ross hadn't let himself think about her at all since their outing to Virginia Beach, but now a vision of her beautiful, smiling face rose before his eyes, and an overwhelming longing poured into his heart. He told himself it was relief at the thought of placing the contents of the cooler into her very capable hands, but either way it didn't take but a second to make up his mind. "I'll call her."

"Oh, boy! Thanks!"

The bathwater was already running by the time Ross finished unpacking the car. Walking around the room, he straightened up some of the mess left over from their predawn departure for the marina while holding the remote to his ear. After four rings he started to get worried. Where the heck was she?

Five rings. Six.

"Come on, Kenzie, answer," he said aloud. "If I have to cook this fish myself—"

Seven. His heart squeezed.

"Hello?"

Kenzie's voice, a little breathless. Ross felt a wave of relief. "Kenzie? It's Ross. I'm not bothering you, am I?"

"I was out in the aviary."

"Are you doing anything tonight?"

"Why?" She sounded wary.

"We just got back from deep-sea fishing. Angus pulled in quite a haul. We released everything except one. He insisted on bringing it home to cook."

"Lucky you."

Her voice sounded warmer, and he felt himself relaxing.

"What kind of fish is it?"

The Silhouette Reader Service™ — Here's how it works:

"Dolphin. Not the bottlenose kind. The game fish dolphin."

"Yeah, I know. Mahimahi. Angus wasn't upset at first, thinking he'd caught Flipper?"

"I wondered about that, but he had no idea who Flipper is."

"Obviously not a popular rerun on the BBC, huh?"

Ross chuckled. He was feeling better all the time.

"So how much does it weigh?"

"About six pounds."

"Wow. Did they filet it for you?"

"Thankfully, yes."

"And you want me to come over and cook it?"

"If you don't mind. I couldn't talk Angus out of the idea of eating it. And the only way I know to cook fish is pan fry them as soon as they're caught."

"This is mahimahi, Ross, not rainbow trout."

"Hey, I'm not a saltwater sportsman, okay?" He gripped the receiver a little tighter. "So, would you mind?"

She hesitated. "Sure *you* don't?"

"Believe me, I'd be forever in your debt."

"Okay. What time?"

"Angus needs to take a nap first. He's exhausted. The boat left at five this morning."

"How about six?"

"Fine. See you then. And thanks." Not until Ross hung up the phone and caught sight of his reflection in the mirror over the wet bar did he realize he was smiling. From ear to ear, like an idiot.

Kenzie was carrying a bag of groceries when she showed up at the beach house a little after six. Angus had been keeping watch for her, and he ran out onto the deck as she came up the stairs.

"Kenzie!"

"Howdy, sport. Boy, did you get sunburned!"

"Are you really going to cook the fish for us, Kenzie?"

"You bet."

Only two days had passed since she'd seen him last, and she couldn't credit how much she'd missed him. As for Ross...

He came onto the deck to take the groceries from her. Tall,

tanned and smiling, he looked warmly into her eyes. "Thanks for coming."

She smiled back, the warmth tingling down to her toes. "Thanks for asking."

She was wearing shorts and a navy T-shirt that made her eyes seem bluer than ever. Her hair was brushed into a ponytail and held back with a dark blue scrunchie. To Ross she looked sweet and natural—a sexy combination that all but took his breath away.

"You look very nice." The understatement of the year.

Her cheeks turned pink. "Thanks."

"You can't imagine how glad I am you agreed to come over."

Oh, she could, because she felt the same way—and not entirely because she was looking forward to cooking dinner for him and Angus. But she wasn't about to tell Ross what the sound of his voice on the telephone had done to her this afternoon. Especially after she'd thought never to hear it again following their day at Virginia Beach.

Angus led her to the refrigerator, fairly bursting with pride. "Here's my fish. I caught it myself. Captain Mike said it was the biggest one he's seen all summer."

Kenzie hid her smile. Fat chance, but as long as Angus believed it, who cared? Still, there would be plenty to eat. She carried the pan to the sink, Angus trotting behind her.

"How are you going to cook it, Kenzie?"

"In a way even you should like. Ever had Mexican food?"

Angus shook his head.

"You're kidding. No tacos, burritos?"

She arched a brow at Ross when Angus shook his head again. "Whatever have you been feeding this child, Mr. Calder? Never mind. I don't want to know. But I may have to report you to the DSS for culinary endangerment of a minor."

"I thought Mexican food was unhealthy. All that cheese and sour cream," Ross defended himself weakly, realizing pizza wasn't exactly the healthiest food, either.

Kenzie washed her hands and began unpacking the groceries. "Not this kind of Mexican food."

Angus pointed. "What are those?"

"Taco shells. We're having fish tacos tonight."

Even Ross wrinkled his nose. "Fish tacos?"

She laughed at father and son's identical expressions. "Scoff if you wish, but wait until you've tasted them." Inwardly her heart was singing. She hadn't cooked dinner for anyone since she'd moved to the Outer Banks. And to have the chance, here in this wonderful kitchen with the golden sunset shining through the windows and the ocean rolling beyond the deck, was like a dream. A dream that included the man and the boy who were leaning against the counter watching her.

"Here, Angus, put these ingredients in the refrigerator," she instructed.

"What can I do to help?" Ross asked.

"You can start the grill. I left the charcoal down in my truck."

Ross went downstairs while Kenzie, humming to herself, began mixing ingredients for the barbecue glaze.

"Can we eat out on the porch?" Angus asked. "We haven't done it once since we got here."

"Sure. Why don't you set the table?"

She handed him the dishes and utensils and watched as he began arranging them carefully. She turned to smile at Ross when he came up behind her.

Ross followed her gaze. "He's so excited."

"It's a big deal, eating a fish you've caught yourself."

He watched over her shoulder as she began dicing a tomato. "What exactly are fish tacos?"

"They're just plain old Tex-Mex tacos, stuffed with fish and salsa instead of ground beef and black beans."

"Hmm."

"Don't be so skeptical. Wait till you try them."

But she'd made the mistake of turning around as she spoke and now she bumped into his wide chest. She tipped her chin to look at him, only to find her eyes level with his mouth. Her throat constricted. Lord, she'd forgotten what he did to her when he was this close.

"What if I don't like them?" he asked, and she saw that his eyes, too, had come to rest on her mouth.

"You can toss them off the deck," she said breathlessly. "The raccoons will love them."

"I'd rather not deal with raccoons again, thanks."

"Or pelicans, either, I imagine."

He grinned, but his eyes continued to hold hers and all at once and for some inexplicable reason Kenzie knew he was thinking the exact same thing she was, remembering the kiss they had shared that night, and what had happened after.

I wish you'd kiss me again, she thought.

"Kenzie—"

His hands were on her shoulders and it was all she could do to hang on to her sanity. Every fiber of her being ached to lift her face to his, to feel those warm, wonderful lips come down on hers, to forget for just a moment who she was and why she was here. Ross's eyes had dropped to her mouth as though he, too, were yearning for the same thing. Desire shivered through her blood in response and she couldn't resist brushing her fingers ever so lightly across his cheek.

Instantly Ross caught her hand in his and brought it to his lips. "Kenzie," he whispered, his breath hot against her skin.

The screen door slammed and Angus came bounding back inside. "I set the table. What can I do now?"

The spell was broken. She turned away quickly, blushing.

"Kenzie? What do I do now?"

She cleared her throat. "The fish can marinate in the barbecue sauce until the coals are ready. In the meantime you can help me make the salsa. Here. Tie this towel around you so you won't get your clothes dirty."

Ross helped Angus onto the bar stool and stood watching as he carefully ladled the marinade over the fish. Angus's brow was furrowed in concentration and the tip of his tongue peeked out of the corner of his mouth. Over his head, Ross exchanged a smile with Kenzie. Not for the first time was he glad that Angus was here to offer distraction.

"I like cooking," Angus said. "What next?"

"The salsa. Here. I chopped the papaya and mangoes at home. Sprinkle some of this on them."

Watching the two of them, Ross felt contentment creeping over him. For tonight, at least, the three of them were together and he wouldn't have to work at his relationship with Angus. Instead he could relax and follow Kenzie's lead in keeping the tone of the evening friendly, impersonal and focused on the boy.

And on these strange things she was cooking for supper and insisting he'd like.

At least in that regard he needn't have worried. Because fish tacos turned out to be among the tastiest things he'd ever had. The tangy, barbecued fish and the sweet papaya salsa tasted delicious mixed with cilantro, lettuce and crispy taco shells. There were sweet-potato fries and margaritas for accompaniment—the one for Angus served without alcohol.

"I could get used to this," Ross teased, reaching for a third taco. "Wish we'd thought to eat out on the porch sooner."

Kenzie leaned back in her chair, enjoying the cool evening breeze. "It's wonderful. I like listening to the ocean while I eat."

"Me, too," Angus chimed in. "Can we eat breakfast out here too, Kenzie?"

Her cheeks grew hot. "I—I won't be here for breakfast, honey."

"Why not?"

Hotter still. "Because I'm going home after I do the dishes."

"Angus and I will do the dishes," Ross added pointedly, but Angus refused to be distracted.

"Why can't you spend the night? There's a hot tub on the deck. You can use it with us."

Ross scraped back his chair. "Kenzie's got to feed her birds first thing in the morning."

"Oh, I forgot."

"And like I said, we're doing the dishes."

Kenzie didn't dare look at Ross. Angus's innocent remark about the hot tub and spending the night had conjured up images she had no right to be thinking. In silence she gathered up the platter and serving bowls.

Angus set his load of dishes next to the sink. "Can we have dessert now?"

Kenzie smiled ruefully. "Sorry, sport. I didn't bring any."

"You promised to make brownies with me someday, remember? How about now?"

She was glad for an excuse to say no. The smartest thing to do would be to go home as soon as possible. "I don't have the right ingredients."

"The grocery store's directly across the highway," Ross said.

When she met his gaze, she could have sworn he was looking a challenge at her.

Her chin tipped. Okay, she'd prove to him—and herself—that she wasn't nervous about staying. That she could ignore the sexual pull and the intimacy between them as though they didn't exist. "You'll have to move your car."

"Why not walk? All three of us?" Ross suggested. "Get some exercise before we eat those brownies?"

"I'll get my purse."

The first stars were coming out as they left the house. At this time of night the store wasn't crowded, and Kenzie sent Ross and Angus to the dairy aisle while she searched for cocoa, vanilla and baking powder.

"I must be crazy," she said aloud. Why had she agreed to stay?

You know why, her conscience answered.

"Oh, hush up."

She'd bake the brownies, write down the recipe for Ross and Angus to use again, then head home. No prolonging the evening after that. And definitely no hot tubs.

Ross and Angus were already waiting for her at the checkout. Angus was grinning impishly. "We bought ice cream for brownies à la mode."

"Ice cream!" Kenzie glanced into the cart. "No way."

Angus grinned at his father. "You were right. She doesn't want the ice cream."

"It's not that I don't like it," Kenzie said, "but—"

"But you're worried about getting fat."

"Excuse me?"

"Dad said we could get the ice cream but that you'd probably say no. He said you'd say you'll get fat if you eat it."

She tipped her chin at Ross. "What sort of stereotypical female nonsense are you teaching him?"

Ross twinkled at his son. "I think she's crumbling."

"How do you know?"

"Because she's trying not to laugh."

"That's not true! Stop looking so smug, Ross Calder!"

"Does that mean we can have the ice cream?"

"No, Angus, it does not. Take it right back to the freezer, please. It happens to be the most fattening brand."

"Know what?" Ross asked, grinning.

She propped a hand on her hip. "No. What?"

"You're very cute when you get mad."

"Oh, so now you're trying to charm me into changing my mind?"

"It's worth a try."

"Can I weigh in with my two cents' worth?"

They all turned to regard the woman behind the checkout counter.

"Please do," Kenzie said, her eyes dancing.

"None of you looks like you need to worry about what you eat. I get families in here all the time fillin' their carts with cupcakes, candy bars, those frozen ice-cream cakes. But you're obviously a nice, healthy family and you're here on vacation, right? So indulge a little, okay?"

Kenzie's jaw snapped shut. That wasn't exactly the response she'd been looking for.

"We'll take it," Ross said. He suddenly didn't look too happy, either.

"She thought we were a family," Angus crowed excitedly as they left the store.

"I know," Kenzie said through clenched teeth.

"But isn't that *neat?*"

Kenzie shot Ross a stricken look.

"It's an honest mistake," he said, shrugging.

But she sensed he felt as uncomfortable about it as she did. Not only because the woman had assumed they were married, but because of Angus's joyful reaction to that.

"I'll empty the dishwasher," Ross said when they got back to the house. "You can start baking."

Without a word, Kenzie showed Angus how to measure the dry ingredients, crack open the eggs, and cream together butter and sugar.

"Now you pour the batter into the pan," she instructed.

"How come you smeared butter and flour in it?"

"So the brownies won't stick. Here, use this to scrape out every drop."

"Can I lick the spoon?"

"Sure." She was feeling a little better after that embarrassing moment in the grocery store. Working in the kitchen always relaxed her.

"Want some?" Angus asked his father.

"Why not?"

Watching Ross bring the spoon to his lips suddenly reminded Kenzie of the kisses they had shared the other night. Of how hot and sexy his mouth had felt on hers. Of how hot and sexy she'd felt in response. And what had happened after.

"Smooth the batter a little, sport," she said quickly. "Yeah, that's good." Sliding the pan into the oven, she dusted off her hands. "Okay. Once the timer rings, take them out and let them cool before you cut them. And don't eat them all at once."

"Aren't you going to have any?" Angus asked.

"It's getting late, sport. I've got to go."

"But Johnny Savage is about to come on! Can't you stay and watch it with us until the brownies get done?"

She'd never been able to resist the pleading in his big blue eyes. And no, she didn't really want to go home to her empty house while Ross and Angus spent the rest of the evening here without her.

"Okay. But only if you promise not to talk while Johnny Savage is on. He's my favorite cartoon."

Angus's eyes went wide. "Really?"

"Really."

Ross's lips twitched. "You're a Johnny Savage fan?"

"Since day one."

"As usual, Ms. Daniels, I find you full of surprises."

Once, a comment like that would have put her on the defensive, wondering what insulting thing Ross was about to say next. But the way he was smiling at her made her breath catch in her throat. There was no question about her staying now. At least for a little while longer.

"Hurry up, Kenzie! It's starting!"

They settled down on the couch in front of the wide-screen TV with Angus between them. But Kenzie couldn't help feeling aware of Ross with every fiber of her being. The more they were together the easier it was for her to imagine things that she had no right to be thinking, wishing for things she had no right to wish for. And remember things that filled her heart with yearning. What was it about this man that threw her off balance and set her pulses racing?

Beside her Angus giggled at something Johnny Savage said to his sidekick, Major Stanton. Kenzie turned to smile at him but ended up locking glances with Ross instead. Without her being aware of it, her eyes were drawn to his lips. Would she ever have the opportunity to kiss them again? To feel those strong, sure hands roving her body? Undressing her, caressing her, driving her crazy with desire for him?

The unbidden thoughts had her all but rocketing to her feet. "Better check on those brownies."

To her relief, they were done. Letting them cool, she began unloading the dishwasher.

Ross appeared behind her. "Let me do that."

"Thanks, but I've seen that episode a hundred times. Where do these utensils go?"

"Here." As he took them from her, their fingers touched. Kenzie tried to ignore the heat that sizzled through her.

I liked you better when I disliked you, she thought angrily. *She'd felt so much safer then.*

"C'mon, Angus," she said aloud, "let's eat the brownies while they're warm enough to melt the ice cream."

They sat at the counter, where Angus's happy chatter served to help Kenzie relax.

"He sure is being silly tonight," Ross observed.

"Blame the chocolate. It acts like a stimulant," Kenzie said.

"Is that right?"

She nodded. "It's toxic to most dogs, too. Which is why you should never give any to Zoom or Jazz, Angus."

"I wouldn't, I promise."

"Is that the sort of stuff they teach you in child-psychology classes?" Ross asked.

Grinning, she helped herself to another scoop of ice cream. A small one. "That, and a whole lot more. Like what goes on in little boys' sneaky little minds."

"Do you know what I'm thinking right now?" Angus demanded with an impish smile.

"Knowing you, sport, anything."

"I'm thinking we should get into the hot tub after we eat our brownies."

Kenzie choked on her ice cream. "Know what I'm thinking?"

"What?"

"That it's late and you should get ready for bed."

"But I took a nap this afternoon."

"For barely fifteen minutes," Ross said without meeting Kenzie's eyes.

"But I don't want to go to bed just yet."

Kenzie had heard that one plenty of times from her nieces and nephews. And she knew just how to get around it, too. "Tell you what. If you get ready for bed without complaining, wash your face and brush your teeth, I'll tell you a bedtime story."

"Really? Can it be one about your birds?"

"I've got just the one," she called after him as he started for the stairs. "About a pelican named Smarty."

"Wait a minute," Ross said, putting the ice cream back in the freezer. "You're not going to tell Angus any embarrassing tales about his old man and his run-in with that pelican, are you?"

"Why not? It's a good way to have Angus see you in a more—eh—human light."

"You've got a mean streak, Ms. Daniels, you know that?" But he was grinning back at her. "And speaking of mean, what is it with that bird? Where did he come from anyway?"

"Smarty? He used to hang out at the Rodanthe pier, a few miles north of here. People fishing there loved to feed him their catches. The little girl whose father ran the bait shop called him 'Smarty Pants,' and I guess the name stuck."

"So how did he get from the Rodanthe pier to your place?"

"Over time he lost his fear of humans and started attacking them whenever he wasn't fed. He actually got to be quite a menace. And dangerous."

"I'll bet," said Ross, thinking of his rear.

"After he picked a fight with a minivan and lost, he ended up in my care with a broken wing. It never mended right, so when I released him he hung around. As you can imagine, he expected me to go on feeding him and got furious when I didn't. The situation got worse and worse and Gordon Harper finally suggested I give him a permanent home in captivity. So now he practically rules the roost, with me as his personal maid, cook and housekeeper."

"Is that the story you're going to tell Angus?"

"With a few embellishments."

"Such as what happened to my derriere the night that creature escaped?"

"Believe me, that will be the highlight of the story."

Angus's head appeared over the railing. "Kenzie? I'm ready."

"Take pity on me," Ross said as she headed for the stairs.

"Don't count on it."

Smiling, he listened to the murmur of Kenzie's voice from above. Angus had gotten into bed without a fuss and now there wasn't a peep out of him.

Ross cleared the counter and wrapped the leftover brownies in tinfoil. He had to smile again, remembering the panicked look on Kenzie's face when Angus had mentioned the hot tub.

His smile faded as his thoughts moved further, imagining Kenzie actually in the hot tub, her tanned skin glistening with steam. Imagining her out of the hot tub and in his bed, looking up at him with those beautiful blue eyes lit with passion.

Ross shook his head to clear it but found her image clinging stubbornly. No doubt about it, he'd been too dangerously aware of Kenzie as a woman tonight. Something about the easy way she'd made herself at home in his kitchen had gotten through his defenses despite the decision he'd made the night he'd made love to her never to allow it to happen again.

Undone by homemade brownies, he thought wryly.

Further wreaking havoc on his self-control tonight was the added fact that Kenzie wanted him, too. It was obvious to Ross in the way she looked at him, in the husky tone of her voice whenever they talked, in the way she couldn't seem to sit still whenever he was near.

Sighing, he massaged the back of his neck. He'd have to send her home the minute she came back downstairs. Because more than anything he wanted to take her to bed again, and that was something he couldn't allow.

Chapter Eight

"You know what I like best about that story?" Angus asked sleepily.

Kenzie smoothed the blankets around him. "What, honey?"

"That my dad laughed after Smarty bit him. I was worried he'd try to hurt him."

"Now why would he do that?"

"Because he gets mad a lot."

Kenzie frowned. "I've never seen him mad, or heard him raise his voice with you. Sometimes he sounds angry, but I don't think he really is."

Angus was silent. Sitting beside him on the bed in the darkened room, Kenzie had a hard time seeing the expression on his face.

"What is it, hon? Why do you think your dad would try to hurt Smarty?"

"Because—because Mum always told me he would," Angus whispered. "Mum always said she didn't stay married to him after I was born because he always got mad and that he didn't like animals."

"She did? Now why do you think she'd say that?"

Angus turned his head on the pillow. "I don't know."

But Kenzie had a pretty good idea. No doubt when Angus had gotten old enough to realize he didn't have a father, he had started asking questions. And Penelope had answered them with unkind lies.

"What else did she say about him? Your father, I mean?"

Angus cleared his throat. "That he didn't want me. That's why he never came to see us."

"I see." Kenzie tried hard to overcome the protective fury coursing through her at this unfairness to Ross. Penelope had been the one who'd kept Ross and Angus apart! How could she have lied to the boy by telling him otherwise? Grimly she changed the subject. "Did you like living in London with your grandparents?"

"I guess." But even though Angus had answered in the affirmative, his tone told the truth.

Kenzie chewed thoughtfully on her lip. "How about Norfolk? You told me you were born there. Did you live there with your mother?"

"My mum came during summer hols."

"Holidays?"

"Uh-huh. But Mum never stayed long, and Grannie didn't like to go there at all. So I stayed there mostly by myself."

"While they went back to London?"

"Uh-huh."

"Who took care of you?"

For the first time Angus seemed to cheer up. "Mr. Perkins did."

"Who's Mr. Perkins?"

"The gardener. He lived in a cottage down the hill. He had a daughter, Claire. She looked a lot like you, Kenzie, and she was nice like you, too. She never got mad at me when I broke something or came home muddy or didn't eat my pudding."

The way his grandparents and Penelope must have done, Kenzie thought bleakly. Angus didn't have to say as much aloud. What he *didn't* say revealed a whole lot more.

And she could easily fill in the rest. Stern and elderly grandparents who thought him a nuisance and sent him off to a gloomy old country house to live, and never allowed him to be rambunctious or to play soccer or do any of those wonderful things that were so necessary to little boys. Add to that an embittered mother who also never seemed to be around and saw nothing wrong with making her ex-husband out to be a monster in her young son's eyes. Maybe Penelope hadn't wanted Ross to have Angus, but she sure hadn't acted as though she was glad to have him, either.

No wonder Angus had opened up to her so quickly on the beach the morning they'd met! Not counting this Claire Perkins woman, Kenzie was probably one of the few grown-ups who'd ever been kind to him.

And as for Ross...Kenzie's heart ached. How could he possibly live down the bad reputation Penelope had given him? No doubt his own fears and inadequacies where Angus was concerned had served to color his behavior so that he did indeed seem cold and frightening to the boy.

Of course, it was possible that she was making too much of the little Angus had told her, but Kenzie didn't think so. And she wondered how Ross was going to undo the years of damage Penelope had done.

"Kenzie?"

"What, sport?"

"Are you crying?"

"Oh, no, honey, not at all. I just got something in my eye." She leaned down to kiss him. "Now go to sleep. It's late and I think you're about halfway to dreamland anyway."

"Uh-huh," he murmured.

She got up and headed for the door.

"Kenzie?"

"Yes, sweetheart?"

"Tomorrow's our last day. Will you come see me?"

"Of course I will. Now, good night."

She closed the door softly and went downstairs. Picking up her purse and other belongings, she headed for the back door. "I had a wonderful time," she called out to Ross as she hurried past the kitchen. "Thanks for having me."

"Wait a minute."

But Kenzie kept going.

Ross caught up with her out on the deck. Grabbing her arm, he turned her around. In the light from the kitchen behind him, he saw the tears on her face.

"Kenzie, what is it? What's wrong?"

"Nothing," she mumbled.

"Bull. Is it Angus?"

"No. Yes. Let me go, please."

"Not until you look at me," he said gruffly.

She raised her eyes to his face.

"You *are* crying." Tenderly he wiped the tears away. "Want to tell me what's going on?"

She'd never heard him use that tone before, never known him to look at her the way he was now. Stupidly, she felt the tears gathering again. But she couldn't bear to tell him, to hurt him the way he'd been hurt that night at her house when Angus had first made them aware of his unhappy past.

"It's nothing, really. It's just hard to say goodbye."

Not a lie but a different truth, only this one made the tears flow faster.

"Oh, Kenzie—" Ross's voice broke on a rough laugh. Lifting her chin, he looked down into her eyes. His touch was gentle and she tried to resist the way it made her feel.

Impossible.

Something in her expression must have changed, because Ross's expression suddenly changed, too. Turning away from her, he thrust his hands in his pockets. "You'd better go."

"Why?" she whispered. "What's wrong?"

"Nothing," he grated. "Oh, hell, everything."

And without warning, he turned around and pulled her against him.

"I can't fight this anymore, Kenzie," he whispered. "I can't fight *you*."

Kenzie gave a little sob of relief as his lips claimed hers in a passionate kiss. At last, at last. Reaching up, she clasped her arms tightly around his neck. The kiss went on and on, a magical thing filled with wonder and delight.

"You taste so good," Ross finally whispered against her mouth. "Like the ocean and sunshine. God, I've wanted this so badly."

His ragged tone awakened a fierce need deep within her. She ached for this man. And cared for him, too. More than she had suspected.

"Make love to me, Ross."

He dragged his mouth from hers. "Are you sure?"

Yes, she was. In fact, she was all but trembling with need for him. "Aren't you?"

His eyes lit with something she couldn't quite identify. Laughter? Triumph?

There wasn't time to think about it, because he swept her into his arms again and mated his mouth to hers. A hot and greedy kiss that left her gasping. He ended it only long enough to ask a hoarse question. "Angus?"

"Sleeping like a baby."

This time he did laugh, a deep, masculine laugh that shivered down her spine. His bedroom was off the kitchen, a high-ceilinged master suite with an enormous bed that sagged sensuously as he laid her down on it and leaned aggressively over her.

His mouth found the pulse at her throat while his hands slid under her blouse. She gasped as his fingers grazed an erect nipple. She hadn't even noticed that he'd undone the buttons. He continued to kiss her as he stripped off her shorts and panties, then shed his own clothes, his hands very strong, very sure.

He brought her closer, letting her feel the length of him once again, every muscle, every angle as his hungry mouth claimed hers. She sighed as he rolled her onto her back and leaned over her, pressing his full hardness against her.

"I'm on fire for you, sweetheart," he murmured against her mouth.

She gasped as he parted her thighs and let her feel how much.

"I've tried not to think about this, about you. But it's been so damned hard."

"I know," she breathed. "Ross, please—"

He turned away briefly, fumbling with the foil packet he had brought, then slowly, slowly, he slid inside. Kenzie arched beneath him and he groaned in response and began to move. Slowly at first, then faster, heating her blood until it coursed like fire through her veins. She caught her breath as the fire spread, filling her senses. Opening herself to him, she could feel the first pulses of impending climax burst within her like exploding stars.

"Ross—" She wasn't sure if she said his name aloud or only in her mind, but he caught her tightly against him at the same moment and together they let passion overtake them.

* * *

"Mmm."

Kenzie closed her eyes and leaned her head back to look at the stars. The water swirled around her naked body, and her mouth curved into a sated smile. "I could get used to this."

"Being in a spa or being naked with me?"

She turned her gaze to his wickedly grinning face. "Being naked in a spa with you, of course."

He chuckled and pulled her against him. Made weightless by the water, her body nestled tantalizingly in the hard curves of his. Leaning her head back against his wide chest, she looked again at the stars.

She didn't know when she'd ever felt so utterly content. As if every need she'd ever had, every want, had been met. And then some.

"Your elbow's poking me in the ribs," Ross said in her ear.

"Sorry." Smiling, she shifted position.

Funny, how nothing about their being together like this was the least bit awkward anymore. Ross had suggested the hot tub after they'd made love and she'd followed him willingly out to the deck to slide naked into the hot, bubbling water.

This time there was no Gordon Harper to interrupt them, no painful admissions from the boy sleeping so deeply upstairs to shatter the intimacy between them. There was just the two of them sharing a rare and enchanting moment of togetherness.

Laying her cheek against Ross's heart, Kenzie traced her fingertips over the muscular curve of his shoulder. "Angus asked me to come see him tomorrow."

"Now why am I not surprised by that?"

"I promised him I would."

"Good. That means there's no reason for you to leave."

Her eyes widened. "You mean, spend the night?"

"Why not?"

"Because it isn't appropriate. Angus—"

"Would be delighted to wake up tomorrow and find you in my bed."

She was sorely tempted, but knew she had to stay rational. "Sorry, no."

"Actually, I wouldn't mind finding you in my bed, either. Only, why wait until morning?"

"Ross! What are you doing?"

Grinning, he lifted her into his arms and carried her easily out of the tub and into the house. "The image of you in my bed kind of appealed to me. So that's where I'm taking you. But not to sleep."

"No?"

"How can I possibly think of sleep with you sitting naked in my lap?"

Kenzie didn't argue. Instead she sighed and wrapped her arms around his neck.

This time their lovemaking was much more unhurried. They allowed themselves to savor long, slow kisses and sensuous touches. To learn what gave pleasure and to be pleasured in turn.

Kenzie learned that Ross's hands could be gentle, as well as strong, and that his lips could leave a trail of fire as they moved from her throat to her breasts and lower still. She learned that stroking him slowly made him catch his breath and then wrap his arms around her as though he couldn't hold her close enough.

She learned that there was an achingly tender side to him and that she was probably falling in love with it, with him.

But she didn't dare say the words aloud. She knew he wouldn't want to hear them. Still, her kisses were sweet and her eyes shone like stars as he slipped into her at last.

"You make me wild, honey," he whispered. "I'm sorry, I can't wait."

Neither could she. Sliding her arms over his shoulders, she pressed close and moved beneath him. Ross groaned as her body instinctively began to match his rhythm.

Their mutual pursuit of release burned into her like a brand that ignited them both and sent them over the edge, Kenzie's arms locked around his neck as she cried out his name.

Afterward she wouldn't let him talk her into staying. Not only because of Angus, but because she was so shaken by his love-making and her reaction to it. In the familiar surroundings of her own home she hoped to regain a measure of control. At least she didn't have to admit as much to him, using her birds as an excuse. If they weren't fed at first light, she told him, they'd wake up her neighbors with their screaming.

Ross seemed to accept that, although he stood grinning somewhat wistfully at her through the truck window when he walked her outside. "Will you come back tomorrow?"

"I promised Angus I would."

"What time?"

"Around two?"

He frowned. "Can't make it any earlier?"

"It usually takes me until lunchtime to care for the birds."

"Then join us for lunch. Where do you want to go?"

"Why don't I bring something over? I love cooking for people and I seldom get to do it. What about chicken or shrimp salad and some homemade bread?"

He propped his foot on the running board and smiled in at her. "That sounds like the perfect plan."

She smiled back, truly happy. "Great. See you tomorrow."

But he made no move to step away from the truck.

"Ross?"

"Hmm?"

"I have to leave."

"Not until you kiss me."

Even though they'd just made love—twice—Kenzie felt the heat creep to her cheeks. "Just a quick one."

Leaning into the truck, Ross put his hand at the nape of her neck and lowered his mouth to hers. It was a long time before he stepped away, and a long time before Kenzie stirred and reached for the ignition.

"See you tomorrow," she said again, and was proud of the fact that her voice didn't waver.

But she could tell from the gleam in Ross's eye that he knew exactly how much his kiss had affected her. Grinning, he stood with his hands hooked in his back pockets as he watched her drive away.

The phone rang just as Kenzie was getting ready to go out to the aviary.

"Hello?"

"Good morning, gorgeous."

"Ross!" Her cheeks heated with pleasure at the sound of his voice, at the memories of last night that flooded through her. Then she frowned. "Is something wrong?"

"Why should there be?"

"It's seven-thirty."

"I didn't wake you, did I?" He sounded apologetic.

"No. But—"

"Good. I'm calling to ask if I can come over."

"Here to my place? When?"

"Now." He chuckled at her obvious confusion. "I'm sorry, I'm not making myself clear, am I?"

"Not really, no."

"I'd like to come over for a few minutes to talk to you. Without Angus. This is a good time because he's still asleep. That fishing trip really tired him out. The housekeeper from the rental agency is here right now and said she'd keep an eye on him for me. He likes her, and she says she knows you. Jake Bodie's sister?"

"Janet? She's super," Kenzie agreed. Thank God, she was thinking, that she'd resisted Ross's urging—and the urging of her own heart—to stay the night at his place. The last thing she needed was one of her neighbors to find her in bed with a renter in one of the agency's cottages. Kenzie's cheeks heated as she pictured the furor that would have caused. She'd never be able to show her face at the Red Drum again; the good old boys who hung out there would never let her live it down.

Not that she cared. Right now all that mattered was that Ross wanted to talk with her privately.

"What's this all about, Ross?"

"It'll have to wait until I get there."

Her heart leaped crazily. She had no idea what he wanted to say. But she knew he wasn't the type of man to play games. Straightforward and to the point, that was Ross Calder. So what was up?

Her mind raced with possibilities as she hurried around tiding up. Traded her working-in-the-aviary T-shirt for a pale blue silk blouse with a jewel neckline. Brushed her hair and put on a little mascara.

He knocked on her door as she was making coffee. She caught her breath as he grinned at her through the screen door. Was there ever a man in this world as good to look at? A man who could make her feel the way she did just because he was standing outside on her back porch?

She hid her sudden shyness by drying her hands on a towel before letting him in.

"You look great," he said softly.

"Thanks. So do you. Come in and sit down. Want some coffee?"

"Please."

She'd never had him alone in her kitchen. He seemed to take up a whole lot more room by himself, as illogical as that was. But without Angus there was nothing to distract her from his masculinity, from remembering the way his kisses, his lovemaking, had made her feel last night.

She poured coffee, got out the cream and set a plate of biscuits in front of him. "I made them yesterday. They're still fresh. Do you want honey or jam?"

"I want you to stop fussing and sit down. But I'll take the honey first."

She returned his smile, relaxing. Taking the chair across from his, she stirred cream into her coffee. "So, what did you want to see me about?"

Was it her imagination or was Ross the one who suddenly looked nervous?

"You know Angus and I are going back to New York tomorrow, right?"

She nodded, not trusting herself to speak.

"Well, I've...um...been thinking a lot about the future. About Angus and how he's going to fit in. Not only at school but with me, the way I live my life. I'm in court a lot and away on business overnight at least once or twice a month." He stirred his coffee and cleared his throat. "The two of you get along so well, and after last night I can't help but think that you dislike me a lot less than you used to."

The way he was grinning at her made her knees feel like jelly. If she hadn't been sure she'd fallen in love with him until now, she knew the moment his crooked, almost uncertain smile warmed her heart.

"You're okay, for a lawyer."

His smile faded and his eyes burned into hers. "I want to ask you something, Kenzie, and I don't want you to answer right away. I want you to think about it first. It's a huge commitment—"

Kenzie's heart stood still.

"—and it's going to change your life. For the better, I humbly hope."

Good Lord, was Ross about to propose to her?

She felt a moment's utter disbelief, then an indescribable joy that surged through her, sweeping away the pain and loss of the last, terrible year. She bit down hard on her lip so she wouldn't make a sound and dropped her eyes to her coffee mug so Ross wouldn't see the jubilant answer there.

"Kenzie—" He reached across the table to cover her hand with his. He sounded as nervous as a schoolboy asking a girl out on a first date. It only made her love him all the more.

She tried to pour all the encouragement she could into her tone. "What is it, Ross? What do you want to ask me?"

His eyes held hers, warm and steady. "Would you come to New York with us and be Angus's nanny?"

Kenzie went still. There wasn't a sound in the tiny kitchen.

"I know it's unexpected," Ross said quickly. "That's why I didn't want you to answer right away."

He got up and began to pace the floor. "It's a big decision and I want you to think it over carefully. But here are some facts that should help. Right now I've got an apartment with only two bedrooms. I've decided to give it up and move out to the suburbs, probably somewhere on Long Island. That way Angus has a better choice of schools and some trees and grass, a soccer field. Your salary won't be stellar, but you'll have room and board and your own car."

"My own car."

He grinned. "Or SUV, if you prefer."

"I already have a car."

"That rusting old truck? No way would I let you drive that on the *LIE*."

"The what?"

"The Long Island Expressway. It's not exactly a place where you'd want to break down with engine trouble."

Kenzie said nothing.

"I haven't mentioned it to Angus. I didn't want him to get his hopes up in case you said no."

Kenzie's heart cramped at the thought of Angus. But still she said nothing.

"You'd be so good for him, sweetheart. You give him the reassurance, the sense of stability he really needs."

Sweetheart. A painful lump formed in Kenzie's throat.

"Not to mention you're a terrific cook and an expert with kids."

The traits of a perfect nanny. Not a wife.

"And terrific in bed." His smile could have melted any woman's heart, but not Kenzie's. Not anymore.

"Would part of my duties include sleeping with my boss?"

Ross chuckled, then sobered as he looked at her. "Kenzie, what's wrong?"

She curled her hands around her coffee mug so he wouldn't see them shaking. "What makes you think I'd come to work for you? I don't need a job. I like the one I have."

"And you can keep it. I'd make sure the new house had a room where you can set up your drawing board and work undisturbed."

She put her face in her hands.

"Kenzie, good Lord, I thought you'd be excited about moving to New York! Look at the place you have now—"

"I happen to love this cottage," she said without looking up. "But it's—it's—"

"It's what, Ross? Small and shabby? Something to be ashamed of? What about me? Do you think offering me a job in New York, with room and board, a car and a salary, is a step up? Is that why you sound so self-righteous, because you think you're doing dirt-poor me a favor?"

"Oh, my God." Ross ran his hands through his hair. "That's not the way I meant it. I thought—"

"Well, you thought wrong."

"Hell, I had no idea—I'm sorry. I thought you'd jump at the chance."

She lifted her chin to look at him squarely. It was hard because she hated to see the genuine confusion in his eyes. She took a deep breath. "You'd better go now."

"What?"

"I'd like for you to leave."

He stared at her. She realized suddenly that he really had no idea why his supposedly wonderful proposal had hurt her so.

Proposal. She didn't know whether to laugh or cry. Could she have been any dumber?

As for Ross's assumption that her house was too ramshackle, that she'd leap at the chance to make decent wages, and then not have a clue as to why she refused...he was behaving just like a lawyer, an insensitive, self-centered, clueless lawyer.

"Kenzie—"

"Please, Ross."

"Okay." He headed for the door, his shoulders bowed. There he turned. "Promise you'll think about it?"

She pressed her lips together, afraid she was going to burst into tears. "I don't have to."

He said nothing else. Just turned and walked out of the door, out of her life.

She walked out of Angus's life pretty much the same way later that day by breaking her promise to visit him in order to say goodbye. Instead she spent the morning cleaning the aviary and treating the birds. But she felt so numb inside that even a savage bite from Smarty didn't hurt.

Afterward she went shopping at Hatteras Landing, a collection of chic new boutiques located at the Ocracoke ferry docks. It was a long drive, but she had something specific in mind. Home again by early afternoon, she packed an overnight bag and forced herself not to listen to the messages blinking on her answering machine, just in case one of them was from Ross.

After loading up the dogs, she stopped by the Harper place to ask the boys to feed her birds. Then she set off for Avon, the dogs sniffing the air from the bed of her truck.

She didn't know any of the people working in the vacation-home rental office, which suited her fine. Carrying in the foam cooler she'd bought at Hatteras Landing, she smiled at the woman behind the desk.

"Hi. I'm a friend of the Calders, staying at the Sea Oats Cottage on Hatteras Lane?"

"Oh, yes. They're due to check out tomorrow morning."

"Can you see that they get this when they drop off the key? It's for Mr. Calder's son, Angus. Something to keep him busy on the drive to the airport."

The woman smiled as she opened the lid and saw the books, puzzles, toys and snacks Kenzie had packed. "What a wonderful idea! Should I say who it's from?"

"There's a note inside."

"Oh, good. I'll take care of it, dear."

Kenzie thanked her and got back in the truck. She planned to head north, across the Chesapeake Bay Bridge Tunnel to Ocean City, Maryland. Her former roommate from college owned an art gallery there and Kenzie had a standing invitation to visit anytime. In fact, Julia's apartment above the gallery had been something of a surrogate home during those dark days of Congressional hearings her father had been forced to attend and before Kenzie had found her own place in Buxton.

Julia had patiently put up with a lot of tears, bleak silences and mood swings back then, so she ought to be prepared for the same thing now.

"Only I'm not going to cry over them," Kenzie said aloud as she turned out of the rental office's parking lot. "Either one."

Which was a lie, because she was doing so already.

Chapter Nine

Kenzie leaned back in her chair and took a critical look at the drawing she'd done. The artwork was good, the inking job even better. Not bad for an evening's work.

The subject matter was sort of depressing, though, considering it involved a recent drunk-driving accident in downtown Norfolk. But all of her cartoons had been somewhat on the dark side since she'd gotten home from Ocean City late last week.

Kenzie sighed and got up to wash the ink from her hands. It was August already and soon it would be Labor Day. Julia had strongly urged her not to attend the family reunion at The Farm.

"You don't need any more heartbreak at the moment," she'd said.

Kenzie hadn't told Julia that her heart was broken, but Julia had decided as much for herself. And it wasn't long before Kenzie was confiding in her the hurt she'd felt when Ross offered her a job as Angus's nanny in order to help her escape the near poverty in which she lived.

Okay, maybe she'd been exaggerating a little, but the hurt she'd felt that morning wasn't an exaggeration at all. She couldn't bear to remember the breathless hope that had surged through her when she had thought Ross planned to propose to her. Every time she thought of it, she'd quail inside and berate herself for being such an idiot. It was easier to hide her hurt behind the anger and betrayal she felt at Ross for making his offer sound as if *he* had been doing *her* a favor.

On top of that, she had to live with the shame of knowing she'd gone back on her promise to Angus of coming to say goodbye, even though she'd dug deep into her pocketbook to buy his farewell present. Had he listened to the tapes she'd given him on the way back to New York? Read the glossy picture book about the wild ponies she'd included along with the drawing pad, colored pencils and electronic game?

Sighing, she turned off the water in the sink. The air conditioner in the bedroom was humming and Kenzie almost didn't hear the phone. Stumbling over the sleeping dogs in the twilight gloom of the hall, she quickly lifted the receiver.

"Hello?"

"Ms. Daniels?" A vaguely familiar voice.

"Yes?"

"This is Delia Armstrong, Ross Calder's business manager. We've spoken once before."

"Yes," Kenzie said, trying to sound friendly and not wary.

"I wonder if you could do me a big favor, Ms. Daniels? Mr. Calder is out of town tonight and I'm here taking care of his son."

Jealousy stabbed at her. She'd never really gotten a satisfactory explanation as to what Delia Armstrong meant to Ross—or Angus. "What's the favor, Ms. Armstrong?"

"Angus has had a fever all day and now he's overtired and miserable. I'm having trouble putting him to bed. Lord knows, I've tried all the tricks that work so well with my grandchildren."

Delia Armstrong was a grandmother?

"I wonder if you'd mind speaking to Angus for me? He's talked so much about you these last few days and I thought hearing your voice might cheer him up."

Kenzie's heart melted. "Gladly."

A moment later Angus's voice sounded on the line. "Kenzie?"

"Hi, sport! You sound awful. Is your head all stopped up?"

"Yeah. I finished working all the puzzles in the book you gave me. I'm sorry you couldn't come see me. How's the bird?"

Kenzie winced. She'd hated lying to him, but she had owed him an explanation as to why she had to leave him a goodbye note instead of coming to visit him herself. Since she couldn't tell him the truth, she'd made up an emergency trip to Ocracoke to pick up an injured osprey. She'd felt certain Angus would understand the urgency of that and forgive her her absence.

Apparently he had.

"The bird's doing great. And Smarty sends his love."

Angus giggled. But he still sounded very weak and ill. Kenzie badly wanted to wrap her arms around him.

"So your dad's away, huh? Is Ms. Armstrong letting you sleep in his bed while he's gone?"

Angus sounded hopeful all of a sudden. "Do you think she'd let me?"

"Why not ask? I got to do that whenever my parents went out of town—but I had to share with my brothers and the dog."

Angus giggled again, then turned away from the receiver. When he came back, he sounded much happier. "She says I can."

"Great. Ask her to leave a light on, too. Tell her I said it's what me and my brothers used to do."

"I will." She could hear the relief in his voice. No, she hadn't forgotten that he was afraid of the dark or that he was reluctant to admit it.

"Kenzie? When are you coming to see us?"

She closed her eyes and swallowed hard to get rid of the painful lump in her throat. "Gee, sport, I don't know. Maybe when it isn't so hot anymore."

"Can you bring Zoom and Jazz?"

"That might not be such a bad idea."

While letting him believe she might visit. Very bad.

She took a deep, shaky breath. "I want you to get some sleep now, okay? It's the best way for you to get better."

"Okay."

"Good night, sport."

"Kenzie?"

"Yes?"

"Will you call me tomorrow?"

She hesitated. "Why don't you call me? Ask Ms. Armstrong to show you how."

"Okay."

"Good night, sport," she said again, and hung up. She sat down on the sofa, tucked up her legs and rested her chin on her knees. She couldn't remember the last time she'd felt this lonely.

And it wasn't just Angus she was pining for.

Delia Armstrong called her back half an hour later. "He's fast asleep. I can't thank you enough. I've never seen him get emotional before, but he was crying his heart out tonight."

Kenzie's own heart squeezed. "Poor little guy. Did he say what was wrong?"

"No. If you ask me, it was nothing and everything coming down on him at once. And having a fever and sore throat didn't help."

"When is Ross—Mr. Calder getting back?"

"Tomorrow night. He's in Philadelphia."

"On a case?" Kenzie asked. She knew she had no right, but she was hungry for news, any news, about him.

"No. He's interviewing a nanny for Angus. She's been recommended by a friend whose children have outgrown her."

"I see."

"Is something wrong, Ms. Daniels?"

"Not at all." Kenzie cleared her throat. "Did he tell you I turned down the same job?"

"He didn't even mention he'd offered it to you." Delia Armstrong sounded surprised. "He's said nothing about you since his return, Ms. Daniels, although Angus has said plenty." She chuckled. "From what I gather you're something of a hero to him."

"Please, call me Kenzie." It was all she could think of to say. Apparently Ross hadn't wasted any time in putting her out of his mind.

"Kenzie, maybe it's none of my business, but do you mind telling me why you didn't accept the offer?"

Because she'd been stupid enough to believe for a tiny, wonderful moment that Ross Calder wanted her to be his wife. Which was absurd, really. She'd only known the man two weeks. Had had a brief affair with him. Hadn't even realized until the last moment that she was in love with him. So why had she been about to say yes without any hesitation at all when she first thought he was going to propose to her?

She'd refused to dwell on that one since then. And she'd not had the nerve to tell Julia that part, either.

"He made some pretty disparaging remarks about my income and my lifestyle," was all she said now. The truth, but certainly not the whole truth.

"Angus told me about your birds and your house and the dogs. It sounds wonderful to me."

Kenzie was starting to like Delia Armstrong more and more. "Oh, it is. And it's my choice to live the way I do. Ross knows nothing about my background. He had no right to suggest I'd be better off accepting his generosity."

"Strange he would put it that way," Delia mused. "He's usually not so tactless."

"Maybe I bring out the worst in him," Kenzie said jokingly. The tears were again dangerously close, so she hurried to finish the conversation. "Glad I could help out with Angus. Please call me anytime you like. And Angus should, too, of course."

"Of course." Delia thanked her again, but she sounded preoccupied.

"Good night, Ms. Armstrong."

"It's Delia. And I hope we—Oh, there's the other line. Probably Mr. Calder checking on Angus. Should I tell him you and I had this chat?"

"Please don't," Kenzie said quickly, and got off the phone.

She poured herself some orange juice after she'd hung up, then stood at the back door looking out into the night. She pictured Ross on the telephone telling Delia that he'd found a wonderful nanny to help raise Angus. Pictured Angus asleep in his father's bed, tousled and feverish and lonely for a mother. Pictured Ross's bed without Angus in it—a big, empty expanse of linens that she would have given anything to share with Angus's father herself.

Lord, she'd made a mess of things, hadn't she?

She hugged herself with her arms, aching.

After a few days Kenzie began to feel a little better. Her longing for Ross and Angus was just as acute as it had been right after Delia Armstrong's phone call, but it helped to stay busy and focus her mind on other things. She had two new patients in the aviary, one of them an owlet that required a lot of nursing and a pelican with an endless appetite. At least he didn't have Smarty's aggressive attitude. But the new arrivals meant that she now spent almost all the time when she wasn't drawing or waiting tables throwing her cast net in the sound or fishing for whiting and croaker to feed her hungry charges.

When the hot August weather started spawning thunderstorms, she spent a lot of time indoors at her drawing board while keeping an eye on the Weather Channel. Hurricane season had started in the spring, but storms on the Outer Banks were most frequent in late summer and early fall. Like every resident islander, Kenzie stayed informed about the weather.

Still, when the storm clouds finally gathered, they came not in the form of a darkening sky but in another phone call from Delia Armstrong.

"Ms. Daniels? Kenzie?"

"Yes?"

"This is Delia Armstrong. We talked a week or so back—"

"Yes, I remember. How are you? Is everything all right with Angus?"

"No, I'm afraid not."

Her stomach felt hollow all of a sudden. "What do you mean? Is he ill? Has there been an accident?"

"No, no, nothing like that. But I need your help. I don't know where else to turn."

Kenzie could have sworn the older woman, who had seemed so calm and capable the few times they'd talked, was on the verge of tears. "I'll be glad to help. Just tell me what you need."

"That's the problem. I don't really know." She paused to blow her nose, confirming Kenzie's suspicions that she was crying. "I'm sorry. It's just that the news is so unexpected."

Kenzie had a hard time keeping her own voice calm. "What news?"

"Oh, dear, I simply don't know where to begin. I suppose I'll have to be blunt about it. It seems Penelope's parents want Angus back."

"Want him back? I don't understand."

"They've filed for custody. Mr. Calder was beside himself

when he got word. He's taken Angus upstate to his brother's. I have no idea what's going to happen next. Ms. Daniels, Kenzie, are you there?''

"Yes. Yes, I am." She took a deep breath to still her tripping heart. "Doesn't Ross have full custody of Angus now?"

"Yes, he does. He became legal guardian when Penelope died. But apparently her parents have contested that.''

Kenzie took another deep breath. "When did Ross find out?"

"Just a few hours ago. That's when he got the phone call from London. Now he's on his way to fetch Angus from the sitter's. He said he's taking him to Cheltenham.''

"Is that where his brother lives?"

"Yes. He didn't say what he plans to do there or how long they'll be gone. Even though he seemed calm I could tell he was distraught. And I certainly don't blame him.''

"But—but there's no way on earth Angus's grandparents can have him back! Ross is a lawyer. Surely he knows the courts usually favor the parents in cases like this?''

"Of course he does." Delia blew her nose again. "But he's a single father and has no way to adequately care for his son while he runs his practice. That's going to count against him.''

"Didn't he hire that nanny from Philadelphia?"

"Angus didn't like her.''

If Kenzie hadn't been so upset she would have enjoyed hearing that. "The custody decision depends largely on the child's testimony, doesn't it? That means Angus's wishes will count a lot, right? I can promise you he won't want to return to his grandparents.''

Delia's voice wavered. "But that's exactly the problem. Things haven't been going very well for Angus and his father lately. Lord knows Mr. Calder is making every effort, but I'm not so sure Angus is—you know—truly happy here.''

"I know," Kenzie whispered. She'd witnessed Ross and Angus's struggles often enough. She took another shaky breath, this time to keep her own tears at bay. "What do you want me to do, Ms. Armstrong?''

"Please, call me Delia. And I wish I knew. But Angus seems so fond of you, and Mr. Calder told me that you had a way of bringing him out of his shell.''

"But how is that supposed to help Angus now?"

"I don't know," the older woman said tearfully. "But I thought I'd call anyway. You seem so capable and levelheaded, and Angus seems to trust you so much."

Deep in her heart Kenzie knew this was true. She could also imagine how confused and uncertain he must feel right now, and how badly he needed someone—needed *her*—to be with him and reassure him that everything was going to be okay.

And as for Ross... Tears stung her eyes. All of the feelings she had thought had been buried when Ross hadn't asked her to marry him came rushing back, filling her heart. A fierce, protective love for this man who had been hurt so often, who didn't deserve to be hurt again. I've got to help him, Kenzie thought desperately. It's got to be me.

"Ms. Daniels? Kenzie? Are you still there?"

"Yes. Yes, I am." She took a deep breath as she made up her mind. "But I won't be for long."

"I don't understand, dear."

"I have no idea how I'm going to help Ross just yet. But I do know that I can't do anything from here. I've got to go to him. To them, I mean. Will you give me their address in Cheltenham?"

"Of course I will." Delia sounded almost jubilant. "Anything else?"

"If you happen to speak to Ross, please don't tell him I'm coming."

"But why not?"

"So he won't try to talk me out of it."

After she'd scribbled down the address, Kenzie hung up the phone and took a few more deep breaths. Then, before her resolve failed her, she dialed her parents' number in Georgetown.

There wasn't much of a chance that her father was home— he played golf every Friday—but even if he was, Kenzie didn't care. She was determined to do something she had promised herself for over a year now she wasn't ever going to do: She was going to ask her mother for money. A lot. Enough to pay someone to look after her birds and enough for a ticket for the next flight from Norfolk to New York. And for anything and everything that might come up after that.

Chapter Ten

Maggie Calder picked the last of the tomatoes and put them in her brimming basket. Back in the kitchen she busied herself washing them and putting them on the drain board to dry. Normally she hummed when she worked in the kitchen, but she didn't feel much like humming today.

Hearing a car turn down the gravel driveway, she went to the bottom of the stairs. "Angus? Your father and Uncle Alex are back."

"I'll be right down."

But it wasn't Alex's police cruiser that pulled up to the house. It was a sleek new car Maggie didn't recognize with rental tags and a young woman with blond hair behind the wheel. Drying off her hands, she stepped onto the porch.

Killing the ignition, Kenzie looped her backpack over one arm. Time to get out of the car and commit to the course she'd set when she left Buxton for New York. No cold feet or second thoughts. She'd come hundreds of miles to help Ross and Angus and she wasn't going to chicken out now.

Taking a deep breath, she stepped from the car.

"May I help you?" The petite woman on the porch was

maybe ten years older than Kenzie. She had shoulder-length auburn hair and was dressed in blue jeans and man's oxford work shirt.

Despite her resolve, Kenzie was momentarily tongue-tied. Now that she was actually here in Cheltenham, she wasn't exactly sure if she was doing the right thing. Delia Armstrong had assured her she was, but Delia didn't know the whole story about her relationship with Ross. Not by a long shot.

C'mon, girl, Kenzie admonished herself. I told you this wasn't the time to get cold feet.

She cleared her throat. "Hi. I'm Kenzie Daniels. I'm a friend of Ross's, and I—"

"Kenzie Daniels?" Maggie's expression cleared. "I feel as if I already know you, what with everything Angus had told us—"

"Kenzie!" A curly-headed missile hurtled toward her from the porch, interrupting Maggie's words.

"Angus!"

It felt good, so good to hug him.

"Nobody told me you were coming!"

"It was supposed to be a surprise."

"Did you bring the dogs?"

"They're staying at a friend's house for a while."

"Did you bring any books to read? How long can you stay?"

Kenzie glanced apologetically at the woman on the porch. To her relief she saw that she was smiling at her warmly.

"Nice to meet you, Kenzie. I'm Maggie Calder, Alex's wife."

Ross's sister-in-law. Kenzie held out her hand. "I'm sorry, I should have told you I was coming."

"No need for that. Obviously the surprise was worth it as far as Angus is concerned."

She looked wonderingly at the boy, as if she couldn't believe the change in him. "Please come in. Ross and Alex are down at the firehouse. They'll be back soon."

She didn't ask why Kenzie was here or how long she was staying. Just led her into the kitchen where she poured her a tall glass of lemonade. "Hope you don't mind sitting here in the kitchen. I've got to get the roast into the oven if it's going to be ready by suppertime."

"No, this is fine. Do you need any help?"

"Not at all. I assume you're staying long enough to eat with us?"

Kenzie nodded.

"How did you find us? We're off the road a ways."

"Delia Armstrong gave me directions. And I asked down at the General Store."

Besides, it hadn't been hard to find the neat white clapboard farmhouse belonging to Cheltenham fire and police chief Alex Calder. The town was so small that the Calders' was one of the only houses on the way out of the village.

"How about some more lemonade? And something to eat?"

Kenzie shook her head no and was about to explain her presence when Angus bounded back into the room, a gray-and-white-striped kitten in his arms.

"I finally found her. She was sleeping on the sofa. Isn't she neat?"

Entranced, Kenzie took the kitten from him. "She's precious."

"Can I take Kenzie out to the barn?" Angus asked eagerly. "I want her to see the chickens, too."

Maggie smiled. "Go right ahead."

Kenzie followed Angus into the backyard. Behind the tidy vegetable garden stood a small shed, painted red like a barn. Wildflowers bloomed in the fields behind it with the mountains rising in the background. Everything looked so lush and green to Kenzie, who was used to the sandy scrub of the Outer Banks.

Angus led her into the shed. "Look, Kenzie, there's baby chicks in the pen. And that big red hen is the one who laid the eggs we had for breakfast today. I named her Friendly French fry because she let me pick her up when we got here and she ate the French fries that were left in the car."

Kenzie had to laugh. "That's pretty clever, Angus."

"Maybe you should get some chickens, too."

"The last thing I need is more birds, thanks."

"I got to look for the eggs this morning, and I get to do it tomorrow, too."

Kenzie smiled at him. "You like it here, don't you?"

He slipped his hand into hers. "It's super now that you've come."

"I'm glad I'm here, too, sport."

She had no more second thoughts about coming—at least for the moment. Angus was clearly happy to see her and Maggie Calder had accepted her presence without question. Hopefully Ross would feel the same.

And if he didn't?

She tried not to think about that.

Maggie was still bustling around the kitchen when they got back. Kenzie was immediately intrigued by the meal preparations taking place at the counter.

"Where'd you get the eye-round?" she asked, indicating the roast. "It's nearly as big as your chicken house."

Maggie laughed. "We've got a butcher right here in Cheltenham. He supplies most of the resorts in the area with grain-fed beef."

"Lucky you." Kenzie sighed.

"Kenzie's a really good cook," Angus said.

"Is that right? Then how about taking a whack at those tomatoes? We've been eating them all summer and I confess I'm bored fixing them."

"Gladly." Kenzie was relieved to help out. She always felt most at ease in a kitchen, and she could use some help calming her nerves. Not only was she still feeling extremely awkward for having shown up unannounced on the Calders' doorstep, but because Ross was due back any moment. She had no idea how he would react to seeing her here. Or how she would react to seeing him.

"Take a look in the refrigerator," Maggie said. "Help yourself to whatever you need."

Kenzie found a wedge of fresh mozzarella cheese and set about cutting it into chunks for a salad. She had already spotted basil growing out in the herb garden and figured Maggie probably had onions on hand. "I'm going to make the dressing from scratch, if you don't mind." She was feeling more relaxed already.

"Go right ahead. And I've been thinking about what to do with you. Where to put you while you're here, I mean. Would you mind sleeping in the study? There's a fold-out couch and—"

"No problem," Kenzie said quickly, feeling a little embarrassed. No need to get nervous, girl, she admonished herself. Deep down, you know you're doing the right thing. Don't you?

"How long will you be staying?" Maggie asked. "Of course, you're welcome for as long as it takes, but—"

As long as what takes? Kenzie thought.

"Aunt Maggie? Can I have some of that string you're tying the meat with? Minnie wants to play with it."

Maggie smiled. "Is that what you named your kitten?"

"Do you like it?" Angus asked.

"As long as you won't be wanting another cat to name Mickey." She smiled at Kenzie as Angus and the kitten left the room. "Ross doesn't like cats."

"I don't think he much likes dogs, either."

"He's not a pet person," Maggie agreed. "Probably because he and Alex didn't have any growing up. I grew up on a farm not far from here. We had all kinds of animals. Alex had no choice about taking some in when we bought this house because I insisted. But he drew the line at kids."

"He didn't want any?"

Maggie smiled sadly. "No. He was worried he'd not be able to...you know, raise them properly. Because of his own childhood."

Kenzie kept her eyes on the tomato she was quartering. "I understand."

"It worked out, I guess, since we found out I couldn't have them anyway. But now there's Angus. I mean, I hope there will be." Her eyes flashed. "It doesn't seem fair, does it? Ross has only had him for a few months and now those—those people want him back."

"They're not going to get him," Kenzie said flatly.

"I wish I could believe that. But Ross said last night that when greed and money are involved, there's no telling what someone like Penelope's father will do."

Kenzie laid down her knife. "Money? I don't understand."

Maggie looked surprised. "Didn't Ross tell you?"

"No."

"It's the reason Angus's grandparents want him back. Apparently Angus's godfather, a distant cousin of Penelope's, has established a large trust for him now that Penelope has died. Whoever Angus's legal guardian is, will control the trust. That's why the Archers want him back. It's supposedly quite a bit of money.''

Kenzie put down her knife, blinded by anger. ''Are you telling me Penelope's father wants Angus back because he's going to inherit a fortune some day? I thought the Archers were rich already.''

''They own a lot of property,'' Maggie explained, ''but Ross says they always lived well above their means. Penelope's lifestyle probably cost her father plenty, too. And the legal entanglements over Angus, as well as Penelope's death, were costly, too, I imagine.''

''By legal entanglements, do you mean the custody battle?'' Kenzie asked. ''Ross told me about it,'' she added, seeing Maggie's startled look.

''He's rarely talked about it to anyone outside the family,'' Maggie said. ''I'm sure you're aware that it was blown out of all proportion by the media, especially because Ross and Penelope were such a power couple in Manhattan during their marriage. Definitely A-list, with the mayor and governor as friends and Penelope a very popular socialite. She was very beautiful and elegant, very polished. A lot of men, important men, enjoyed being seen with her. Small wonder the custody proceedings made headlines.''

''Poor Ross,'' Kenzie whispered. More than anyone, she knew just how badly the white-hot spotlight of publicity could burn.

''The media frenzy got so bad, especially in London, that a reporter actually broke in to the house and took pictures of Angus taking a nap,'' Maggie added heatedly. ''Ross was beside himself. He was worried things would go even further and someone would end up hurting his son.''

Kenzie closed her eyes to blink back the tears. ''And in the middle of all that, Penelope was killed in that plane crash. How Ross must have suffered!''

Maggie opened the oven door. ''Let me get this rotisserie going. Then I want to show you something that'll help you understand what it was like for Ross.''

What she brought back downstairs with her a few minutes later was a scrapbook bulging with newspaper clippings. ''I saved every one. Ross doesn't know I have them. He'd be furious. It was a terrible time for him.''

Kenzie sat down at the kitchen table and began flipping through the pages. Headlines from the London newspapers leaped out at her, as did glossy photographs of Ross and Penelope in happier days, Ross in a tuxedo, Penelope in a glittering gown. Ross looking young and carefree and utterly handsome, Penelope classically beautiful. Angus had inherited her turned-up nose and bright blue eyes.

''Why did you save these if you knew Ross would be angry?''

''I—I thought maybe they'd help Angus understand someday what happened between his parents.''

The headlines grew increasingly hysterical as Kenzie worked her way toward the back of the scrapbook. Breathless confessions, unfair speculation, outright lies screamed for attention at the top of every page. The photos were grainy, as if the subjects had no longer posed for them willingly but had been shot on the sly. And there was the picture of Angus asleep in his nursery, a close-up of his dark, tousled hair and chubby boyish face.

Kenzie stared at it, remembering Maggie saying that the photographer who had taken it had broken in to the room like a common thief. She closed the book, swallowing back her tears. Ross's decision to fight for Angus made perfect sense in light of all this.

Kenzie handed the scrapbook back to Maggie. ''What does Ross intend to do?''

''He definitely plans to fly to London, but when that will be he hasn't said. And we've decided not to prod. Alex felt it would be better to give him some space first. That's why they're at the firehouse today. He's helping set up for the fair. It's our biggest fund-raiser of the year.''

''Actually, we're back,'' said a voice from the hall, and a tall, dark-haired man who could only be Ross's brother stepped into the kitchen. He smiled at Kenzie. ''Hi. I'm Alex Calder. I was wondering whose car was parked out front.''

She fought hard to squelch her sudden panic. Finally the time had come to explain why she was here. Did she even know herself what she was going to say? Forcing herself to smile back at him, she reached out to shake the hand he extended. ''Hi, Alex. I'm—''

Her words trailed off. Ross had entered the kitchen behind his brother. Kenzie's heart swelled with a joy that was tempered by pain at seeing him looking so tired. If she hadn't been sure she'd fallen in love with him back home in Buxton, she knew it now. Knew it with a certainty that made her knees go weak. Even though she knew he didn't love her in return...

Sure enough, she saw him freeze at the sight of her. For a charged moment their eyes met. Then Ross scowled. "What in hell are you doing here?"

Maggie put a hand to her lips. "Oh, my! You didn't know she was coming?"

Ross's eyes snapped to his sister-in-law's face. "Do you know who she is?"

"Yes, I do. I mean, no, I guess I don't. She didn't exactly say." She looked at Kenzie, utterly bewildered. "I assumed you were here about Angus."

"I am. I've come to help in any way I can." As Kenzie said those words, she knew all of a sudden she knew what she was going to do. How she could help the boy she'd come to care for and the man she knew without a doubt that she loved. Smiling brightly, she again held out her hand to Alex. "How do you do? I'm Kenzie Daniels, Angus's nanny."

The silence in the kitchen was broken by a giggle from Angus, who was in the living room playing with his kitten. The sound seemed to bring everyone back to life.

"Nanny?" Alex Calder's eyes went from Kenzie's face to Ross's. "You didn't tell me you'd hired a nanny."

"Actually I turned down the job when he first asked," Kenzie said.

"And now you've changed your mind?"

"That's right."

"But what—how did you—" Maggie began.

"Will you excuse us a minute?" Ross interrupted, taking Kenzie's arm in a not-too-gentle grip. Out on the back lawn, well out of earshot, he finally let her go. "What are you doing here?"

Kenzie kept the bright smile pasted on her face even though

he didn't sound glad to see her. "I've changed my mind about your offer. Delia told me the job was still open."

Ross's eyes glittered. "I should have known."

"Don't be angry with her. It was my idea."

"I should have known that, too."

She hid her hurt by maintaining the smile. "You should be glad I'm here."

He ran his hand through his hair. "My God, Kenzie, do you have any idea what's going on?"

"Yes, I do. That's why I came. You'll make a much better impression on the judge by having full-time care for Angus. Someone with a master's degree and only a bit shy of a doctorate, no less."

Ross stared at her. "Is that why you changed your mind about accepting my offer?"

Her chin tipped. "Why else?"

Ross could think of a hundred different answers, but he didn't voice them. He was still reeling from the shock of walking into Alex's kitchen to find her there. From her almost defiant announcement that she now worked for him. And especially from what the sight of her had done to him inside.

No, he hadn't forgotten for a minute how beautiful she was. How sexy her smile and how warm and welcoming the light in her eyes.

What he'd forgotten was the way just her presence seemed to make any bad situation seem all right. How hard it was to feel alone with her around. She was calm and she was strength and Angus had become aware of that a lot sooner than his father had.

Okay, so maybe Ross had always sensed as much about her, too. He'd just been too stubborn and arrogant to admit as much. Had preferred to keep her at arm's length and convince himself that she was only making the situation between him and his son worse.

Well, he'd be a fool to deny that he needed her now. Just knowing she was here made him feel optimistic for the first time since that early-morning phone call from London had swept the ground from under his feet.

The corners of his mouth turned up in a wry smile. "I'm

sorry. I should be thanking you for being here, not cross-examining you.''

Kenzie wasn't sure if she felt all quivery inside because he seemed to have accepted her presence so readily or because of the way he was smiling at her. Either way, she dropped her eyes from his. ''And I should have let you know I was coming.''

''Now that you're here, are you really going to stay? I mean, have you accepted my offer?''

''For as long as it takes to get you and Angus through the custody hearings. With a few contingencies.''

He thrust his hands into the back pockets of his jeans. ''Such as?''

''This is not going to be a live-in situation. I'll rent an apartment or hotel room nearby. I'll get Angus ready for school in the mornings, cook dinner and stay until you come home at night. Weekends you're on your own, unless you're out of town on business.''

''I see.''

Annoyed, Kenzie felt herself blushing. ''It would look better to the judge.''

''Right.''

She could feel his eyes nailing into her. Both of them knew it had nothing to do with appearances and everything to do with the fact that they had gone to bed together on two occasions.

Two. Kenzie was determined to keep it that way. By refusing to move in with Ross and Angus, she had sent an unmistakable signal that there wasn't going to be a next time. She had no doubt that Ross had gotten the message.

Loud and clear, apparently. ''New York isn't the Outer Banks,'' he growled. ''Are you sure you can afford to live on your own?''

''I can. Besides, I'll need a place for Zoom and Jazz.''

''But—''

''Kenzie!'' Angus burst between the two of them and threw his arms around her waist. ''Uncle Alex says you're going to be my nanny! Is it true? Is that why you're here?''

Over his head, her eyes met Ross's. ''If your father says yes.''

''Dad?''

For a minute Ross didn't say anything. He looked as though he was struggling with something inside himself. And again he looked so worn and tired that Kenzie had to tighten her hold on Angus so she wouldn't go to him and put her arms around him. She must remember never to do that again.

"It's true, son."

Angus whooped. "Wait'll I tell Ms. Armstrong!"

He's the reason you came, Kenzie thought tearfully, watching him run back to the house. She looked at Ross and her heart squeezed. All she could do was pray she'd have the presence of mind to go on believing that.

"There's a lot left to iron out," he said, avoiding her gaze.

"I know."

"Can it wait until tonight, when Angus is asleep?"

"Definitely." She hesitated. "It's going to be okay with him, isn't it? I mean—they're not going to get him back?"

"No."

She shivered, not so much with worry for Angus but because of what it did to her when Ross looked like that. He was suddenly so self-assured once again, so aggressively male, and she couldn't help but respond in a purely female way.

She forced her thoughts back to the subject at hand. "So what happens next?"

"The papers were filed in a London family court. I've got a few days to respond."

"Is that why you came here? To consider what to do?"

He nodded. "And now that you're here I have more options. Like keeping Angus here until it's over. I don't want any publicity. No cameras, no reporters. No circus sideshow like the last time."

Her heart turned over at the bitterness in his tone. What would it take to wipe away those awful memories? "I'll stay here with Angus as long as I need to, and as long as Maggie and Alex will have us. This way you can concentrate on making your case with the judge."

"I plan to go back on Monday. No sense in trying to do anything over the weekend. And I did promise to help with the fair." He hesitated, then looked at her with a smile tugging the corners of his mouth. "Kenzie?"

"Mmm?" She was half lost in the sweetness of watching him smile.

"Thanks."

She shook off her daydreams. "For what?"

"For being here. For agreeing to help out."

"Glad to do it."

But she'd had to swallow hard and force herself to sound casual. She wanted so badly to put her arms around him, to tell him he could go ahead and smile all he wanted because he wasn't alone anymore.

Instead she followed him back into the kitchen, fully aware that it wasn't going to be easy working for Ross loving him as she did. She could only hope her feelings for him wouldn't affect her previously carefree friendship with Angus.

To her relief, nothing in that regard had changed. When Ross and Alex went back to the firehouse a few minutes later, Kenzie found herself slipping naturally into the easy relationship she'd had with Angus back in Buxton. Furthermore, Maggie Calder refused to treat her like her brother-in-law's employee, and by the time they'd gotten dinner ready they were chatting like old friends.

Maggie watched admiringly as Kenzie seasoned the gravy for the roast. "Angus was right. You're a demon in the kitchen."

"I've always loved to cook."

"Ross is lucky, then. He lives on TV dinners and spaghetti from a can. Cooking's not a skill he ever had to learn. When he was married, he and Penelope ate out every night. When they gave parties she'd hire a caterer."

"Did they give a lot of parties? I can't imagine Ross being very social."

Maggie sighed. "He was a lot different in those days. Before their marriage soured, I mean. Sometimes I see a glimpse of the old Ross when he plays with Angus or when Alex teases him about something. But now, well, I'm just glad you're here. Angus already seems much happier. I hope you'll have the same effect on Ross."

"What effect?"

Ross and Alex had appeared in the mudroom and were taking off their jackets.

"Kenzie's a terrific cook," Maggie said easily, changing the subject. "I'm hoping she'll fatten the two of you up."

"It does smell delicious in here." Alex kissed his wife and

grinned at Kenzie. "We don't always eat like this. We're just celebrating the fact we've got company."

"Family," Maggie corrected.

"Family. Pardon my semantics, dear."

Kenzie wondered if Ross had been more like his smiling, good-natured brother when he'd first married Penelope Archer. She remembered the newspaper clippings she'd seen of the handsome, carefree attorney with his beautiful young wife and wondered if there was a chance Ross might be coaxed into being that way again.

Fat chance. Not with the curveballs life had been throwing at him.

She studied the two men during supper. Alex was taller and a little heavier than his brother and going handsomely gray at the temples. He seemed utterly content in his role as fire and police chief of this tiny upstate New York town and longtime husband to Maggie. He told jokes throughout supper that had all of them laughing and didn't mind at all when Angus's kitten, Minnie, clawed her way up his pants leg for a handout.

By contrast Ross seemed to wear his masculinity much more uneasily. Restlessness seemed to crackle around him like electricity. It didn't help that he looked much too disturbingly handsome for Kenzie's peace of mind in a navy sweatshirt and faded jeans. Or that she couldn't help watching him as he ate or laughed in response to something his brother had said.

No, it wasn't going to be easy working for a man you wanted with every fiber of your being.

But Kenzie had come to New York with her eyes wide-open. Maybe she couldn't right the wrongs in her own family, but she was going to do all she could to help Angus and Ross. So what if she had to fight her feelings for him at the same time? She was a mature, self-disciplined woman, easily up to the challenge.

"The fair starts tomorrow morning, Kenzie," Alex said. "Can we count on your help?"

"Maggie mentioned something about it," Kenzie remembered. "What exactly is it?"

"It's our annual Saturday fireman's fair. A major fund-raiser for us and fun for the kids. We can always use another volunteer."

Kenzie smiled. "What do you want me to do?"

"I'll introduce you to Claire Holliday tomorrow," Maggie said. "She coordinates everything. But there's plenty for you to do. You can serve concessions, be a bingo runner, sell tickets..."

Alex took another helping of the tomato-and-mozzarella salad. "Or help in the barn. Angus told me you're good with animals. By the way, this is delicious."

Kenzie's nose wrinkled. "Farm animals? I'm not too good with those."

Alex chuckled. "Neither is Ross. You should have seen him trying to pen up the chickens this afternoon."

"Hey, don't look at me," Ross said. "I'm a lawyer, not a farmer."

"Can I help with the pony rides?" Angus asked eagerly.

"We'll see," said Ross.

"I know one thing you can do," Kenzie told him, "and that's take a bath."

"Now? But it's not even dark yet."

"You can play outside for half an hour if you like. Then we'll have that bath and read a little before bedtime, okay? But first take your dishes over to the sink."

"What about dessert?"

Maggie put a hand to her lips. "Oh, dear. I forgot about dessert."

"The raspberries were looking mighty ripe out in the garden," Alex said.

"Raspberries?" Kenzie's eyes shone. "They don't grow down South."

"Let's go pick some!" Angus cried. "Can we, Aunt Maggie?"

"Go on," Maggie said. "Take the colander along. Would you help him keep out of the thorns, Kenzie? I'll see if there's some ice cream in the freezer. And you two men can clear the table in the meantime."

But Ross and Alex stayed seated after the room emptied. Alex poured himself more iced tea from the pitcher.

"Okay," Ross said into the silence, "go ahead and ask me. I know you wanted to earlier, and I appreciate your giving me some space. But I'm ready for cross-examination now."

Alex crunched on a piece of ice. "You know what I'm thinking."

"That I do. Yesterday I told you I was having trouble finding a nanny. Today one shows up unannounced at your door."

"A twenty-first-century Mary Poppins by the look of her. Angus seems thrilled. Where'd she come from?"

Ross explained briefly.

Alex frowned. "I don't like the sound of that. What does she do for a living? Or did, before you hired her?"

"She's the editorial cartoonist for a Norfolk newspaper."

"Even worse. I don't like it, Ross. No background check, no references..."

"Stop being a cop, Alex. Delia's the one who got in touch with her and told her where to find us. She's nothing if not thorough."

"I've said for years she would've made a great police detective." Alex sounded relieved. "But I still think it's strange."

"What? Her accepting the job after turning me down? Or showing up unannounced?" Ross's lips twitched. "You don't know Kenzie."

"It's more the look on your face when you first saw her. I've never seen you look that way before."

"She took me by surprise," Ross growled.

"Yeah," Alex said, "she must have."

"Trust me, anybody would've been caught off guard. She made her refusal quite clear the day I first offered her the job."

"Knowing you, she was asked with all the tact of a lawyer."

"Now you sound like her."

Alex looked smug. "My point exactly."

Scowling, Ross got to his feet. Alex had always been too observant, which was what made him such a good cop. And that's why he'd be better off not discussing Kenzie with Alex any longer. "Are we going to clear this table or not?"

But later, watching Kenzie herd a reluctant Angus upstairs for his bath, Ross thought about what his brother had said. Had Kenzie turned him down because he'd presented his offer in a tactless manner? He knew that he'd offended her—hurt her, even, but he still didn't know why.

All he knew was that he'd made the offer because he hadn't wanted to say goodbye to her. To face the difficult task of taking

Angus back to New York and raising him by himself. Not when Kenzie made it so easy. Not when being around her was so much sweeter than being alone.

Okay, maybe Alex was right and he'd presented his case less diplomatically than he should have. Maybe he'd pushed a bit too hard after she'd initially turned him down. And maybe he hadn't been entirely truthful with himself as to why he cared so much that she'd said no.

But it wouldn't be wise to analyze that. Kenzie was here now, and Angus was happy, which made Ross happy, too. In fact, he was feeling downright optimistic for the first time since getting that call from London. No way would Angus want to go back to England now that Kenzie was here.

And he was secretly glad that Kenzie wasn't going to be a live-in nanny. Because Alex really was too darned observant. It wasn't only surprise Ross had felt at seeing Kenzie in the kitchen with Maggie. In that unguarded moment when his eyes had first met hers, he'd been overwhelmed by memories of their lovemaking. Overwhelmed by the knowledge that he wanted her still. Badly. Maybe worse now because he not only desired her but needed her, as well.

On the other hand, he was a grown man. Mature and in control, especially over his own libido. And he wasn't about to risk losing the most perfect nanny Angus could have by luring Kenzie back into his bed.

Besides, Kenzie had made it clear in so many words that that part of their relationship was over. A fleeting pleasure, a vacation fling. All he'd have to do was remember that.

No problem, he thought. No problem at all. He only hoped he'd be able to keep convincing himself of that.

When Kenzie came back downstairs, she found Ross and Alex watching TV in the living room. Maggie was reading a book.

"Angus wants you to come upstairs and say good-night," she told Ross.

"Does he?" Ross sounded pleased.

"How'd you get him into bed so easily?" Maggie asked. "He's not been very cooperative with us."

"Good nannies never reveal their secrets," Alex teased.

"There's no secret to it," Kenzie insisted. "Just think how

many different beds he's had to sleep in for the last few months. And Angus isn't very comfortable in a strange bed.''

Alex frowned. ''Poor kid. I never thought of it that way.''

Maggie, seeing the helpless look on Ross's face, put down her book. ''Are you sure you don't mind sleeping in the study, Kenzie? I've made the bed in there and put clean towels in the bathroom. You'll have to shower upstairs since it's only a half bath.''

''I'll be fine. Thank you. What time do we have to be at the fairgrounds tomorrow?''

''Around nine.''

''Do you mind if I go jogging now?''

''A fitness freak.'' Alex shook his head. ''You and Ross both. But you'll be fine. There's plenty of moonlight and the only danger you'll encounter on Cheltenham streets is a stray possum. They can be dangerous if you trip over them.''

Maggie grinned. ''Or worse, if it turns out to be a skunk.''

Kenzie laughed. ''I'll be careful.''

Actually, she was looking forward to some exercise after being cooped up in the car for most of the day. After flying into Newark International Airport and renting a car, she'd driven all the way up to Cheltenham on crowded interstates, spending more than an hour bogged down in traffic outside Albany. She'd taken a food break at a truck stop for a greasy hamburger and fries, which was another reason she was looking forward to running. Besides, it would do her good to put on her Walkman and forget about everything for a little while.

Like the fact that she'd turned her entire life upside down with the simple, impulsive words she'd said to Alex Calder: ''Hi. I'm Angus's nanny.''

The country lane that wound past the house was wide and deserted, the moon bright enough to show her the way. She didn't see a possum, but she did hear something rustling in the tall grass by the roadside. When she stopped to investigate, a raccoon lifted its masked face to her before slipping away.

When she came back to the house, the downstairs was empty. Maggie had left a light burning and a note saying they'd gone to bed. There was no sign of Ross.

Kenzie could hear a TV on behind one of the closed doors when she went upstairs to shower. After she'd washed her hair and dried off, she wrapped a towel around her and gathered up her belongings.

Stepping out into the hall, she came face-to-face with Ross, who'd just emerged from Angus's bedroom with Minnie the kitten. They stared at each other for a moment before Ross spoke.

"I'm locking her downstairs. She was sleeping on Angus's pillow and I don't want her waking him. How was your run?"

Kenzie tried to ignore the fact that she was naked but for a towel. Thank goodness it was a big one. "I enjoyed it," she said calmly. "The air's so much fresher here. And it felt good to run uphill for a change."

"I can imagine." He cleared his throat. "I know we still need to talk, but can it wait until tomorrow? It's late."

Kenzie smiled wryly. "And I'm not exactly dressed for it."

"I know."

The way he said it made her realize that he was very much aware of her bare legs and shoulders. And no doubt aware that the towel covered only part of the rising swell of her breasts. Despite herself, she found herself remembering how strong and sure his hands had been when he had caressed her breasts while making love. How gentle he had been, and how she had burned for his touch.

Heat rushed to her cheeks. "Good night."

"Kenzie—"

She didn't wait to hear what he was going to say. She hurried downstairs and locked the study door. Trembling, she pulled on her nightshirt. Okay, he'd caught her off guard this time, and she was tired following what had, in truth, been a very stressful day. She'd not react the same way next time. In fact, there wasn't going to be a next time. Tomorrow she'd ask Maggie for a bathrobe.

She was stupidly close to tears as she crawled into bed. Maybe her eyes had been wide-open when she'd made the decision to come here, she thought. Only, she'd not quite realized what she was letting herself in for.

Chapter Eleven

The fairgrounds were actually a collection of baseball, soccer and football fields located behind the Cheltenham firehouse. The largest field had been set up with rides, including a Ferris wheel and a carousel. Another field held the midway with colorful booths and stuffed animals for prizes. There were concession stands and a bingo tent. A barn and corral beyond the fields teemed with dairy cows and horses.

Angus was almost jumping up and down with excitement. "I didn't know it was so big! Can we go on the bumper cars?"

Kenzie laughed and hugged him to her. "There'll be plenty of time for everything, sport. Don't worry." But she, too, was looking forward to some fun. Lord knows, they all needed it.

Even though the fair wouldn't officially open until noon, the grounds were crowded with volunteer workers. Everyone seemed to know everybody else, and quite a lot of the locals—including some very attractive women—greeted Ross like a long-lost friend.

Kenzie was astonished at herself for feeling jealous. Ross didn't help matters by being utterly charming. In fact, he was behaving much more open and friendly with these women than he ever had when he'd first met her. And certainly not at all like a man who only two days ago had been dealt such a hard blow by his ex-in-laws. She tried not to let it bother her, but it did. And it didn't help her ego any when the women who were sizing her up immediately lost interest in her the moment Maggie introduced her as Angus's nanny.

So what did she expect? She was Ross's employee, not his date.

And if she was going to work for Ross, she was going to have to get used to awkward moments like this. No doubt he was actively dating a lot of women back in Manhattan, and Kenzie might even be asked to baby-sit Angus while he went out to dinner with someone else.

The thought was depressing.

She told herself to snap out of it. No reason to be down, what with the morning air fresh and cool and not a cloud in the sky. Hatteras had been hot for so long now that she had welcomed the chance to put on a pair of jeans and leather hiking shoes and a knitted green sweater. She hadn't been to a country fair in years and she was going to enjoy herself, no matter what.

Maggie led them into the barn where Alex and Ross excused themselves to meet with some of the volunteer firemen setting up a ring for the judging. Kenzie was introduced to Claire Holliday, an older woman with graying hair and glasses and a clipboard crammed with notes.

"Heck, yeah, we can use an extra hand. Nice to meet you, Kenzie. Mind helping out at the ladies auxiliary serving up lunch? It's our biggest moneymaker and the lines are always long."

"I'd be glad to."

"Great. Come on over around ten and we'll get you started."

"But who's going to go on the rides with me?" Angus asked.

"We'll take turns," Maggie said. "But first you can help me at the cake raffle booth."

"What's that?"

"You put a quarter on a number and they spin the wheel. If it lands on your number you get to pick out a cake to take home."

"No problem helping out there, huh?" Kenzie teased.

"No way," Angus said happily.

They wandered into the agricultural building to look at the rabbits and baby pigs. Kenzie especially liked the dairy calves while Angus was drawn to an exhibit that explained all about milking.

"Wanna give her a go?" asked the burly man holding the dairy cow's halter.

Angus shook his head shyly. "You do it, Kenzie."

"Me? I don't know how to milk a cow."

"Can't visit Cheltenham and not learn how to milk a cow," the man said, grinning.

"Please, Kenzie?"

Kenzie sat down reluctantly on the stool. The cow turned to look at her.

"Don't be scared. She's just checking you out."

Kenzie had been bitten by pelicans and clawed by raptors. She wasn't in the least bit afraid of this gentle-eyed creature. But milking turned out to be much harder than she imagined. And it didn't help that a small crowd gathered to watch, including Ross and Alex, who wandered over from the other side of the barn.

"Don't squeeze," she was told. "Strip."

Like removing blanched almonds from their skins or forcing the last bit of anchovy paste out of the tube, Kenzie told herself.

The transition from barnyard to kitchen did the trick, but no one was more astonished than Kenzie when a foamy white stream shot into the bucket. Angus squealed, everyone else applauded, and Ross reached down to help her to her feet.

"Nice going," Alex said. "Around here we respect women who know how to milk."

Kenzie smiled at him although she was distracted by the fact that Ross still hadn't let go of her arm. "I'll keep that in mind when I start looking for another husband."

"Oh? Did you have one before?" Alex asked with sudden interest.

Ross tightened his hold on Kenzie's arm in order to turn her away. "Quit being a cop, Alex."

"No, it's okay," Kenzie said. "I was engaged to be married about a year ago, but it didn't work out."

"Oh?" Alex said again.

"My fiancé dumped me just before the wedding."

Alex suddenly looked pained. "I'm sorry."

"I'm not," Kenzie shot back. "Not anymore."

"Hey, look," Alex said, relieved. "There's George Richardson. He said he might be up this way today. Excuse me."

"Who's George Richardson?" Kenzie asked as Alex hurried off.

"State senator. He and Alex were roommates in college. And I'm sorry about just now. After nearly fifteen years on the force Alex can't always remember when to stop interrogating people."

"It's really okay."

Was it? Ross watched, frowning, as Kenzie and Angus knelt in front of a pen filled with fluffy yellow chicks. Why would any man choose not to marry her? And was the broken engagement the reason that had prompted such a vibrant and life-loving woman to move into an isolated marsh-front cottage, pouring her considerable energy into caring for wounded birds instead of finishing the doctorate in a field she obviously loved?

Kenzie came up behind him and gently touched his arm. "Ross, please stop being mad at your brother."

"I'm not," he said, more aware of her hand on his sleeve than his own simmering anger.

"You are. And it's truly okay. Yes, I was hurt when Brent called off the wedding, but I'm not anymore."

Brent. What a preppy, pretentious name. Ross disliked it intensely. Somehow he'd have to make this up to Kenzie. She didn't deserve the hurt she'd suffered.

But there was no chance to talk to her about it. Maggie showed up just then to take Angus to the cake booth and Kenzie headed off to the lunch shed on the far side of the field. Ross himself had volunteered to work the front gate, and for the next two hours he handled ticket sales, greeting Alex and Maggie's friends and neighbors with what he hoped was a sincere-enough smile.

But the moment he was free he headed over to the shed bearing the sign, "Cheltenham Ladies Auxiliary."

A long line of people was waiting to be served and Ross joined them because it gave him the chance to watch Kenzie through one of the Order Here windows. She was flipping burgers like a natural and chatting with the other cooks as though she'd known them all her life. She had tied an apron around her waist and Ross liked watching the way the strings dangled below her jean-clad hips and how her French braid bobbed as she moved. He got a glimpse of her smiling face every time she turned to hand a finished burger plate to the ladies working the counter.

"Who's that woman you keep staring at? I never seen her before."

Ross turned to find one of Alex's young police officers behind him. "That's Angus's new nanny," he said coolly. And no way he'd been staring.

"How long's she staying?"

Ross frowned. While he genuinely liked Tom Peters, he could sense where this was headed. "We're going back to Manhattan first thing Monday morning," he said, emphasizing the first word.

"She married?"

"Engaged, I think."

"Oh." Tom's sudden frown was worth the lie.

Kenzie smiled when she saw Ross reach the head of the line. Laying down her spatula, she stepped to the window. "May I help you, sir?"

"Yes, ma'am." Ross wondered if Tom Parker had noticed that she'd personally come over to take his order. "I'd like a burger and a chocolate malt."

"Fries or coleslaw, sir?"

"Slaw."

She brought him an extralarge helping, and Ross stepped aside a little to make sure Tom Parker could see.

"That'll be twenty dollars, sir."

"For a burger and shake?"

She batted her lashes, looking adorably innocent. "This is a charity event, sir. A big-city lawyer like you can be counted on to make a big donation, right?"

The other women stopped what they were doing to laugh.

"That was cheap," Ross muttered, pushing the twenty-dollar bill across the counter toward her.

"But very generous."

He couldn't resist her dancing eyes. "Okay, okay. Care to join me for lunch?"

Her face fell. "I can't."

"I'll gladly make a generous donation for your meal, too."

"Go on, Kenzie," one of the women said. "For another twenty bucks we'll be glad to spell you."

They sat down together at one of the picnic tables.

"Thanks," Kenzie said. "I was starving."

"I'll bet. It's after one o'clock. Not working too hard, are you?"

She shook her head.

Ross took a bite of his burger. "This is delicious."

"That's because it's local, grain-fed beef, and those are home-grown tomatoes. And the freshest milk I've ever had. That's why the shakes taste so good. I could get spoiled living here."

Ross had to smile at her dreamy expression.

"I confess I totally misjudged the kind of people living here, too," she went on. "For a small village this place has incredible diversity. Believe it or not, the lady I've been flipping burgers with is a retired aeronautical engineer from Lockheed Martin. And the woman in the blue sweater just published her third nonfiction book. This one's about Sir Thomas Aquinas, of all things. The woman next to her is one of Alex and Maggie's nearest neighbors. She milked sixty cows before coming here this morning and she's still running circles around me."

"It's this mountain air. And the fact that the people here are pretty healthy. The nearest fast-food joint is twenty miles away. No way they're going to stick to poor diets."

"Of course, there are exceptions."

Ross turned around to follow her gaze. "Holy cow."

Angus was hurrying toward them carrying a cake the size of a basketball covered with poisonous-looking lime-green frosting.

"Look what I won at the cake raffle!"

Kenzie's nose wrinkled as he set it proudly in front of her. "What is it?"

"A mint-chocolate-chip cake. Aunt Maggie let me pick out the one I wanted."

"Obviously."

"Can I have some now?"

Kenzie cast a helpless glance at Ross.

"Why not save it for after dinner, son? That way your aunt

and uncle can have some. Maybe Alex can use it to patch the holes in his roof,'' Ross added in an undertone to Kenzie.

"Are you talking about my cake?'' Angus asked suspiciously.

Kenzie and Ross exchanged glances, then burst into laughter.

"Hey,'' Angus exclaimed, "you're friends now, aren't you?''

The laughter stilled.

"What do you mean, son?''

"You never seemed to like each other before, but you do now, don't you?''

"Yes,'' Ross said deliberately. "We do.''

Kenzie got up quickly, her cheeks flaming. "Let me get you some lunch, sport.''

"Okay.''

She was glad for the distraction as Angus tried to choose between a hamburger and a chili dog. There had been no mistaking the husky tone of Ross's voice just now, or the fact that it had shivered through her like a physical touch. Kenzie had promised herself that she would stay immune to this man's voice, his charm, the fact that she had fallen in love with him.

Okay, so obviously it was going to be a little harder than she thought. And the best thing to do about that right now was to avoid Ross as much as possible.

But that proved difficult, especially when Alex pushed an envelope across the dinner table at Ross that night.

"What's this?''

"Tickets to dinner at Beechwood Manor. Edie Parker's holding a fund-raiser for George Richardson tomorrow. You know he's up for reelection next year.''

"Then why don't you go?''

"I've got station duty tomorrow night. You, on the other hand, are free to represent the family.''

Ross pushed the envelope back across the table. "No thanks.''

Alex frowned. "You haven't accepted one of Edie's invitations in years.''

"You know why,'' Ross said, scowling.

"I sure do. And it's high time you got on with your life, at least for Angus's sake.''

"Do I have to go to a dinner?'' Angus asked, dismayed.

"No, son. Your father does."

Ross turned to his sister-in-law. "How about you, Maggs? Don't you want to go?"

"No thanks. We've been to hundreds of those. I'll watch Angus, and you take Kenzie."

Kenzie looked up quickly. "I don't think so."

"Why not?" Alex demanded.

"You'll have a great time," Maggie added. "Beechwood is gorgeous."

Kenzie shook her head, smiling to take the sting out of her refusal. "No, I really can't."

"Edie Parker's chef is one of the best in the business," Maggie went on. "Half the restaurants in Manhattan have been trying to lure him away."

"Ouch," Kenzie said. "You fight rough."

Maggie grinned. "Then why refuse?"

"Because I only brought two pairs of jeans with me."

"What if I found you something decent to wear?"

Kenzie smiled at the diminutive woman. "You're very sweet to offer, Maggie, but we're not exactly the same size."

Maggie wasn't at all daunted. "If I can find you something to wear, something truly appropriate, by tomorrow night, will you agree to go?"

"Sure," Kenzie said, confident it was a bet she couldn't lose.

Maggie and Alex exchanged glances. "How about you, Ross?" Maggie asked innocently. "Alex ought to have something in his closet for you."

"Something from a former, more fitter age," Alex added with a grin, patting his stomach.

"How long ago would this 'former age' be?" Ross asked dryly. "If you're trying to set me up in a plaid suit with wide lapels and bell-bottom pants—"

"You got something against my seventies wardrobe?"

"Other than the fact that it's full of mothballs and was ugly, no, grotesque, even in the seventies? Nothing at all."

Kenzie joined in the laughter, not at all worried that she'd end up attending a fancy dinner party with Ross. She'd been to scores of fund-raisers in her lifetime and knew that nothing short of a cocktail dress for her and black tie or tails for Ross would be appropriate for an evening with a senator.

No way Maggie was going to pull that one off.

Or at least that's what Kenzie thought, until she came out of the shower after a run the following morning to find her small room filled with garment bags and shoe boxes. Maggie stood in the midst of them, looking smug.

"What's all this?" Kenzie demanded, even though she already suspected.

"The dresses you're supposed to try on for this evening."

Kenzie had put on fresh jeans and a sweatshirt upstairs in the bathroom—just in case she ran into Ross on the way out again. Now she took her time hanging up her towel and brushing her damp hair in the small half bath next to the study. Maybe if she stalled long enough the dresses would be gone when she came back.

But of course they weren't. And Maggie had already unzipped the bags, revealing a rainbow of shimmering silks, velvet, chiffon and sequins.

Kenzie stared. "What—where—"

"I've got a friend in Lake George who's a bridal consultant. I drove down this morning and borrowed some of her creations. We're not really a backward little dairy town, you know. A lot of very influential people have summer houses around here."

Influential and wealthy. Kenzie fingered a strapless gown of ice-blue silk. Her mother had introduced her to haute couture at a very young age and she knew quality work when she saw it.

Lord help her, after all this time wearing nothing but shorts and ink-stained T-shirts, she was dying to try it on.

"That's the first one I grabbed when I thought of you," Maggie said approvingly. "Sandra says it looks best on tall, slender blondes. Go on, see if it fits."

It did. Like a second skin.

"Look how the fabric shimmers when you move. And it rustles, too, like a whisper."

Kenzie frowned. "An expensive whisper."

Maggie sighed. "It's perfect for you."

Kenzie fought temptation with all her might. "A slit skirt like this calls for heels, Maggie. You can't possibly—"

"I took a look at your shoe size while you were out running. Here." Maggie stacked the shoe boxes onto a table next to the mirror where Kenzie stood. "Nine pairs to choose from, all the right size. One of them just has to work."

Naturally there was a pair of sexy sling-backs that fit Kenzie perfectly and looked absolutely fabulous with the gown.

"Last but not least," Maggie said, and placed a rope of shimmering pearls around Kenzie's neck. "These were my grandmother's. Since I'm the only daughter, they came to me. My brother got the farm. I've never cared." She stepped back to survey the effect and sighed with happiness. "They're gorgeous, Kenzie. So are you. How can you say no to being served dinner by Chef Anton Barrieman while dressed the way you are?"

Looking at herself in the mirror, Kenzie swallowed hard. "I'm not sure about this."

"Oh, come on! Why not? And think of all the trouble I went to to put this outfit together for you."

"That's what worries me. Why did you?"

Maggie's expression grew serious. "Okay, I admit, I had an ulterior motive. Alex and I both did."

"Oh?"

"To push Ross a little. Force him to reacquaint himself with people who used to see a lot of him. Normally we wouldn't insist, but now there's Angus to consider. These are influential people, Kenzie, and you never know when you may need their help."

"I see." And because she did, Kenzie couldn't exactly refuse.

Ross was wearing a superbly cut black tuxedo when he joined her in the living room later that evening. Kenzie's heart nearly quit beating when she saw him in it. "Dashing" and "drop-dead gorgeous" were words that leaped instantly to mind, because he looked even better than James Bond at the gaming tables in Monaco, sipping a martini while surrounded by fabulously beautiful women.

"Oh," was all she could say.

Alex appeared behind his brother, grinning proudly. "Were you expecting a *Saturday Night Fever* disco suit?"

"Something like that," she said lamely.

"So was I," Ross said, although his eyes were fixed on Kenzie. "How did you manage this with your policeman's salary, bro?"

"Don't you recognize it? I wore it to your wedding."

Ross finally looked away from Kenzie to frown at his brother. "My wedding? To Penelope?"

"Who else? I figured it's as good a time as any to relaunch it into society. And it complements your escort perfectly."

Escort? Kenzie's face reddened. Good Lord, Alex and Maggie didn't consider this a date, did they?

Apparently the same thing had occurred to Ross because he, too, suddenly looked embarrassed. "You'd better get a coat. It's cold."

The gown had a smartly cut little jacket, and Maggie handed it to Kenzie without a word, although Kenzie noticed that she was biting her lip as though trying to hide a smile.

Wait a minute...

She tried to catch Maggie's eye, but Maggie wouldn't cooperate. Kenzie scowled, thinking back to what Maggie had said about attending tonight's dinner for Angus's sake. Was that really the truth or a lot of baloney? Were Maggie and Alex trying to deliberately set her and Ross up on a date? No way! She'd die of embarrassment if that were the case.

"Ooh, Kenzie!" Angus was looking down at them through the stair rails above. "You look so pretty! Like a princess!"

"Thank you, sweetheart." At least this particular Calder was being straightforward with her.

Ross didn't say anything as they drove down the quiet streets of Cheltenham. But when they stopped at an intersection to wait for a slow-moving tractor to pass by, he twisted in his seat to look at her.

"Seems we lost the bet, doesn't it?"

"Thanks to Maggie. I honestly didn't think she'd pull this one off."

"Neither did I. Especially not—" He broke off and looked away.

"Not what?"

He didn't answer until he'd pulled onto the two-lane highway. "She said she'd find something suitable for you to wear. But that's the last word I'd use to describe you right now."

Kenzie's throat tightened. "Oh?"

Actually, dozens of words had leaped to Ross's mind the moment Kenzie had entered the living room looking like a vision in the slinky blue gown. Her upswept hair had accented the beauty of her face, and the low-cut neckline had drawn attention to the slenderness of her shoulders and the long, slim column of her throat. Pearls and strappy heels, sheer stockings and a glimpse of long, shapely legs had only made his pulses race faster.

They hadn't slowed since.

What to say to her when mere words weren't enough? How could he tell her she was the most beautiful woman in the world without revealing from the tone of his voice that he wanted her more than anything?

He cleared his throat. "I think Angus described you best."

"As a princess?"

He thought he heard a trace of disappointment in her voice, but didn't have time to dwell on it because he needed to concentrate on passing the lumbering tractor ahead of them. It took a while on the narrow, hilly road, and by then the whitewashed fence marking the beginning of Beechwood's pastures had appeared through the twilight.

They joined a long line of cars inching down the manicured driveway. The stone manor house was ablaze with lights, and a pair of attendants was directing the cars to a roped-off lawn.

"It's enormous," Kenzie said wonderingly.

"Four generations of Parkers have had plenty of time to build additions." Ross parked the car, cut the engine and turned to look at her. "Are you going to be okay with this, Kenzie?"

"You mean, because we were kind of roped into it by Alex and Maggie?"

"That and the fact that this probably isn't your usual cup of tea."

"Meaning I'd be more at home in a roomful of Hatteras fishermen?"

Even though she'd spoken lightly, he thought he saw a trace of hurt in her eyes. Darn it, that's exactly what he'd meant, but he hadn't intended it to be an insult. He'd intended it as reassurance, to let her know that he understood that she might be feeling a little intimidated but that he was going to stick close to her side all evening. Being married to Penelope had made him a pro at this sort of thing, even after all these years without practice.

"Maybe I should try this again," he said roughly. "You don't look like a princess, Kenzie, and you'd look equally at home in the Sultan of Brunei's palace as in the Red Drum Café."

"If not a princess, then what?"

"Hmm?" He hadn't heard the question. He'd been watching the way the corners of her mouth had turned up when she smiled.

"You said I don't look like a princess."

"No. That's what Angus said. And he's got good taste for an eight-year-old. But to a man like me—"

Too late he realized he was treading on very thin ice. Because, to be honest, she looked nothing like an ethereal, out-of-reach princess to him but rather a sensuous, utterly desirable woman who made his pulse race like nothing before in his life.

He was in deep trouble and he knew it. Not only because he couldn't admit what he'd been about to say without revealing his feelings to her, but because he was feeling this way about a woman who had selflessly given up everything for the duration of the custody hearing to work for him as his son's nanny. How was he going to resist her once they started spending time together in his home when he could barely think for want of her out here in the car in this darkened garden?

He passed a hand across his eyes. "Look, Kenzie—"

"Excuse me, sir." A valet was at the driver's-side door. "May I take your keys?"

Ross had forgotten how efficiently Edie Parker kept her staff trained. Another valet was already opening Kenzie's door in order to help her out.

In silence they went up the stone path to the brightly lit house. Someone else was there to take Kenzie's jacket and direct them toward the reception hall. Ross had been at Beechwood Manor often enough to have looked his fill of Edie and Nathan Parker's priceless collection of artwork and early American antiques. Gold and bronze, silver and polished mahogany gleamed wherever you turned.

To his surprise, Kenzie wasn't drinking in any of it. Not the sweeping double staircase or the imported marble floor, the Venetian glass or the arrangements of flowers cascading from every waxed sideboard and occasional table. She was studying the people standing in a knot at the end of the hall waiting to be received by the Parkers and their guest of honor, and, to Ross, she appeared rather nervous.

A sudden need to protect her overwhelmed him. Moving closer, he offered her his arm. When she took it, he briefly covered her hand with his own. He felt her tremble at his touch and knew a flash of anger at his brother. Why had he ever let Alex talk him into coming tonight? He should have known that Kenzie would feel totally out of her depth in this place, even though she had no reason to. She was easily the most beautiful woman here, but of course he'd bungled it when he'd tried telling her as much out in the car.

"Just smile and shake hands," he said in her ear as they joined the other guests. "Edie Parker's the one in the sequined dress. I'll introduce you and all you have to do is thank her for the invitation."

"Okay," Kenzie whispered back, touched that he felt the need to protect her. In truth she *was* feeling a little anxious, but not because she felt intimidated in surroundings like this. Rather, she was worried she might run into someone she knew, a family friend or an associate of her father's who was familiar with her past and wouldn't think twice about bringing it up in front of Ross.

"Why, Ross!" Edie Parker, a striking older woman, seemed truly delighted when they finally reached the front of the line. "I'm so glad you could come. It's been much too long. Nathan has been asking for you and so has George."

Ross murmured the expected response, introduced Kenzie and then ushered her past Senator Richardson and his wife into the crowded drawing room. "There, that wasn't so bad, was it? How about a drink?"

"Yes, please."

"White wine?"

Her nose wrinkled. "I'm afraid I need something stronger."

He grinned. "Wait here."

As soon as he had their drinks, he hurried back, but voices hailed him and he was forced to stop and trade pleasantries with people he hadn't spoken to in years. To his relief, Kenzie was still standing in the alcove where he'd left her, but she wasn't alone. Ross scowled as he recognized Travis Sutherland. In the past, the millionaire software developer had cast his roving eye on Penelope, even though both had been married at the time. But Penelope had known how to deal with his kind; Kenzie would be at his mercy.

Ross quickened his pace, a heated rush of defensive male instinct pounding through his veins. But before he could reach them, Sutherland whirled and brushed past him. Ross could have sworn the man was blushing.

He handed Kenzie her drink. "What was that all about?"

"Nothing, really. Apparently he didn't at first understand the meaning of the word 'no.'"

"He does now, from the look of it. What did you say to him?"

"If I told you, I'd no longer be a princess."

Chuckling, he touched his glass to hers, then started to say that no one he knew had ever succeeded in rattling Travis Sutherland. But Kenzie wasn't paying him any mind. She was staring across the room at a small group of men conversing by the terrace doors.

"Good Lord. Is that Stumpy Friedman?"

"Who?"

"The gray-haired guy leaning on the cane."

Ross looked. "Who's Stumpy Friedman?"

"Ross. He's only won three Pulitzers for political cartooning. He's syndicated in just about every newspaper in the country. Justifiably so. He's absolutely the best there is."

"Edie Parker's known for her interesting mix of guests."

"I've got to meet him."

"Then I'll get her to introduce you."

But Kenzie was already walking toward him. Ross watched her speak to the group of men, saw them laugh at something she said and move obligingly aside to include her. Then she was shaking hands with Stumpy Friedman, saying something else that made him laugh again. Seconds later they were chatting like old friends.

Ross didn't join them. Instead he sipped his drink and watched. Enjoyed the way the light from the chandeliers glowed in Kenzie's blond hair. At the way the ice-blue silk draped her body like a caress. At the long, sexy column of her throat that was exposed every time she tipped back her head to laugh. And marveled at how utterly at ease she seemed.

What a woman. He was glad now that Alex had convinced him to bring her here. This was the first time he and Kenzie had ever been anywhere together without Angus—and he was enjoying it, so much so that he found he could put his worry about his son completely out of mind. Another first. And all because of her.

Someone came up to talk to him. Ross exchanged pleasantries, his attention still on Kenzie. Someone else took his place. An older man with graying temples.

"Hello, Ross."

"Charlie."

Ross was wary now, Kenzie forgotten for the moment. Charlie Alden was a partner in his old Manhattan law firm.

"Haven't seen you at Edie's for a while."

"I've been busy."

"So I heard. Got your own practice now. In Brooklyn, right?"

"Queens."

"Ah." Charlie's gaze followed Ross's. "That the lady you brought tonight?"

"It is." Ross was warier than ever. While he didn't believe Charlie had been one of the partners who had abetted Penelope's scheme to ruin him, he'd never been entirely sure. "Her name's Kenzie Daniels."

"What's she do?"

"She's a political cartoonist."

Charlie's brows rose. "Not the one from the *Norfolk Messenger*?"

"That's right."

"I'll be damned. Can you introduce me?"

"Sure."

Apparently Kenzie had fans. The small group surrounding her and Stumpy Friedman had grown by the time Ross and Charlie joined them. Kenzie beamed when she saw Ross and slipped her hand through the arm of the young man with the ponytail standing beside her.

"Ross! Come meet Jon Franklin. Do you know who he is?"

Besides being the man standing just a little too close to Kenzie for Ross's liking? "No."

"He's the head writer for *Pocket Comics*. And he does the voice of Major Stanton. You know, the character from Angus's favorite cartoon?"

"Right. Nice to meet you."

"Likewise." Jon Franklin drew a business card from his pocket and handed it to Kenzie. "I've got to go. Promise you'll call if you ever decide to make the switch to animation?"

"You bet."

Ross put his hand on her arm. "Kenzie, this is Charles Alden. We used to practice law together."

"Oh." Kenzie looked at him searchingly. Ross wondered suddenly how much she knew about his past. Had Delia ever told her what had happened between him and the partners of his old firm?

But at the moment Ross was more interested to hear what Charlie wanted to say to Kenzie. To his astonishment the first thing he asked about was her father. Although Ross thought he saw a shadow flit across her lovely features, Kenzie answered with a smile that he was fine, and Charlie immediately went on to compliment her on her drawings. After voicing enthusiastic agreement with most of her views, he self-consciously asked for her autograph.

"I'll be damned," Ross said once Charlie had gone away.

"What? Did you think I was going to chew him up and spit him out because he's a lawyer, too?"

He grinned. "Something like that."

But he knew that he owed her an apology. A big one. Because he had underestimated her badly. How could he have imagined even for a moment that she'd not know how to handle herself in a situation like this? Hadn't he told her just a little while ago that she'd be just as comfortable in a sultan's palace as in a Hatteras café? And what about her father? He was curious as to how Charlie Alden knew the man. What else didn't he know about this warm wonderful woman?

He cleared his throat. "Kenzie, I—"

"Ross! Ross Calder! How long has it been?"

He forced himself to smile at the couple bearing down on him. Evan Holmes and Ruth Bartlett-Holmes, Penelope's favorite interior designers. He reminded himself that he'd made the decision to reestablish contact with people like these for Angus's sake. Alex had been right; he couldn't go on hiding from the world forever.

On the other hand he wanted to get Kenzie off somewhere alone, to apologize for what he'd said earlier about worrying that she'd not fit in. He'd meant only to prepare her for the sometimes overwhelming spectacle that was a Beechwood Manor dinner party. Instead he'd ended up sounding like a snobbish, insensitive lout while Kenzie, it seemed, was not a stranger to functions like these or to the people who frequented them.

But when the pleasantries with Evan and Ruth Holmes had been exchanged and the couple had moved away, Ross found that Kenzie, too, had vanished. Where in heck had she gone? He went from room to room in search of her with no luck, despite the fact that she definitely stood out in a crowd.

After a while Ross began to wonder if maybe she'd gotten fed up with the noise and confusion and fled out to the garden. Then he began to wonder if maybe she hadn't gotten fed up with *him* and gone back to Cheltenham. A little later he started to worry that something had happened to her. Had she fallen ill? Slipped and hurt herself on the slick marble floor?

Heartbeat accelerating, he began searching through the more private quarters of the house and asking questions of the staff. Finally, a server with a tray of hors d'ouevres steered him toward the kitchen.

Controlled chaos was the best way to describe what was going on in the high-ceilinged room. Meats were roasting in the huge commercial ovens and men and women in uniforms were pounding, mixing, slicing and measuring at several stainless-steel workstations under the direction of a burly man who could only be Anton Barrieman.

"Ross, hi!"

A cheerful wave from Kenzie, who was standing at the butcher-block table slicing mushrooms with a long, sharp knife. Ross's heart cramped with relief.

"Sorry for running out on you. I came in to take a peek at what we're having for dinner and somehow ended up helping."

Chef Barrieman gave her a worshipful smile. "Thank goodness for that. We are shorthanded tonight."

Ross couldn't tell if the other man was looking at Kenzie that

way because of her clinging silk dress or because of her aston-
ishing skill with the knife. Hopefully the latter. He realized he
had to say something, even though he was close to speechless.
"The only place I've seen anyone slice mushrooms like that is
on the Food Channel."

"She is a natural." Chef Barrieman blew Kenzie a kiss, then
gasped. "Fenwick! You idiot! You must not whip the butter like
so!"

Undaunted by the chaos around her, Kenzie finished slicing
the mushrooms, then started on what seemed to Ross a mountain
of zucchini. He watched for a moment, wanting to say so many
things and not knowing where to start.

"You are really something," he said at last.

She slanted him a grin. "In what way?"

"I thought you'd be intimidated by your surroundings, the
people here. But you passed muster with the Parkers and Senator
Richardson, traded quips with your hero, Bunky Friedman—"

"Stumpy," she said, laughing.

"—been asked for your autograph and now welcomed into
Anton Barrieman's inner sanctum."

"Are you surprised?" she teased.

"I was at first. And that was a big mistake."

"Oh?"

He cleared his throat. It was now or never. Kenzie didn't look
as if she was about to abandon Anton Barrieman in his hour of
need for a private conversation outside on the lawn. "That last
morning on Hatteras—at your house, remember?—you accused
me of being a snob. Of prejudging you. Well, I did it again
tonight. But God knows I won't do it again. You're one-of-a-
kind, Kenzie. And I'm an idiot for not realizing it sooner."

Her knife stilled as she lifted her eyes to his burning blue
ones. "Do—do you mean that?"

"No. Yes. Actually, I'm even more of an idiot than you think.
I've realized it all along but was just too stupid to admit it to
myself."

"Ross—"

Suddenly he couldn't stand it anymore. "Let's get out of
here." His voice was rough. "We need to talk."

She followed him out without another word. He gripped her
elbow as they hurried through a rear service entrance and down

the steps to the lawn. Far away from the lighted footpath he pulled her into a bower of trailing roses. The drugging scent, the darkness surrounded them, making words unnecessary. Even before he reached for her, she was in his arms, her slim, silk-clad body pressed against the length of his.

Passion exploded. His mouth found hers and he was kissing her possessively, greedily. All night he'd had to share her with someone; he wasn't about to share her again. They were alone now. No distractions, no interruptions. They had all the time in the world.

But not the patience.

Without lifting his mouth from hers, Ross trailed his hands down her bare shoulders to her back. Unzipped silk whispered as it dropped in a shimmering pool on the grass. Kenzie moaned as his hands found her breasts, as his mouth moved hungrily to take their place.

The dark tuxedo suit blotted out the white pool of her dress as it, too, landed in the grass. Arms around each other, they sank down among them. Ross's body was all hard angles and planes in the dim moonlight. And it fit, ah, it fit so perfectly that Kenzie sighed when she opened herself willingly to him at last.

Another sigh, a low moan, and he was a part of her. Filling her. Moving inside her in a way that made her clasp her arms about his neck and pull him closer still.

"Kenzie," he whispered, his breath hot against her temple.

But he didn't say anything else. He didn't have to. Already she could feel the thundering of his heartbeat and the answering throb of her own heated pulse through her veins. She held him close as they climaxed together, the pounding of her heart forming words all its own: *I love you, I love you, I love you.*

Chapter Twelve

"Shh! Don't make so much noise! Someone will hear us."

"That didn't bother you a little while ago, did it, Ms. Daniels?"

"Oh, really?"

"Yes, really. You were—eh—quite caught up in the moment, if I recall."

Kenzie turned her back to him. "You weren't exactly subtle yourself." He could hear the laughter in her voice. "Zip me up, please."

Instead of complying, he dropped a kiss onto the naked curve of her shoulder.

"Ross!"

"Okay, okay. Here, hand me my coat. And don't worry. They'll all have gone in to supper by now."

Still, Kenzie hesitated as she stepped out of the bower. Ross thought her caution adorable. Ten heated minutes ago she'd not given a second thought to scattering her clothes all over the grass, uncaring of who might see or hear.

Then again, neither had he. Lord, he'd never lost his head like that before.

"Come on." Taking her hand, he pulled her across the lawn. Another minute and he'd have her dress off again.

The terrace was empty when they reached it. Through the tall windows they could see the guests seated at candlelit tables in the ballroom. They were all looking toward the head of the room, where Edie Parker or Senator Richardson was probably giving a speech.

"Looks like there are some empty chairs in the back," Ross said. "We can probably sneak in without raising a fuss."

"Wait." She caught at his sleeve.

"What?"

"You've got some grass on your coat."

"And you've got rose petals in your hair."

She dusted off his coat, he plucked the petals from her hair, then bent his head to kiss her upturned mouth.

Her eyes shone. "You're shameless, Ross Calder."

"Smitten is more like it."

"Careful," she warned, "you're under a spell. And spells always end at midnight."

His eyes burned into hers. "No, they don't. You're not a princess, remember? So fairy-tale rules don't count."

No rules did at the moment. Tomorrow they would go back to being cordial with each other. They would resume their roles as employer and employee and focus on nothing but their respective responsibilities toward Angus.

But not tonight. Maybe the evening was enchanted after all.

Or maybe I am, Ross thought. He'd been burning for Kenzie all night. Had battled to deny it from the moment she'd appeared in his brother's living room looking like a vision. And never in his life had he been so carried away by desire that he'd thrown caution to the wind and made love with someone in a bower of roses.

But even though his desire for this woman had been gloriously sated, a strange thing had happened. He wanted her still. And not just in *that* way. Nothing would give him more pleasure right now than to escort Kenzie into the ballroom, enjoy her company at dinner and afterward dance with her, because Edie Parker's fund-raisers always included entertainment by a big-band orchestra for guests who didn't want to turn in early.

Where once charitable evenings like this had bored him to distraction, he wanted this one to last.

He put his hand in the small of her back. "Let's go in. I'm starving."

Was it his imagination or did she shiver at his touch? "Me, too."

Senator Richardson had just finished his speech. During the applause, they made their way to the back of the room. Someone waved to Kenzie as she passed a nearby table, a platinum-haired woman whose voice was drowned out by the lingering applause but who blew Kenzie a kiss and mouthed, "Wonderful to see you, darling! How's your mother holding up?"

"Fine," Kenzie whispered back, but she was looking decidedly uncomfortable.

"That was Nina Bradford," Ross said, surprised.

"Um, yes. Do you know her?"

"I most certainly do. Penelope never appeared in public unless she was wearing a Nina Bradford original."

"Oh."

"How is it that you know her?"

Kenzie fidgeted. "She went to Vassar with my mother. They've been friends for ages." In fact, Nina Bradford was Kenzie's godmother, but she wasn't about to tell Ross that.

"Your mother. You've never told me a thing about your family."

They were interrupted by their table companions, who greeted them with introductions all around, and then by the waiters carrying in the first course. Kenzie was grateful for the distraction. She didn't really want to tell Ross about her family, especially not about her father, whose unlawful actions still filled her with shame. Thank goodness the few people here tonight who knew who she was hadn't managed to reveal her identity to Ross— for surely Ross, too, would remember last year's titillating scandal involving Republican front-runner Burton Daniels III.

On the other hand, did she have any reason to keep her family skeletons hidden any longer? After all, she should be confident enough in their relationship by now to trust that he wouldn't condemn her the way so many other people had, and to understand the pain she had endured because of what she'd done, both publicly and privately. Wouldn't he?

Then again, she didn't want to think about Ross right now, even though it was hard not to with him sitting so broad shouldered and solid beside her. She could feel him in every fiber of her being, in fact. Just his nearness reminded her of the fury of his lovemaking and her passionate response to it.

Lord, she loved him. Loved him so much it hurt.

But she couldn't tell him so.

Or could she? Would he want to know or would he be angry with her for distracting him from his worries over Angus?

Angus. How on earth could she care properly for Angus if she had fallen so hopelessly in love with his father?

I've got to get out of here, Kenzie thought, paying no attention to the friendly chatter of the woman seated on her other side. She had too much to think about, too many feelings to sort through. And she realized she wasn't quite ready yet to explain her family to Ross after all. While she hoped he had come to care for her a little, she couldn't be sure that his feelings wouldn't change after he'd learned how she'd betrayed her own father.

Ross laid a caressing hand on the back of her neck. "You okay?"

She closed her eyes at the wonder of his touch. The urge to run away was suddenly gone. "Yes, I am."

"Then you'd better start eating. After all, you helped prepare it, didn't you?"

She smiled and picked up her fork. Whatever happened tonight was suddenly fine with her. As long as she and Ross were together, she didn't mind if the evening never ended.

It turned out to be wonderful. Kenzie had forgotten how much she enjoyed dining on gourmet food while sipping outstanding wine and chatting with charming and witty table companions.

And to dance with Ross. To feel his hand in the small of her back and his body close to hers as they moved in perfect rhythm around the ballroom floor. She was smitten and she knew it and for once she didn't care.

"Kenzie?"

She lifted her head from his shoulder and blinked, suddenly aware that the latest dance, a deliciously slow number by Cole Porter, had ended. "Hmm?"

"I think it's time we said good-night."

She glanced at her wristwatch. "Four o'clock! Oh Lord, I had no idea...."

"Neither did I." Ross still hadn't let go of her, and he kept an arm about her waist as they went back to their table to collect their things.

Looking around her, Kenzie realized that the crowd had thinned over the past few hours. Oh, there were still plenty of couples out on the dance floor, but a lot of people were yawning and the bartenders had unclipped their bow ties and taken off their jackets. Near the front of the room, Stumpy Friedman was holding court at a table littered with wine bottles while Senator Richardson was doing the same at a table comprised of lawyers and elected officials Kenzie knew by sight but not by name. Powerful men, as her father had been. Still was, she reminded herself hurriedly, then looked around nervously for Nina Bradford.

She'd been so wrapped up in Ross's company that she'd forgotten about her godmother. But it looked as if Nina had already left, and Kenzie sighed gratefully at the thought. For once her luck had held.

"Tired?" Ross whispered in her ear.

"Yes," she whispered back, although she wasn't. She felt as if she'd been walking on a cloud all night. She could have gone on dancing with Ross for another hour. Or two, or even three. Maybe I'm an enchanted princess after all, she thought, returning his smile with a tender one of her own.

Ross was still holding her as they said good-night to everyone and thanked the Parkers for their hospitality. And he didn't let her go until the valet had brought around their car and he'd helped her in.

They didn't speak as Ross drove away, but it was a warm and comfortable silence, the kind each wanted to savor for as long as they could. How easy it was to forget your troubles, Ross thought, on a night like this, with a woman like this.

Earlier that afternoon he had made plans to leave for New York City in the morning. Now he found himself wondering what he and Kenzie and Angus should do together when the sun came up. Go hiking? White-water rafting? Or spend the day lazing around on Alex and Maggie's front porch?

The endless possibilities made him smile. For the first time since getting that phone call from London he had something to look forward to. Just knowing Kenzie was here made all the difference in the world.

He turned to look at her. She had leaned her head back against the seat and closed her eyes. Ross longed to touch her but wasn't sure if she was awake or not. And if she had fallen asleep, was she dreaming about him? God, he hoped so. It had never been more important to him than it was right now to know whether or not Kenzie cared for him. That she'd stopped viewing him as the heartless lawyer and failure of a father she'd accused him of being on Hatteras Island. He thought he'd blown his chances for good after she tossed him out of her house that last morning when he'd stupidly offered her a job.

He winced as he always did whenever he recalled that awful encounter. Few things in his life before or since had caused him more regret. Even now, when Kenzie had changed her mind about becoming Angus's nanny, he was still aware of how badly he had failed her by suggesting she needed the money—needed him, to make something out of her life. But he wasn't about to fail her ever again.

A tenderness he'd never known before overwhelmed him. No, my darling, he thought, I'll never let you down again.

A faint ray of pinkish sunlight filtered through the blind and fell across the bed. Instantly awake, Angus pushed back the covers. Smiling, he remembered what he was going to do today. It was something he had decided last night after watching Kenzie and his father get in the car and disappear down the driveway. Kenzie had looked so pretty, his father so happy. And he'd known right then what he had to do.

Still, even though he was terribly excited, there was an uncomfortable knot in the pit of his stomach. He wished he had someone to talk to about it. You didn't try to get two people to marry each other without help. Especially when, for a long time, he'd been so sure they hated each other. Every time he'd so much as mentioned Kenzie's name, his father had changed the subject or, worse, told him he shouldn't be seeing her anymore.

Angus had been too scared of his father while staying at Cape Hatteras to ask outright if Kenzie could join their family. All too well he could remember his mummy telling him, whenever he'd ask, that his father was bad tempered and impatient and not the least bit interested in his son. So he hadn't dared.

Sometimes he missed his mum, a little. But she'd never really been a part of his life because she'd always been going off to parties or traveling to Spain or Malta with her friends. He'd hated staying alone with his grandparents, who were so cranky about his presence in the house that he wasn't even allowed to own a football, let alone bring one indoors.

Those times when his grandparents had also gone away on holiday and sent him to Norfolk to stay were the times Angus had been happiest.

"Why can't I live with Claire and Mr. Perkins?" he'd demanded tearfully not long after Mummy had died, terrified of the thought of going to live with his father.

"Because your father wants you now," his grandmother had snapped.

"Heaven knows we can't have a grandson of ours being raised by a gardener and his daughter," his grandfather had added sternly.

Unfortunately, Angus had realized right away upon meeting his father that Mum had been right about this tall, silent man who'd treated Angus as though he didn't really want him around. At least in New York there was Miss Delia, who was warm and friendly and tried really hard to make Angus feel at home.

And Kenzie. Besides Claire, Angus had never met a woman who gave hugs so freely, who seemed to truly like his company and was fun besides. Certainly none of the teachers at boarding school, or his grandparents or even his mum had made Angus feel that they truly wanted him around or that they liked him and were interested in what he said and thought and did.

Something in his heart always felt warm and good whenever Kenzie was there. And he thought maybe his father felt that way now, too. Because ever since they'd gotten back from their trip to Cape Hatteras Angus had started to wonder if maybe his father wasn't lonely. If maybe he didn't miss Kenzie a little, too.

For a long time now he'd been working up the courage to talk to his father about her. To try and put into words how much better he felt when Kenzie was with them. How much better his father seemed to feel.

But then, just a few days ago, something had happened, only Angus didn't know what. He knew only that his father had become as distant as in the days before they'd met Kenzie, and that he hadn't talked at all on the drive up to Uncle Alex and Aunt Maggie's house. He knew that the three of them talked about him at the kitchen table whenever they thought he wasn't around. Angus had no idea if he was in trouble or not, and he'd been too scared to ask.

But then Kenzie had shown up, all hugs and kisses and calling him "sport," a nickname he loved, and right away Angus had known everything was going to be okay. Surely his father, too, had come to realize how much they needed her?

His heart knocked against his ribs as he pulled on his jeans and sweatshirt. It was much too early to be getting up, but he was too excited to go back to sleep. The way his father had looked at Kenzie last night...maybe, just maybe...

Then again, did he really think he could fix things between them? What if his father and Kenzie weren't really in love? After all, there was no soft laughter or kisses between them like Uncle Alex and Aunt Maggie shared whenever they were together.

Angus's stomach tightened in fear. Oh, yeah? What about the way they'd laughed together when he'd shown them the cake he'd won at the fair? Or the way Dad had looked at Kenzie when they'd left for the party last night? That, most of all, had convinced Angus that something magical was going to happen. After all, Kenzie hadn't looked like a fairy-tale princess for nothing. And although Angus didn't really believe in fairy tales anymore, he couldn't help remembering that "happily every afters" always happened at the end of a ball.

Okay, his father and Kenzie hadn't exactly gone to a ball, according to Aunt Maggie. But didn't a dinner party count?

Though he'd waited up for them as long as he could, he'd finally fallen asleep. So that meant that even though it was superearly right now and the sun was barely up, he was going to wake up his dad and talk to him. Man to man. Explain what he felt and what he wanted and why it made sense for Kenzie to become his mum. Kenzie had always talked to him about his thoughts and feelings and how it was okay not to hide them, so that's what he was going to do with his dad, no matter how much his heart might be pounding at the thought.

His head came up at the sound of a car turning into the driveway. Scrambling onto his bed, he looked out of the window. A van with a strange satellite dish had pulled up on the lawn. So had another one, and an SUV and two cars. Each one of them had big signs painted on the sides. "News Channel 12," Angus read on one of them. "WSSR-TV," he read on another.

People were spilling out of the cars. Some of them had microphones. A lady in a blue blazer was combing her hair and putting on lipstick. Another one was talking to a man with a camera and pointing to the house.

The porch door slammed. Angus saw his uncle walk down the driveway. He was dressed in his police sweats and wearing house slippers on his feet, like he'd just woken up and hadn't had time to get dressed. Angus watched him talk for a while with the people on the lawn. He didn't look at all happy. In fact, he was scowling, and at one point gestured angrily toward the house.

Downstairs the telephone rang. It was a long time before he heard his aunt Maggie answer it. When she hung up, it rang again. Angus could hear her voice filtering up the stairs. She sounded mad.

Something's happened, he thought numbly. Something bad.

Without bothering to take off his clothes, he scooted back into bed and pulled the covers over his head. The happy moments he'd spent dreaming of having Kenzie for his mum were forgotten. That all-too-familiar feeling of uncertainty, of some vaguely anticipated doom, crept over him once again.

The way it had before they'd finally told him Mum was very, very sick.

When they told him she'd died.

When they told him he was going to go live in a country he'd never been to with a father he'd never seen.

When his father had woken him up very early a few mornings ago and brought him here without a word of explanation.

"Kenzie," he whispered, tears starting in his eyes. "Where are you?"

* * *

Kenzie had been dozing when Ross's car turned down the lane heading out of Cheltenham Village, but his muffled oath made her sit up with a start. Pushing the hair from her eyes, she gasped when she saw the cars and vans parked on the street in front of Alex and Maggie's house.

"What is it?" she demanded, thinking instantly of Angus. "An accident?"

Ross jerked the car to a halt. "Those are news trucks, not ambulances."

"They're blocking the road. How can we get past them?"

"I don't want to get past them," Ross said grimly. "I have a feeling I know why they're here."

"Oh, Ross, no! You can't think it's because of Angus and you!" Dismayed, Kenzie laid her hand on his arm. The muscles were rigid with tension beneath her fingertips. "Your brother is the chief of police," she argued calmly. "I'll bet he has news crews in his front yard all the time."

"I don't know that for sure." Slowly Ross pulled the car up under an overhanging tree well out of sight of the front yard. "I'm going to sneak around back."

"I'm coming with you." Kenzie's heart was hammering as she gathered up her belongings. What had happened? Were Maggie and Alex all right? Was Angus safely asleep in his bed? The need to assure herself was overwhelming.

"Ready?" Ross asked.

"I'll try."

While she had plenty of experience dodging staked-out camera crews, she wasn't sure she'd be able to run fast enough in her heels and tight-fitting gown to make it around back before she and Ross were seen. Fortunately a pickup truck appeared around the bend on the far side of the Calder house just then. All of the cameramen, reporters and photographers turned expectantly as it approached, and Kenzie, wasting no time, followed Ross across the field behind Alex and Maggie's house. He helped her climb through the fence railings and, hand beneath her arm, pulled her toward the back door.

Kenzie's heart was tripping by now. Even though she'd seen no evidence of an ambulance or paramedics, she couldn't help fearing the worst. If only she and Ross hadn't stayed so long dancing at the Parkers! Or taken the long way home through the dark pine forests and past a silent lake steaming with mist under the graying light of dawn. It had been pretty at the time, and very romantic, but now she wished fervently they'd not made a point to dawdle so much.

"Alex! Is everyone all right?"

Ross's brother had jerked open the back door for them. "Considering the fact they've been camped out there for a while now, we're fine."

"Where's Angus?"

"Still asleep as far as I know."

"Who are they? What do they want?"

Alex's hard gaze settled on Kenzie. "Why don't you tell us?"

"Me? I—I'm afraid I don't understand."

"No? Then maybe I should clue you in. Seems that somebody at the Parkers' place recognized the daughter of Burton Daniels III last night." He shifted his gaze to Ross. "You know Burton Daniels, I presume? The lawyer who lost the Republican nomination last year because of some offshore hanky-panky with questionable campaign contributions?"

"Yes, I remember," Ross said impatiently. "What's that got to do with—" He broke off, a stunned look creeping across his handsome, unshaven face.

"That's right, bro. This is the same Burton Daniels's daughter who won that Pulitzer Prize for exposing her father's perfidy in a political cartoon. What a bittersweet award that must have been, huh, Kenzie? So what did you do with the money?"

"I—I gave it to a nonprofit that provides medical care for kids on Hatteras Island," Kenzie whispered. "And—and used some to build the aviary. But—"

"Is *that* why they're here?" Ross interrupted, as though just coming around to believing it. "Not because of me? The fact that Pen's parents want Angus?"

"Not a breath of that yet, Ross. No, it's Ms. Daniels here, whose mere presence is pretty big news for a town our size," Alex growled. "And why not, considering the Daniels family usually sticks to the Washington and Newport social circles? Far as I remember they also like rubbing elbows with presidents and foreign statesmen, and playing polo with Prince Charles—"

"That wasn't—my brother Burt was a Rhodes scholar," Kenzie said desperately. "He was invited by a colleague—"

"If you could page through the back issues of all those glossy magazines Penelope used to read, Ross," Alex interrupted, "I'll bet her family appeared in any number of them."

"But why should that matter?" Kenzie cried.

Alex jerked his thumb over his shoulder. "Because *they're* out there waiting to talk to you. Wanting to know how it feels to be back on the social circuit after all but dropping off the face of the earth. They want a statement from you, too, Ross, about how she happened to pop up at a Republican fund-raiser as your date." Alex looked disgusted. "They asked me how it feels to have such a 'celebrity' for a houseguest. Naturally I didn't comment."

Kenzie looked at him, too numb to speak.

"Maggie has already fielded three calls from Senator Richardson's staff," Alex went on. "They're waiting to see what kind of fallout this is going to have. Sometimes notoriety can help a campaign. Sometimes it can tarnish an otherwise blameless reputation. At any rate, they're not pleased that you didn't give them some advance warning."

"I would have appreciated some, too." Now Ross's eyes were burning into hers, and, unlike Alex's, his expression had the power to wound.

Kenzie twisted her hands together. "I'm sorry. Truly sorry. I should have told you, but—"

"Damned right, you should have." He towered over her, eyes glittering now that the shock was wearing off. He seemed even angrier than Alex. "Maybe then I would have known better than to offer you a job as Angus's nanny, not made a fool of myself suggesting you needed a job, you, the daughter of Burton Daniels, of all people! No wonder you brushed me off that day!"

Kenzie fought back the tears. "That's not why I turned you down! And I'm here now, aren't I?"

He nodded toward the street. "And so are they! The last thing I need right now. Media scrutiny! Don't you remember that publicity ruined my chances with Angus the last time? No telling how long it'll be before some intrepid reporter for *E!* or *Entertainment Tonight* digs up some dirt on the guy who escorted you last night, like finding out that I have a juicy past of my own. If you've cost me my son, Ms. Daniels—''

Kenzie recoiled in horror.

''Ross.''

Kenzie didn't wait to hear what Maggie was going to say as she appeared in the hallway behind them. Whirling, she ran to the back door.

''Wait a minute.'' Alex, his anger defused in the face of her pain, had her by the arm. ''Where you going?''

''To give them what they want,'' Kenzie said. ''Then maybe they'll pack up and leave all of you alone.''

''You can't handle them.''

''Try me.''

Alex's voice was filled with remorse. ''Look, kid, I know you're usually tough. But you ain't so tough right now. Mainly thanks to me, I think.''

Tears stung her eyes at the sudden sympathy in his tone. He was right. Her shoulders slumped.

''Go to bed,'' Maggie said, putting an arm around her. ''You look exhausted.''

''But—''

''Alex can wait the vultures out. No need for you to hang around. Maybe they'll be gone by the time you get up.'' She gave Kenzie a gentle push. ''Now, scoot.''

Kenzie cast a helpless glance at Ross. What she saw on his face made her bow her head and hurry from the room.

Ross started after her, but Alex whirled and jabbed his forefinger into his brother's chest. ''Hold it right there! Back off that woman or I'll lock you up for being an ass!''

''Now wait a minute! I have as much right to get mad at her as you do! Even more!''

''No, you don't!''

''Is that so?''

''Yeah, that's so, because she's not in love with *me,* you idiot!''

''I have no idea what you're talking about,'' Ross snapped. ''Besides, what are you getting so worked up at me for? I'm not responsible for this!''

''And neither is Kenzie!''

''So all at once you're on her side, eh?''

"I am, now that I realize she didn't do this deliberately. You saw her face, Ross. She didn't know this was going to happen!"

"She didn't want to go to Beechwood in the first place," Maggie reminded him gently. "Maybe she suspected she'd run into someone she knew."

Ross thought back to the warm welcome Kenzie had received from the many guests who seemed to know and admire her, including Nina Bradford, one of the country's greatest fashion designers and who Kenzie had breezily dismissed as a college chum of her mother's. And Charlie, his old law partner, had even asked about her father, meaning Charlie had known all along who Kenzie was while Kenzie had chosen to keep him...and Angus...in the dark. His sense of betrayal grew. "She should have said something before we left. Given us some hint of what she'd be bringing down on our heads!"

Alex folded his arms across his wide chest. His anger had vanished completely the moment he had seen Kenzie's hurt, exhausted expression. Now it was Ross who needed calming down. He didn't think he'd ever seen his brother look so stunned—or angry—in his life. "And just what did she bring down on our heads? A coupla TV crews with nothing better to do in a town where nothing ever happens. So what?"

Ross stared at him disbelievingly.

Alex shrugged. "If you knew how many times we've had reporters camped out on our lawn—"

"Alex, come on! It goes with the turf! You're the chief of police, for cripes' sake!"

"Right. So you gotta believe me when I say this is nothing to get bent out of shape about for you, me, Maggs or Kenzie."

Ross glared at his brother. "But what about Angus? Have you forgotten what happened to him the last time the media got involved in my life?"

"But this is different, Ross," Maggie said pleadingly. "You told us the courts always favor the parents in suits like this. So there's no way the Archers are going to get Angus back no matter what the newspapers may print about last night."

"And if they find out I had an affair with the daughter of the notorious Burton Daniels III? Who happens to now be my son's nanny, no less? How do you think that'll play to the judge when it comes to assessing my fitness as a father?"

Maggie's cheeks heated, but Alex merely shook his head. He might only be a small-town cop, but he knew human nature through and through. "Don't overrate the scandal, Ross. It'll probably appear in a few magazine issues, maybe win a brief mention on some television gossip program. So what? You know damned well this thing with Angus won't come to trial. Your private life is immaterial."

"I can't risk that," Ross said tightly.

Alex stared thoughtfully at his brother's retreating back. "Know what I think?"

"What?" Ross snapped.

"I don't think you're mad at Kenzie for jeopardizing your chances with Angus. You're too good a lawyer to believe that's actually going to happen."

"I'm not mad at Kenzie. *You* were mad at Kenzie."

"I told you, it was only because I thought she'd done this to us on purpose. That she was some spoilt, attention-hungry rich girl."

"Like Penelope," Maggie whispered.

"Exactly. And the second I realized she wasn't, I was able to put the whole thing in perspective. Which you need to do, too, Ross. This is really no big deal."

"The hell you say."

"I do. And I happen to think you're mad at her for another reason than because you think her notoriety will ruin your chances of keeping Angus."

Ross glared at him. "Is that right?"

Alex crossed his arms in front of his chest. "Yeah, that's right. I think your anger at her for not revealing her background has nothing to do with the harm she may have caused Angus. It's much more personal."

"Oh?"

"Yeah. While it was hard enough to tell her you loved her before, it's going to be near impossible now, isn't it?"

Now it was Ross's turn to cross his arms in front of his chest. His eyes blazed into his brother's. "That's ridiculous."

"Oh, come on. You know it isn't. You couldn't bring yourself to admit it on your last day of vacation. Not to her, probably not even to yourself. So you settled for offering her a job as

Angus's nanny. The coward's way out, but a good way to keep her around.''

Maggie's hands flew to her cheeks. Ross took a step toward his brother. ''You calling me a coward?''

Alex shrugged. ''It's understandable, considering how badly you got burned by Pen. It's enough to send any man's heart scurrying for permanent cover. But I'm convinced you're also mad now because you misjudged Kenzie's background and her upbringing so completely. I'll bet the allowance Daddy Daniels gives her is four times the nanny's salary you offered her. Not only that, but now you've got to come to terms with the wealthy woman she really is. To accept what you are, too. Granted, you've come a long way in building up what Penelope destroyed, but you're no prime catch as far as a Washington Daniels is concerned.''

''Alex!'' Maggie whispered. ''That's unfair!''

''It's not what I think, Maggs. It's what Ross believes of himself.''

''Bull,'' said Ross.

''Really?''

Ross passed a hand tiredly across his eyes. When he looked up, the fight seemed to have gone out of him ''Okay, let's say you're right. Hypothetically speaking.''

His brother snorted. ''You want hypothetical? Let's just toss out a big one, okay? Say you went to her and apologized for being such a jerk in making that ridiculous claim that she may have jeopardized your custody of Angus. Say you told her you don't give a damn that she's rich or that she exposed her father as a criminal—something that took a hell of a lot of courage, I might add. And then humbly ask her to marry you—something you wanted to do the day you left Hatteras only you were too cowardly to admit to yourself that you were in love with her back then. And don't forget to add how afraid you are she'll turn you down because you're not the wealthy, successful attorney you were when you were married to Penelope, because that's eating at you right now, too, isn't it?''

''You're lucky, Alex. I'm too sleep deprived to sock you one.''

''And the mudroom's too small for fighting.''

Ross smiled without humor. "Okay. One more hypothetical question."

"What?"

"Supposing you're wrong? About my feelings for Kenzie?"

"Give me a break. Knowing what goes on in people's minds is the mark of any good cop. Besides, you're my brother. I know you too damned well."

"Ross." Maggie's hand was on his arm. "You look as done in as Kenzie. Why not go upstairs and rest? The two of you can talk later."

He struggled with the temptation. Struggled with his anger and despair and, above all, with the knowledge that every little thing his brother had said was true.

God, he wanted to tell her. So much so that it hurt. But Alex was right: He *was* a coward. He was scared to death she'd turn him down, and he didn't think he could deal with her rejection. Not after Angus had rejected him time and again. Not after suffering through the string of failures that had plagued him for years: the loss of his partnership in his Manhattan firm, the loss of his marriage and the dreams that had gone with it, even the abandonment by his father so many decades ago. And he certainly had no business proposing to Kenzie after overdramatizing the significance of the TV crews parked outside the door.

On the other hand, there was nothing he wanted more at this moment than to let her know how much he needed her. How deeply he loved her and how hard he would strive to make her love him in return.

"Dad!"

They all looked up, startled. Angus rarely called his father that. Ross went down on his knee. "What's wrong, son?"

"Kenzie's gone! You've got to get her back!"

"Gone?"

Angus nodded, his face pressed against Ross's shoulder. "She came to say goodbye. She said—she said she loved me very much but that she couldn't stay with us anymore. She said it was because she'd done something bad that might hurt you and me if the TV people found out. Then she went to talk to the people outside. I saw her hug one man with a big camera around his neck and then she drove away with him in his car. Why would she do that? Why would she think we cared that she did something bad?''

Ross and Alex exchanged glances over his head.

Maggie came back into the room. ''He's right. Her things are gone.''

''Did she leave a note or anything?'' Alex demanded.

''No. Just the gown and the pearls. What else did she say, Angus?''

''Nothing.'' Angus's face was streaked with tears. ''Can you get her to come back, Dad?''

''Not if she's made up her mind to go.''

''Please?''

Ross smoothed the hair from his son's brow. ''I'll try.'' Even though it was obvious to him that everything Alex had said was now a moot point anyway.

Angus must have heard the doubt in his voice, because suddenly he locked his arms around Ross's neck and hugged him tightly. ''You can get her back, Dad, I know you can. Because you can do anything.''

''I'll try, sport,'' Ross said again, his voice unsteady as love for his son and for the woman both of them needed all but overwhelmed him.

Chapter Thirteen

The law firm of Burton Daniels III occupied three floors of the historic Rayburne-Carter building not far from Capitol Hill. Kenzie's father had leased the downstairs retail space to several high-end clients, including a fashion designer and an award-winning bistro. Kenzie skirted both after she'd paid the cab driver and headed for the imposing entrance off the side street.

She tried to ignore the knot in her stomach, but it wasn't easy. She had no idea how her father or her oldest brother would receive her. She didn't think they'd make a scene in front of the staff or call security to have her thrown out. Would they?

It doesn't matter, she reminded herself. What mattered was that her brother Burt was one of the finest family-law attorneys in the country. Whatever damage she may have done to Ross's chances of keeping Angus, Burt would know how to fix it. Her jaw clenched. Heaven help him if he refused.

Still, the knot in her stomach tightened as she punched the elevator button. Memories of the last, awful confrontation she'd had with her father and brother in this very building were turning her knees to jelly.

But not her resolve. All she had to think of was the anger of betrayal in Ross's voice when he'd confronted her at Alex and Maggie's earlier this morning. "If you've cost me my son, Ms. Daniels—"

Equally painful had been the bewilderment on Angus's face when she'd gone upstairs to say goodbye. And hardest of all to bear was the way the cameras had clicked and the microphones were shoved in her face when she'd slipped outside to deal with the reporters—just as Alex had predicted.

She'd not have gone outside to speak to them at all if she hadn't recognized Vince Abrams among the crowd. A freelance photographer for magazines like *Town & Country* and *Vanity Fair*, he'd attended numerous shoots at her parents' house in Georgetown and even at The Farm. While Kenzie had never liked being in the limelight that was cast by her parents' social and political prominence, she'd always liked Vince Abrams, who was nice, never intrusive and had a great sense of humor.

She'd been so glad to see a familiar face in the crowd that she'd readily accepted his offer to talk somewhere private. And over a pot of coffee at an interstate restaurant she'd told him not only what she'd been doing at the Richardson fund-raiser the night before, but also about Angus and her fear that she'd somehow jeopardized his father's chances of retaining custody of the boy.

And after talking to Vince for a while, she'd come to realize that the only way to deflect any damage she may have caused was to, in her words to Vince, "trot out some big guns of my own."

Her oldest brother, Burton Daniels IV, was about as powerful a form of ammunition as Kenzie could imagine. His high-profile custody clients included a number of Hollywood stars and Washington insiders, and his most recent case had involved a Maryland heiress whose ex-husband, a billionaire Arab oilman, had tried to abduct his children from their private American school and fly them to Yemen. Returning the kids to their mother had been an act of utmost skill for Burt because both the Yemeni and U.S. governments had gotten involved in what had turned out to be a delicate exercise in diplomacy.

Kenzie figured that Sir Edward Archer's greedy attempt to get his hands on the title that Angus may or may not inherit would be a piece of cake after that one.

Vince had been kind enough to drive her all the way to LaGuardia Airport and arrange to have her abandoned rental car picked up in Cheltenham. She'd caught an afternoon flight to D.C., and now here she was, emerging from the polished brass elevator in front of the Daniels law offices.

"Oh, God," she whispered.

Through the beveled glass windows flanking the double mahogany doors, she could already see her brother Burt striding toward her. Tall and dark like all the Daniels men, he had that same grim look on his face that their father had worn when he'd kicked Kenzie out of this very building more than a year ago.

Burt must have seen her via the security camera in the lobby. Well, he sure hadn't wasted any time in meeting his enemy at the gate, had he?

Kenzie thought of Angus and Ross—the one thing that could give her courage. She took a deep breath.

The door crashed open.

"Kenzie! There you are! I was just going out." Burt had her by the arm and was propelling her toward the stairwell. "No time for the elevator. Did Tad reach you or was it David?"

"I—um—"

"Doesn't matter. I've got my car out front. Hurry up, will you?"

"What's—what's going on?" she panted, trying to keep up with him on the stairs.

"It's too early to tell. Dad's waiting on the doctor now. She's been brought up to I.C.U. and—"

"Mom? Has something happened to Mom?"

"Didn't they tell you?"

"No! What is it?"

"A heart attack. I just heard about it myself. Let's go. Dad says she's been asking for you."

Kenzie didn't remember much of the trip to the hospital. It took a while, thanks to downtown Washington traffic. She said nothing the whole way and Burt had to concentrate on his driving. He didn't even think to ask her why she'd shown up so quickly at the office.

In fact, no one seemed to question her presence. David and Tad, who were already waiting in the I.C.U. lounge, had the same reaction as Burt: they assumed she'd shown up in response to some family member's frantic call.

"Glad David found you," Tad said, hugging her.

"I've no idea how Stuart got hold of you so fast," David said, squeezing her arm, "but I'm glad you're here."

"Any news yet?" Burt demanded.

"Dad's talking with the cardiologist right now. We should hear any minute."

Kenzie collapsed in a nearby chair. No doubt about it, she was in shock. It was too much to take in after everything that had happened last night and this morning, after the exhausting trip by car and plane to get back to D.C. She could only sit and stare numbly at the floor. The fact that she'd been welcomed back into the family fold so easily meant nothing. Her mother—

"Dad!"

Her brothers were on their feet, crowding around him. Kenzie had another shock at seeing him. Had he always had so much gray in his hair? Could somebody age that quickly in a year?

He caught sight of her just then and froze. Kenzie looked back, her heart in her throat. Then he held out his arms to her. Automatically, with a muffled sob, she went to him.

"Kenzie. I'm glad you're here."

His familiar voice, the smell of his expensive aftershave, washed over her, making her want to burst into tears.

She swallowed hard. "What about Mom?"

Her father's drawn face relaxed a little. "It's not as bad as we thought. Palpitations, not a heart attack. Dr. Patek said something about fine-tuning her pacemaker. But they want to keep her overnight, just to be sure."

"Can we see her?" asked Tad.

"No. She's resting now. But I want to tell her Kenzie's here." His eyes sought his daughter's. "You'll be staying?"

"Of course!" She had to speak around a really big lump in her throat. "As long as I'm needed."

The lounge doors swung open just then and Kenzie's brother Stuart, her sisters-in-law and all her assorted nephews and nieces surged in. There was a lot of noise and confusion as everyone reacted with joyous disbelief to her presence.

"Kenzie!"

"What are you doing here?"

"How'd you get here so fast?"

"Are you home for good?"

Smiling faces, both adults' and children's, surrounded her. Little arms embraced her and kisses were rained on her cheeks. Tears stung her eyes as she admired a nephew's new tooth and marveled at the toddler who'd been a baby when she left.

A nurse stuck her head in the door. "Please keep it down. This is Intensive Care, you know." But she didn't sound very angry.

Dr. Patek obligingly returned to answer everyone's questions. Then Burt's wife, Dana, raised her hand for silence. "It's almost suppertime. Let's head over to Grassio's for pasta and check on Mom on the way back."

"Good idea. Come ride with us, Kenzie."

"I'll follow in a minute. I want to wait for Dad."

Stuart's wife gasped. "Is that a good idea?"

Tad slid an arm around his sister's waist. "It appears they've reconciled."

"Hallelujah," said Dana.

"I was—um—a little surprised myself," Kenzie admitted.

"He's a different guy these days," Tad explained.

David snorted. "Community service has a way of doing that to you."

Kenzie's eyes widened. "Community service! Mom never told me."

"Yup. Two hundred hours of pro bono legal work performed for the Public Defender's office and other places like that. Mom probably didn't want you feeling responsible for Dad's having to defend crack addicts and homeless mothers."

The way Ross did. Only, Ross had chosen to continue in that field even though his legal expertise was attracting more and more high-profile clients these days. Maggie had told her so the other morning at breakfast...was it only three days ago? Kenzie shook her head, feeling as if an eternity had passed since then.

"You okay, Kenz?" Tad asked.

"I'm fine. And I think pro bono work like that is the finest thing a lawyer can do. All of you'd do well to take a page from that book."

"She's right." Burton Daniels had returned to the lounge in time to hear his daughter's impassioned words. "As a matter of fact, we're planning a lot of changes at the practice in that regard.''

Kenzie's eyes widened. "You are?"

"Burt can fill you in on all the facts at dinner."

"You're not coming with us?" Tad asked.

"I'd rather stay here with your mother. However, I will say one thing."

All eyes were on him as he came forward and laid his hand on Kenzie's shoulder.

"It's about those community hours I put in."

"I'm sorry," Kenzie whispered. Her heart was hammering in her throat. Was it possible that she'd misread her father earlier? Had she been forgiven or not? Oh, God, not this after losing Angus and Ross. She'd not be able to bear it.

"You don't owe me an apology, Kenzie. In fact, I owe you one. And my heartfelt thanks."

"Y-you do?"

"That's right. Thanks to you I've spent the last year working with homeless families, abused mothers, runaway kids. Through their suffering, I've come to appreciate the rare blessing of an intact, loving family. It made me realize how stupid I'd been for keeping the Daniels clan from being one of them. There's no excuse for what I did to you, Kenzie, none."

His voice wavered and he coughed and tried to look stern. "I broke the law. You upheld it, despite how difficult it must have been. Can—can you ever forgive me?"

"Oh, Dad. There's nothing to forgive."

Kenzie could feel her heart breaking with joy as her father enfolded her in his familiar, bearlike embrace. And with sorrow because another family she knew, a small one consisting only of a father and a son, was not similarly blessed.

She stayed behind while the rest of the family headed off to eat. She wasn't ready yet to be part of their noisy gathering.

She didn't have to wait long. Her father came back into the lounge less than ten minutes later. He was clearly surprised to see her waiting. "I thought you'd gone to Grassio's with the others."

"I was hoping I'd get the chance to see Mom."

"She's sleeping. They kicked me out, too."

They looked at each other. For a long time neither spoke.

"So," Kenzie said at last. "Is this it? Just like that we're reconciled?"

Her father winced. "Forget Grassio's. I'm taking you to Holloway's. We need to talk."

The restaurant owner seated them at a private table in the back where they wouldn't be disturbed. After they'd ordered, her father shook his head. "I'd almost forgotten how direct you are. No nonsense and right to the point. You would've made an outstanding lawyer."

"You've said so before. In fact, it was the last thing you said to me the day we...um...parted ways."

He put his face in his hands. "Lord, I remember." After a minute he gave her a faint smile. "Know what? I'm glad you didn't study law. Because then you'd never have discovered your talent for cartooning. Lampooning me in that Easton newspaper was the best thing you've ever done."

"But—but Dad, you were furious when they published that drawing!" It was the understatement of the year.

"I was at first. Now I realize it was the beginning of my redemption."

"Excuse me?"

He smiled at her. "Sorry. Didn't mean to sermonize. But the pull of political ambition is hard to explain. I used to be an ethical man. But I woke up one day not long after you'd left home to realize I wasn't one anymore." He sighed. "I have no excuses for what happened. I wanted to win that nomination, and backing from the Delderfeld bank would have filled my campaign chest. For the first time in my life I allowed greed and ambition to get in the way of common sense."

"Kind of like giving yourself over to the Dark Side of the Force, huh?"

He smiled, and the tension between them eased. "Believe me, it wasn't easy breaking free. In fact, it was damned hard. Not only did I have to pay my debt to society and keep the practice alive, I had to deal with the family—and that was toughest of all."

"I'm not following you, Dad."

His eyes held hers. "You have no idea how hard they all campaigned in your behalf. Your brothers didn't let me forget for a minute that I was the one who'd broken the law, not you.

Their wives were just as bad. And Alida! Good Lord, the woman nearly drove me mad. Your mother, on the other hand, never said a word. Not one. But her silence was a constant, accusatory shout. I finally had to insist your name not be mentioned in my presence again. It was that or completely lose my sanity.''

He hesitated, then went on brokenly, ''We missed you, Kenzie. *I* missed you. Our lives have been so empty without you. It was wrong of me to take out all my anger and disappointment—and shame—on you. I was planning to tell you as much even before your mother got ill.''

''Oh, Dad.''

She took his hand across the table.

Their food came. It was easier to talk while they were eating. And by the time the dishes had been cleared away the awkwardness between them was largely gone.

While her father had a cup of coffee, Kenzie went to the rest room to wash her hands and try to make some order of her untidy hair. When she got back, her father was just pocketing his cell phone. ''That was Stuart. They're still at Grassio's. He checked with the hospital and your mother's sleeping comfortably. Looks like she'll be discharged tomorrow.''

''Dad, that's wonderful!''

''Good thing we left the hospital when we did. Stuart says the news crews are parked out front. I suppose I'll have to issue a statement come morning.'' He cleared his throat. ''What about you? Can I take you home?''

Home. The word had never sounded so good to Kenzie. She realized all at once how exhausted she was. ''Yes, please.''

''Before we go, while I have you here alone, there's one more thing I need to say. It's about Brent.''

''Oh?''

''You've heard he got engaged again?''

''To an interior designer from Baltimore.''

''Yeah, well, apparently that didn't work out. He was asking about you the other day, Kenz. I'm not going to interfere, but I want you to know that whatever happened between the two of you was entirely my fault. I—I said some unfair things to him. And to his credit, he remained loyal to the family throughout.''

''To himself, you mean.''

''Now Kenzie—''

"Come on, Dad! You know perfectly well that your long-standing reputation here in Washington was good enough to get you past the—uh—the mistake you made. But if there was any sign that the firm wasn't going to weather the storm Brent would've bailed in a heartbeat."

"Kenzie, please give him a chance. I know you're bitter, but—"

"Actually, I'm not. Maybe at first, but not anymore."

"You spent a year in North Carolina—"

"I know, I know, licking my wounds in exile. That's what Tad said whenever he tried to goad me into coming home. But there's no chance Brent and I will ever reconcile, even if that's what he wants. Don't look like that, Daddy. You did me a huge favor, actually. I'm not in love with Brent anymore. I don't think I ever was." Her voice dropped to a whisper. "Back then I didn't know what love is."

"Kenzie, are you crying?"

She blinked. "No, Daddy, I'm not. But while we're here and we have some privacy, I want to ask you for a favor. Two of them, actually."

He reached for her hand. "You name it, sweetie."

Kenzie took a deep breath. "First of all, I want you to make a contribution to the Dare County Raptor Center in Manteo, North Carolina. A big one, because they're going to get a few more birds than they counted on once I shut down my aviary."

"Your aviary? Honey, I don't understand."

"I'll explain later, when we have more time. Right now the most important thing is the second favor."

"Shoot away."

"It's a legal matter. I need you and Burt to put your heads together and help out a...a friend."

The next few days were much more hectic than Kenzie had expected. Even though her brothers and their families left once her mother came home from the hospital, there was little in the way of peace and quiet. Word had gotten out that Kenzie was back in town, and the phone calls and visits never stopped. Friends and acquaintances she hadn't seen since last year all seemed to be clamoring for attention.

Worried that the noise and activity would prevent her mother from resting, Kenzie finally agreed to accept some of the invitations she received. One of them was to a barbecue out in the Maryland suburbs over the weekend, where another of the guests turned out to be Brent Ellis. Because both she and Brent were long-standing friends of their hosts, Kenzie had prepared herself for the possibility of running into him, but she still uttered a muffled oath when she spotted him striding toward her that Saturday afternoon across the manicured lawn.

He looked absolutely gorgeous. Polo shirt and perfectly draped designer slacks, expensive loafers on his feet. Blond hair blow-dried just so and his devastating smile aimed straight at her.

"My God, Kenz, you look beautiful."

She let him kiss her cheek, even hugged him back, but she was anxious to return to the pool house to play hide-and-seek with the restless pack of kids who'd been invited, as well.

Thinking about them, she didn't pay a lot of attention to what Brent said. She was only vaguely aware that he was telling her how glad he was that she and her father were reconciled, how it was time to put the past behind them and think about the future. Did she have plans? Was she home for good?

"I'm not sure," Kenzie said truthfully. There'd been some discussion to that effect around the dinner table last night. Burt and Stuart wanted her to return to school and finish her Ph.D. Tad's wife suggested opening a restaurant. Others voted for a permanent commitment to cartooning.

"Whoever thought all your doodling would lead to a successful career?" David had teased.

"I just doodled to while away the hours in geometry class," Kenzie confessed. "I never dreamed it would take me anywhere, either."

But everyone assumed she was back home for good, that she was planning to take up where she'd left off as though the last horrible year had never happened.

Not surprisingly, her mother was of the mind that Kenzie take some time off before making any decisions. In her opinion her daughter looked much too thin and drawn.

"It's understandable, considering the scare you gave us," Kenzie said firmly.

"All the more reason to unwind a little. No sense in rushing things."

Alida was of a similar mind. "You rest up first, then worry about tomorrow. And when you decide what to do, be sure it makes you happy."

Happy, Kenzie thought now, half-listening to Brent describe a piece of property he had just purchased somewhere along the Potomac River. How was happiness possible without Ross? Without Angus?

At least her father had readily agreed to help out as far as the custody suit was concerned. Yesterday morning he and Burt had asked her a number of questions, all of them along professional lines and therefore easy to answer without giving herself away. She had no idea if either one had been in touch with Ross yet. She hadn't had the courage to ask, and neither of them had said another word about it.

"Suppose you could come see it sometime?"

She blinked at Brent. "What?"

"The property. The architect is drawing up plans, but I'd certainly like your feedback first."

"Oh, Brent, I'm not sure that's a good idea."

He gave her the devastating smile that she'd always gone weak-kneed over before, back when she'd been so certain she was in love with him. She knew better now. So much better.

"Why not? We could make an afternoon of it. Pack a lunch and eat down on the dock. Did I tell you it's deep water? I'm thinking of buying a yacht."

Not a boat, a yacht. She could imagine the guys at the Red Drum Café snickering over Brent's choice of words.

The Red Drum Café...

Like a thunderbolt she suddenly realized what she wanted to do. "It sounds perfect, Brent, but I can't. I'm leaving for Hatteras in the morning."

"Whatever for? There's no reason to hide away out there anymore."

"I wasn't hiding."

Okay, maybe a little, at the beginning.

"Then why go back?"

"My dogs are there. All my stuff."

"Then let me come with you. I can help you pack."

The last thing on earth she needed: Brent Ellis setting foot in her run-down cottage. Pawing through the personal effects of the life she had made for herself there. His presence blotting out the precious memories of Ross and Angus she wanted so badly to protect and cherish.

She took a deep breath and looked at him kindly. "I appreciate the offer, Brent, but no. I don't see any reason to take up where we left off last year."

"Ouch."

"Brent, I'm sorry, but——"

"Hey, no problem."

She had to hand it to him, he recovered quickly. "Thanks."

"Why don't you give me a call as soon as you get back?"

Nope, he hadn't recovered. Hadn't even paid her words any mind. He was so sure of himself, he didn't for a minute believe she wasn't going to fall for him all over again.

Which was ludicrous. She'd never be able to look at another man without comparing him to Ross. Not the angry, silent Ross who'd tried so hard to hide his feelings, his fears and love for his son from her and the rest of the world. But the Ross who had opened up to her little by little; had learned to trust his instincts for fathering, laughed with her after a rampaging pelican had taken a bite out of his rear and then kissed her until the world had turned beneath her feet...

"I'm not sure I'm coming back."

She'd spoken lightly to put him off, but as soon as she uttered the words she wondered how much truth was in them. Maybe none, but she knew all at once that she needed to get back to the Outer Banks as quickly as possible. Surely she'd find a measure of peace while watching the sun set over the sound? Learn to live with the yawning emptiness in her heart by staying busy caring for her birds? Find a way to laugh without pain while shooting the breeze with her friends down at the marina and in the Red Drum Café?

"Kenzie, don't be silly."

She stood up on tiptoe and kissed his square, manly jaw. "I'm sorry, Brent, but I won't be back for a while. And even if I wasn't going, you should know the truth. There's someone else in my life now. Someone...someone very special. In fact, there are two of them."

"You're joking, of course."

"No, I'm not. Goodbye, Brent. All the luck in the world with your house."

And she meant that, truly.

She could feel his eyes on her as she left him standing there on the lawn. In just a few seconds the fact would sink into his handsome head that he had been rejected. He, Brent Ellis, gifted attorney, manly hunk and senator-to-be. Rejected by his ex-fiancée, of all people. If she hurried, she'd have enough time to make her apologies to Colin and Frannie Fields, her hosts, and get into her car before he came after her.

But it was close. She heard him calling her name as she reached the back porch. Luckily Frannie was just coming outside with a freshly diapered baby on her arm. In a rush, Kenzie explained where she was going, gave both Frannie's and the baby's cheek a kiss, then slipped away around the rhododendrons before Brent had time to catch up.

Chapter Fourteen

The sun was still high in the sky when Kenzie drove her father's car across the Oregon Inlet bridge on her way to Buxton. The moment she saw the surf rolling onto the shore, she knew she'd made the right decision. Much as she loved being home again with her family, she badly needed some time to herself. The events of the past week had swept her along in such a mad rush that now she wanted nothing more than to take stock of everything that had happened—and to think about her future.

At least her encounter with Brent had convinced her of one thing: She'd never really been in love with him. "Infatuated" was a better word for what she'd felt, and infatuation wasn't worth fighting for.

Nor was it the basis for any kind of commitment. You didn't choose to spend your life with a man just because he was handsome and carefree and your father approved of him. You spent your life with a man who filled some hollow part inside of you, made you whole, and who you made whole in turn. Someone who transformed your weaknesses into strengths and your lonely hours into fulfillment.

Surely she had come to matter to Ross in at least one of those ways? Could a man who had opened his heart so completely when he'd made love to her be totally uncaring otherwise? She refused to believe it. And she *had* to believe his anger and disappointment the morning after the Beechwood fund-raiser had been a reaction to the news crews outside the house, to memories of what had happened when he'd tried taking Angus away from Penelope.

Not for a minute would Kenzie let herself believe that something else had made Ross lash out at her that way. Not dislike or even hatred once he'd found out the truth about her past. Still, panic clawed at her whenever she considered that he might loathe her now for being a "Washington Daniels," a woman cut from the same cloth as his former socialite wife.

"But I'm not like Penelope!" Kenzie said aloud. Surely Ross had learned as much about her!

Then again, none of that would matter if Ross had never cared for her to begin with.

But I can make him care, Kenzie thought passionately. I know I can.

In fact, she was going to do everything in her power to win his love.

Speeding down the highway toward Buxton, she took stock of her situation. A year ago she'd driven across this same stretch of road brokenhearted and uncertain of her future. A few weeks before that she'd still been living at home with her parents, attending graduate school and letting her curriculum and her parents' and Brent's wishes decide the course of her days.

But she'd grown up so much since then! No way was she the same woman who had arrived on this island crying and desperately alone. And no way was she coming back here a second time to hide away from the outside world. She had built a new life for herself here, one that had made her happy. Surely this strong, resilient Kenzie would have no trouble fighting for Ross Calder's love?

The good Lord knew she had to try. And at the very least she had to make certain that her blundering in Cheltenham hadn't cost him his son.

"We'll do what we can about that," Burt had assured her when she'd left. "It shouldn't be a problem."

She wanted so badly to believe he was right.

She tried not to think about Ross as she drove through Avon and past the cottage he had rented with Angus. Tried not to remember their unexpected encounter at the Red Drum Café.

But it was hard. She'd never realized before how much a part of this world he had become.

Her pickup truck was parked next to the front porch of her house. Everything else looked the same. Hopefully Gordon had gotten the message she'd left on his answering machine and would have the freezer stocked with mullet for her birds. She was much too tired after the long drive from D.C. to go fishing now.

She wasn't going to pick up Zoom and Jazz until tomorrow, either. Instead she was going to sack out on the back porch for a while, then take a long walk on the beach. Then a light supper and a turn at the drawing board, then bed. The thought of such familiar, undemanding routine made her smile.

She opened the front door and stepped inside. Her smile promptly faded.

"What the—?"

There were fresh flowers in a vase on the coffee table. Freesias, her favorites. Gordon Harper was the only one who knew she was on her way home. Where on earth had he gotten them and why on earth had he done so?

She stopped short inside the kitchen.

The table had been covered with a clean linen cloth and set for two. More flowers had been arranged in the center. Something was simmering in a pot on the stove. The oven light was on.

"Hello? Is anybody here? Gordon?"

The screen door slammed.

Kenzie whirled.

Ross Calder. Filling up her small kitchen the way he always did. Smiling at her in a way that made her breath catch.

"There you are," he said softly. "Just in time for supper."

"Ross! What—"

"Put away your things. Wash up. We eat in two minutes."

"But—"

"It isn't much. Hamburgers and roasted corn, macaroni and cheese. Alida wanted me to cook something more elaborate, but this was about as fancy as I dared to get."

"Alida."

"I've been in touch with her by phone. She's guided me through the whole process. You know what a lousy cook I am, and I wanted this to be special."

"Special?"

"Kenzie. You're talking in echoes."

"I don't know what else to say."

"Then don't say a thing. Go wash up. Are you hungry?"

"Yes, but—"

"Good. I'll have everything ready when you get back. Oh, wait. Before you go—"

He took her face in his hands. Tipped her chin so that he could drop the lightest and sweetest of kisses on her lips. "Welcome home."

She felt his smiling gaze upon her as she tottered off to the bathroom.

True to his word, he had dinner on the table when she returned. Nothing looked burned or undercooked or otherwise inedible.

Ross, smiling and oh so self-assured, waved her into a chair. "Alida told me exactly when you left Georgetown, so it was easy to estimate when you'd get here. My only worry was that you'd stop for dinner along the way."

"I wasn't hungry."

"But you are now."

"Yes. No. I mean—" She shook her head. She wasn't sure what to say, what to think, especially what to feel. "Ross, where's Angus?"

"In New York with Delia. He agreed when I explained why it was better for me to come alone."

"And why did you come?"

Suddenly it was his turn to look uncertain. "Um, well, I was sort of saving that for dessert."

"You made dessert?"

"Actually, Alida couldn't convince me to try. Burgers and macaroni are one thing, cakes and cookies are too ambitious for me at this point. So I went to the Gingerbread House for bear claws."

Like the ones they'd eaten the first time he and Angus had

ever set foot in her kitchen. Kenzie put down her fork, tears stinging her eyes at the memory. "Ross, why are you here?"

The phone rang. Ross reached for the receiver before she could. "Hello? Angus! I had a feeling it'd be you. Couldn't wait, huh?

A pause, then Ross chuckled. It was a deep, pleasant sound. "I know. Me, too. No, I haven't asked her yet. Give me time and I'll call you back, okay? What's that? Sure will. I love you, too. Bye."

He sat down again, smiling. "Angus said to tell you hello."

And if Kenzie had heard right, had also told his father he loved him. She met his gaze without smiling back. "What's going on here, Ross? What did he want you to ask me?"

Ross's smile faded. "What I should have asked you the first time around."

"I'm not following you."

He cleared his throat. Kenzie got the feeling he was trying to regain some of the assurance he'd felt before Angus's phone call. Her own throat felt raw, her breath hard to catch. She laced her fingers together because suddenly they were shaking.

"Do you remember what I said to you the last time I set foot in this house, Kenzie?"

"Of course. You offered me a job as Angus's nanny."

"A display of cowardice I'm still deeply ashamed of."

"Cowardice? What do you mean?"

He balled his hands into fists. "I came over here that morning with one thing in mind—to keep us from saying goodbye. The thought of going back to New York alone with Angus was intolerable. And of course the best way to avoid that was to ask you to marry me. But I chickened out. There were so many arguments against it. We'd known each other barely two weeks. I hadn't exactly been Mr. Congeniality. I knew you'd come to care for Angus, but I wasn't sure how you felt about me. So I did one of the stupidest things I've ever done. I offered you a job instead of my heart."

"Is that what you wanted to give me?" Kenzie whispered.

His eyes were windows to his aching soul. "Would you have accepted it?"

Overwhelmed, she bowed her head. "Only if you never asked

for it back. That morning at Alex and Maggie's, when the reporters came—''

''God, Kenzie, I never meant any of that. They didn't matter. What did was the possibility that you'd never want a man like me. A lousy father and a struggling attorney isn't worthy of a Washington Daniels.''

Kenzie leaned back in her chair, too stunned to laugh or cry or find the strength to throw something at him.

''But Angus seems to think I am. That's why he urged me to come down here to see you. We both agreed I should come alone, though. Your feelings for my son are obvious, but we Calder men are a package deal, Kenzie. You can't have the one without the other.''

''I can't?''

''No.''

''Then I suppose I'll have to.''

''Have to what?''

''Marry you. I assume that's what you came to ask me this time?''

She had to smile at the stunned look that crossed his face, then catch her breath at the fierce joy that replaced it, a joy that seemed to well up from the very depths of his being.

''Kenzie, you mean it?''

''I've never been more serious in all my life.''

All of a sudden he had pulled her out of her chair and she was in his arms. It was like a homecoming, his mouth covering hers in a kiss that wiped away all the uncertainty and pain, and she clung to him, feeling happier than she had ever dreamed possible.

''Kenzie,'' he finally whispered against her lips, ''I love you. I missed you so badly. When I realized I'd driven you away—''

''You didn't. You couldn't. I went home to get help for you and Angus. Because I loved you so much, too.''

He kissed her again, then lifted her wordlessly in his arms and carried her to the bed. Laid her down with a gentle strength that touched her to the soul. His heart was in his eyes as he drew the straps of her tank top away from her shoulders and kissed the warm hollow of her throat.

''Oh, Ross.'' Blissfully she closed her eyes and wrapped her arms around him. Right then and there she vowed silently that no one would ever hurt this wonderful man again. That he would know nothing but happiness and caring and unconditional love for the rest of his days. He had suffered enough and deserved no less. And neither did she.

"Ask me again," she whispered against his mouth.

He lifted his head. "What?"

"To marry you."

He laced his fingers through hers, then brought her captured hand against his heart. "Kenzie Daniels, I love you more than I thought it possible to love any woman. I need you more than I've ever needed anyone. You make me laugh. You make me complete. You make me feel I can do anything I want. And what I want is you. For me. For always. And for Angus. I want us to be a family. I don't care where we live. Here or in Washington or New York. Even the moon would be all right by me. And I don't care how many birds and dogs and other critters will have to share the house with us. Just say you'll marry me. Will you?"

"Those last two words would have sufficed," she said with a laugh, although tears had sprung to her eyes. "But yes, yes, I will," she whispered, blinking them back.

He didn't have to tell her how her words made him feel. He showed her, with his hands, his lips and his words, murmuring endearments as he slipped the clothes from her body, worshiping every inch he exposed, learning every curve and plane and shadowed hollow all over again, letting her know how much he had ached for this—for her.

She sighed his name as he slid into her at last. Pulling him close, she wrapped her arms about him and took him deep, whispering how much she loved him and what his kisses, his touch did to her.

He groaned. "Sweetheart, you make me wild when you talk like that."

"Show me," she challenged.

He did, stroking in and out of her in a way that made her senses reel. Her hips rose up to meet his savage thrusts, matching them as she mated with him in a timeless ritual of passion and love.

And just as quickly the tantalizing promise of release danced through her veins, leaped between them and swept them both away.

Afterward he propped himself up on the pillows and held her nestled against his chest. He didn't speak.

Kenzie, overwhelmed, didn't, either.

But eventually she said, "What on earth prompted you to call Alida?"

His chest rumbled as he chuckled. "Your father thought it was a good idea."

"My father? When did you speak to my father?"

"Let me see. Once this morning, once yesterday and at least twice early last week."

"Last week!"

"I talked with your brother, too."

"About what?"

"Burt and I spent some time comparing notes on the British family court system. We both agreed on a strategy for having the custody suit dismissed. After making a few overseas phone calls to some barristers in high places, Burt gave me the go-ahead to phone Penelope's parents."

"Nobody said a word about any of this to me! This morning when I left, Burt promised he'd look into it. Instead you'd both taken care of everything! Why didn't he say so?"

"Because he'd agreed not to say anything until you and I had a chance to talk. Your father, too."

"So you phoned the Archers in London." Kenzie digested this for a moment in silence. "What did they say? What's going to happen to Angus?"

Ross lowered his head to nuzzle her ear. "There are a few things left to iron out, but Angus is definitely staying in America. With me. With us."

"Oh, Ross, I'm so glad." She laid her head against his heart, her own so full she thought it might burst. "But wait a minute—"

"Hmm?"

"You said you talked to my father after that. A number of times. What about?"

"You."

He must've known she'd try to jump up, because he tightened his arms around her so she had no choice but to stay settled where she was. "He's one impressive guy, your dad. No wonder you turned out so headstrong and uppity."

"Oh?"

Ross chuckled. "There's no beating around the bush with the man. He's every bit as to-the-point as you are."

"Ross! You said the two of you talked about me! When was this?"

"The first time he called me. It must've been the night of your mother's heart attack. Right after he'd taken you out to dinner and you'd asked for his help with Angus."

"He called you that night?"

"Pretty much the minute he took you home, I think."

"To ask questions about the case?"

Ross chuckled again. "No. In fact, he wanted to chew me out. Said you'd returned home to Washington looking about as miserable and brokenhearted as when you'd first left a year ago. He said it didn't take a genius to figure out what was wrong. While he said he wasn't about to cross-examine me about your personal life, he did say he hoped I had a good reason for dumping an exceptional woman like you. He—whoa, sweetheart! Lie back down. No reason to look so mad!"

"Ross! That was between you and me! Something personal! How could you! How could he?"

"Shh. Come here. Lay your head down like you did before and just listen."

"But—"

"Please?"

Impossible to resist the invitation in those sexy blue eyes. Smiling despite herself, she settled back into his arms.

Ross waited a moment to see if she truly meant to behave, then chuckled softly. "That's better." He cleared his throat and his voice grew husky. "The first thing I said back to your dad on the phone that night was excuse me, but I hadn't dumped his only daughter. Dumping suggested I'd *had* you to begin with, which certainly wasn't the case. And the reason for that, I told him, was because I'd been too stupid and cowardly to grab on to the best thing that had ever happened to me the moment it— you—stepped into my life."

She trailed a tender kiss across his cheek, still unable to believe what she was hearing. "You're too hard on yourself, Ross."

"No. I *was* stupid. And cowardly. There were so many chances during our time together when I could easily have said something. Just opened my mouth and told you how I felt. Instead I hid from my feelings, hid from you. Every single time I asked you to keep away from Angus, told you to stop interfering in his life, I was really trying to keep you out of mine. You were starting to become much too important to me, Kenzie. And I was scared you didn't feel the same."

Tears stung her eyes. "Who can blame you? From the way I acted you must've thought I despised you. But I was hiding, too," she confessed in a whisper.

He brought her up against his hip and tangled his legs with hers so that no part of her went untouched. Once they were locked so intimately together, he turned his head to look deeply into her eyes.

"I know. But your father knew it first. He told me it didn't take a particularly keen eye to see that his daughter had fallen hopelessly in love. He said he was willing to take on the case with Angus and help us get back together, but only if I promised to do right by you."

"Right by me?"

"He meant he wanted to make sure you'd be happy. That this—Angus and I—were what you wanted. That's when I told him what I had in mind. That I wasn't about to let you go again and that I was going to ask you to marry me the moment I saw you again, no matter where, no matter when. That I was willing to let you pursue any career you wanted. Drawing, television writing, finishing your Ph.D., whatever. I told him I'd even started harboring a secret dream that you'd show an interest in helping me out in the firm—becoming a child advocate or something like that. But whatever you decided to do, I promised him—and myself—that I'd give you no reason to ever be disappointed or unhappy with the decision you'd made. That I'd care for you and cherish you and love you to the end of our days."

Kenzie was silent for a moment, struggling to swallow the boulder-size lump in her throat. "And you're telling me the two of you planned all this the first time you talked?"

"More or less. That's why I didn't follow you to Washington right away, though believe me I wanted to. Instead Angus and I cooked up this scheme. We figured you'd be more receptive to giving me another chance here, after you'd had some time to think things through at home."

"That's why Angus called you earlier? To find out what I'd said?"

Ross chuckled. "Actually, that was the third or fourth time he called. I promised him before I left that I wasn't going to come back without you, but I think he was nervous about my ability to deliver. I was, too," he confessed roughly. "I don't know what I would've done if you'd say no."

So that explained the flowers. The home-cooked meal—an ambitious one by Ross's standards. Kenzie's heart swelled as she realized how carefully he'd planned to make her homecoming special.

Ross must have been following her thoughts. "Angus suggested I cook for you. He said you always seemed happiest in the kitchen."

"He's a regular heartbreaker." Kenzie lifted herself up on one elbow and ran her finger lovingly down Ross's lean cheek. "Just like his father."

"An older, wiser father, thanks to you."

She traced the outline of his full, sexy mouth. It was starting to sink in that this man was going to be her husband. That she could touch him whenever she wanted. Wherever she wanted. She forced her thoughts back to their conversation. "Thanks to me? What do you mean?"

Ross captured her hand in his and held it tightly. Momentary pain flashed in his eyes. "Angus was...upset when you left. There was no calming him down until I agreed to go after you. No, wait, don't look so stricken. You did us a tremendous favor by leaving."

"I did?"

"You sure did, sweetheart. By being the common ground that finally brought Angus and me together."

"How is that possible?" she choked.

"Think about it, honey. Before you came along I had no idea how to talk to Angus. I had no frame of reference about fathers and sons. But I'd seen how *you* talked to him, so that's the way I talked to him about you.''

''What—what did you say?''

''Actually, once I got started I told him everything. How he'd been the smart one for falling in love with you right away while I'd been a jerk for denying it. How I'd made something as easy as saying 'I love you' much harder than it was because I'd never had a father who'd said it to me. That after seeing you hug him, kiss him, tell him you loved him like it was no big deal I'd come to realize it really wasn't at all hard to do.''

Kenzie lifted her eyes to his. ''And what did he say?''

Ross swallowed. ''This morning when I left for the airport he said, 'I love you, Dad,' like he'd been saying it all his life. Like he'd been thinking for some time that I wasn't the monster his mother had led him to believe, but that he'd needed me to prove it once and for all. But I don't think he would ever have said it without you unlocking the pieces for him, little by little, whenever the two of you were together. And a woman like that, a woman like you, is too precious to let slip through either of our fingers.''

Kenzie blinked back tears. ''And that's what you came here to tell me? With Angus's blessing?''

''Absolutely. I wanted to come see you the second your father let me know you were there in Washington, but he suggested I give you time. I didn't want to, but now I agree it was the right decision.''

''I had a lot of things to sort out,'' Kenzie admitted, thinking of her mother's illness, her reconciliation with her father, her final conversation with Brent.

''Your father kept me apprised of what you were up to, so I knew when you made the decision to come back to Hatteras pretty much the moment you did.''

''He never once let on,'' Kenzie marveled. She didn't know whether to laugh or cry or be utterly furious. ''Just wait until I get my hands on him!''

''He's a tough old bird,'' Ross said with a chuckle. ''And truly sorry for what happened between the two of you. Although I can't say I feel the same.''

''What?''

He lifted her hand and tenderly kissed each fingertip. ''Because if you'd never come here to the Outer Banks, Angus would never have crash-landed his kite on you. And then I'd never have met the prickly, lawyer-hating, family-values-preaching woman I now freely admit is the love of my life. And will soon be the mother of that son and, I hope, any other off-spring that care to show themselves in the years to come.''

He was teasing her, she knew, but his voice had grown husky, and she knew, too, that this was his way of saying something that came straight from his heart.

''Oh, Ross.''

But she couldn't say anything else. There were no words for what she felt right then.

Nor any reason to say them. As Ross lowered his mouth to hers, she knew by the look in his eyes that he understood the way she felt. And that he felt the same. For now, and for always.

Epilogue

A warm September sun filtered through the trees. Out on the bay, an oyster boat putted south against the tide. On the strip of sandy beach below the sprawling white farmhouse, a group of children in bathing suits screeched with pleasure as they splashed through the water under the watchful eyes of several grown-ups.

Kenzie, coming down the back steps with a tray of cutlery and napkins, saw that one of those grown-ups was Ross. He was standing in the shallow water with his pant legs rolled up, arms across his chest, dark head thrown back as he laughed at something her brother Stuart had just said.

Her heart swelled as it always did whenever she laid eyes on her husband. Smiling, she set the tray down on one of the picnic tables.

Dana, her oldest brother's wife, hurried over to help. "Barbecue's almost done. And Dad's getting ready to dump out the crabs."

No Labor Day celebration at the Daniels farm was ever held without a traditional Maryland crab crack or a barbecue for those who didn't care for seafood. Kenzie's stomach growled with pleasurable hunger. Behind her, Tad and Burt were taking seemingly dozens of ears of roasted corn off the grill while Alida was dishing out the coleslaw.

Kenzie smiled, watching Beatrice Archer, Angus's English grandmother, help Delia Armstrong spread the newsprint on the table where the cooked crabs would be dumped and then cracked with wooden mallets and special crab knives to yield their succulent meat. Earlier, Beatrice had expressed doubt that she would care for them, but had gamely agreed to try.

Her husband, Sir Edward Archer, was seated with Kenzie's parents under a shady oak tree not far away. The Archers and the senior Daniels had taken to each other from the start. Ross had joked that his ex-in-laws always recognized fellow blue bloods the moment they met, but Kenzie knew he was pleased. She knew, too, how much he'd worried about this visit, which he had agreed to only after she'd insisted.

"They're Angus's grandparents, Ross," she had reminded him when first presenting him with the idea. "They've lost their only daughter. They shouldn't have to lose him, too."

Especially after admitting, in one of the letters Kenzie had started trading with them back and forth across the Atlantic after she and Ross had gotten married last October, that they had initiated the custody suit only out of concern for Penelope's son.

Ross had been utterly dismissive when Kenzie had told him this. But gradually, as the letters continued and she got more and more glimpses of the sad, lonely couple living behind those pages, she'd come to understand their point of view. Yes, it was true that Angus had received a princely trust-fund sum from his godfather, but it was concern for him alone once the blinding grief at their daughter's death had faded a little that had promoted the Archers to want him back.

Thanks to Kenzie's letters and the first, awkward telephone calls between New York and London that had followed, the air had been largely cleared.

But Kenzie, too, had secretly worried about this first meeting, held on purpose during the boisterous Labor Day family gathering at The Farm rather than at the more intimate—and therefore potentially more awkward—Calder home on Long Island.

They needn't have worried. Yes, the Archers were every bit as stiff and correct as Angus had described, but after a week in the company of noisy Daniels children and their pets—Angus had insisted that Jazz and Zoom accompany them from New York—they were actually starting to mellow a bit.

"We'll have them swinging from the chandelier at Mom and Dad's in no time," Tad had said after the Archers had been coaxed into joining a rowdy game of water polo their first day at The Farm. Both of Angus's grandfathers had acted as captains, and Sir Edward had actually done a cannonball off the float after his team had won. No one had looked more surprised than Mrs. Archer at this shocking behavior, except maybe Angus.

Seeing the look on the boy's face had convinced Kenzie that she'd done the right thing in trying to draw Penelope's parents into their grandson's new life. Family was what mattered most, she thought now, stealing a glance at her own parents, who were playing the perfect hosts to their English guests under the trees.

They seemed to genuinely like each other, Kenzie thought gladly. And maybe her parents' outgoing ways would serve to warm them up even more.

One step at a time, she thought. It's only their first visit.

But she had the feeling there'd be more.

A big, gentle hand landed on her shoulder and a pair of very sexy lips was suddenly nibbling on her neck.

"Ross! I'm busy here."

"I know. That's why I came to help."

"Then fold these napkins, please. Put them under the cups so they won't blow away."

"Not until you kiss me."

She lifted her face obligingly.

"Mmm. Can I have another one?"

Smiling, she obliged again.

"One more?"

"Now, Ross."

Sliding his arms around her hips, he drew her closer and kissed her anyway.

"You are so stubborn," she protested, glad that he was.

"And you are so irresistible."

They smiled at each other. Kenzie could hardly believe that next month they would be celebrating their first anniversary. She felt as if she'd been with Ross forever, so well did they get along, and so easy and natural was their love.

"I feel I've married my best friend," she'd confessed to her mother a few months ago, when Alicia Daniels had called to see how the move into the new house on Long Island was coming.

"That's the secret to marital longevity. Once the passion fades, the friendship'll carry you to the grave. Not that your father and I are cold fish yet, mind."

"Mom!" Kenzie had protested, even while blushing because the word "passion" had reminded her of Ross's lovemaking. Why, just this morning before he'd left for work...

"So you're adding a home office?" her mother had continued.

"For me, yes. That way I can be here when Angus gets home from school. Of course, I'll have to be in court a few times a week and meet with Ross at the office to discuss our cases, but—"

"Are you sure it's a good idea, the two of you working together? I couldn't imagine trying to practice law with your father."

Kenzie laughed, almost able to hear her mother shudder over the phone. "I won't be practicing law with Ross. I'll be advising him. Working with those clients of his who are minors or have custody of minors."

"I still wish he'd accepted that offer to rejoin his old firm. Your father did say they're among the best in Manhattan."

"Ross intends to be the best in Queens, Mother."

"And I'm sure he will be. Now, as for that addition. Have you thought about a nursery? That extra bedroom next to Angus's seems so small to me."

"It's a house, Mom, not a manor. And old bungalows like ours always have small rooms. That's why we're building an addition, although we plan to keep it as unobtrusive as possible so it doesn't interfere with the original lines of the house. And as for a nursery, that third bedroom is adequate for now. Besides, we don't need one yet."

On the other hand...

"What are you thinking about?"

Ross's tender whisper broke into Kenzie's thoughts. He had

wrapped his arms around her and was holding her close, his eyes dancing into hers.

"I was thinking about the little speech you plan to make before dinner. And whether Angus has blabbed yet."

"What's that mean? Blabbed?"

Angus had wiggled his way between them, making sure to be included in his parents' embrace.

"Angus! You're soaking wet!"

"If you really love me, Dad, you'll hug me, wet or not."

"Cheeky brat," Ross said, grinning and obliging.

"What's 'blabbed' mean?" Angus persisted.

"Spill the beans," Kenzie said, then laughed when he still looked confused. "You'll get used to American slang soon enough, sport, I promise. But what it actually means is, have you told anyone our secret yet?"

His eyes grew round and his voice dropped to a whisper. "About the baby? No way! You said not to tell anybody until supper!"

"Which should be right about now," Ross said. "Looks like Alida is waving everyone over."

Angus slipped his arms around Kenzie's waist and laid his cheek against her still-flat belly. He'd been doing that a lot since finding out last week that he was going to be a big brother, to hug the baby and let it know how much it was wanted, he'd said. "Won't they all be surprised!"

Kenzie ran loving fingers through his tousled hair. "Would you like to tell them?"

"Me? But I thought Dad was supposed to."

Ross grinned. "If you'd rather, son, that's fine with me."

Angus was silent for a moment. Then he took them each by the hand. "I've got a really good idea. Let's all go and tell them together."

And so they did.

* * * * *

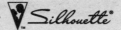

If you enjoyed what you just read,
then we've got an offer you can't resist!

Take 2 bestselling love stories FREE!
Plus get a FREE surprise gift!

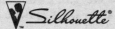

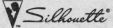

SPECIAL EDITION™

A captivating new book by author

Lynda Sandoval

ONE PERFECT MAN

(Silhouette Special Edition #1620)

After fourteen years of avoiding even
the remote possibility of entanglements
that might put his daughter in a vulnerable
position, Tomás Garza willingly brought
beautiful Erica Gonçalves into his house,
into all their lives, even if only for business
reasons. She was here, and the memory
of her, he knew, would linger even
when she'd left.

What had he been thinking?

*Available June 2004
at your favorite retail outlet.*

COMING NEXT MONTH